MEN IN LOVE

M/M ROMANCE

Edited by Jerry L. Wheeler

Riding the Rails

The Dirty Diner

Tricks of the Trade

Visit us at www.boldstrokesbooks.com

MEN IN LOVE
M/M ROMANCE

Edited by

Jerry L. Wheeler

A Division of Bold Strokes Books

2016

MEN IN LOVE: M/M ROMANCE

ISBN 13: 978-1-62639-736-1

THIS TRADE PAPERBACK ORIGINAL IS PUBLISHED BY
BOLD STROKES BOOKS, INC.
P.O. BOX 249
VALLEY FALLS, NY 12185

FIRST EDITION: APRIL 2016

CREDITS
EDITOR: JERRY L. WHEELER
PRODUCTION DESIGN: STACIA SEAMAN
COVER DESIGN BY JEANINE HENNING

CONTENTS

INTRODUCTION: HOW MEN ROMANCE

Jerry L. Wheeler

In my case, I was romanced by an outfit.

My late partner, Jamz, was an astute man, totally aware of himself and the effect he had on others. And he dressed accordingly, leaving nothing to chance. He considered the placement of every hair, no matter what color it was that week, as important a part of his ensemble as his shoes, shirt, pants, or choice of jewelry.

We met sleazy, in the arcade of an adult bookstore. Oh, don't look so shocked. It happens, and, yes, some of those relationships last lifetimes. His first words to me were…well, let's just say they were a proposition. I accepted. We had sex in the theatre, but then he walked me out to my car and kissed me in the parking lot, two occurrences that rarely happen with tricks. We exchanged business cards, and three days later, he called me for a proper date.

I did not get the gay guy clothes gene. I can take Armani and make it look like Sears off the rack, so I gave minimal thought to my outfit that Saturday night. I was more worried this was going to go like the last nineteen dates I'd been on in the last two months: awkward, unfulfilling, and laden with an atmosphere of excruciating boredom. At exactly six thirty, my buzzer rang.

When I opened my apartment door, I noticed again how tall he was. And how handsome. His reddish-gold mullet—shush, it was in fashion then—almost gleamed in the light from the hall fixtures. He wore black motorcycle boots, black jeans with a black leather wallet on a platinum chain, and a studded belt. His forearms were hairier than I'd remembered, and he had a lot of tattoos I hadn't noticed before.

But for all the menace he projected, his smile was wide and his eyes were bright, and that's when I noticed his T-shirt. It, too, was black, with the sleeves rolled up. On the front was the logo from *The Partridge Family* TV series of the 1970s, beneath which read: *C'mon Get Happy*. It was the perfect contradiction. I smiled and fell in love, right there in the doorway of my apartment.

"That's what you were supposed to do," he told me months later when the subject came up for whatever reason.

"You mean you wore it on purpose?"

"Hell yes, I wore it on purpose. Took me two days to get it right."

"Why?"

"I figured if I wanted to catch a writer, I had to tell a story."

Did I also mention he always knew the right thing to say? Yeah. That.

The eighteen authors gathered for *Men in Love* all have their own stories to tell. Some are poignant and hopeful, like Thom Collins's tale of a renewed affair in "Love in Portofino" or Kassandra Lea's sweet "When the Sun Shines," or our opener, "Range of Motion," 'Nathan Burgoine's portrait of a relationship founded on healing as much as love.

Some authors chose to look at how relationships start, like the blind date of Michael Bracken's "Bathhouse Backstabber," the catfishing of Megan McFerren's "Firebrand," the chef reality TV showdown in Dale Cameron Lowry's "American Master Bakers," and the surprise shifter ending of Erzabet Bishop's eerie "Wilde," not to mention a slight bit of time travel to help out a first date in Matthew Bright's "What a Coincidence."

We haven't left the middle of the relationship unaddressed, either. Both Vinton Rafe McCabe ("The Essentials") and Maryn Blackburn ("The Second Time Around") use romance and routine for very different effect. In both of these superficially disparate tales, we see couples who have unconventional standards for romance, but their happiness and satisfaction are tangible regardless. And speaking of unconventional, we couldn't do a romance anthology with just couples, so Colton Aalto provides "The Missing Piece" of a triad.

That, however, isn't our only foray into the unconventional. Jerry Rabushka's "Crewman," about love among housepainters, and R. W. Clinger's "Photo-Love and Seven Ways to Get the Guy" both have memorable first person voices, as does Evey Brett's "Security Breach." Gregg Shapiro's "6th & E" explores the effect of temptation on a relationship, and Kevin Klehr's "Conversations with an Angel" looks at how parents and family can affect a romance. In the case of Richard Natale's "The Seven Forty-Five," however, we see how two men who meet on the commuter train strike up a romance that could very well end them both. Our closer is a lovely piece by George Seaton, "Continuum," which is both reflective and hopeful.

So, get comfortable and make sure to have the tissues handy as we take a long, heartfelt look at *Men in Love*.

And, you know, I still have that *Partridge Family* T-shirt.

JW
Denver 2015

Range of Motion

'Nathan Burgoine

H ey, Billy, isn't that your bike bunny boy?"

I hid my reaction behind a glower at Mick, my least favorite coworker at the gym.

"Don't call clients that," I said. "And don't call me Billy."

I waited so it wouldn't look like Mick had managed to yank my chain if he was bluffing. When I figured I wouldn't seem too obvious, I turned to look at who'd just walked through the gate. We gave our members keycards so they could swipe themselves in, and at first I thought I might be looking at the wrong person, or that Mick had indeed been teasing me, but no. It was the guy I'd been hoping to see for nearly four months.

No suit. And was his hair shorter?

"See?" Mick said. I hadn't fooled him with my casual look. "Bike bunny boy."

Mick used the term "bike bunny" for all the women at the gym who came in, did cardio on the stationary bikes, and then left without touching anything else. I tried to take the high road with Mick, who always stopped just short of crossing the line with his comments or jokes or calling me Billy even though he knows I prefer William, but some days were harder than others. Mick had been bad enough when he'd clued in that I was gay, but once he'd realized I'd developed a crush on a client, he'd delighted in it. Mick had started calling him "bike bunny boy" and declared he was being inclusive, not offensive.

Bike Bunny Boy—it annoyed me that I'd started thinking of him by that name, too—had stepped into the changing room, and I took a second to bring over two applications to the computer. Mick, noting the arrival of two young women, left the front desk. I waited till he was out of view to pull up a list of the names of the clients currently swiped in.

I'd tried this before without luck. Two months ago, when I'd realized Bike Bunny Boy hadn't shown up in a while, I'd tried to search him out, but a lot of people worked out every Tuesday, Thursday, and Saturday. I couldn't find a pattern that was quite right from my recollection. I'd heard another client call him Benny in passing, but when I searched the database for Benjamin, Ben, or Benny, I got no hits that seemed right. The birth date was obviously wrong, or the last visit date wasn't right. Searching out a client was also something of a problem if I was working with Mick. It broke the rules and made me feel a bit like a creepy cyberstalker, but something about this guy made me want to step out of my comfortable life. I'd never minded being single before, but one look at him and I was risking my job.

He was attractive, sure, but he wasn't a model or anything. He was lean, with the body of a runner or a bicyclist, and he had collar-length brown hair that just started to curl at the ends. His eyes were a rich hazel, though they looked a little lost under his strong brow. Clean shaven, he looked young, but he often arrived in a suit. I was convinced he worked in one of the nearby office towers, so I guessed he was in his late twenties at least. I liked that he changed into an old T-shirt and a pair of sweatpants, not some sort of logo label workout outfit, and that his shoes were obviously well worn and chosen right. When he ran on the treadmill, he didn't put on headphones and seemed to pay attention to everything he was doing. It was the same on the bike and his rare bouts with the elliptical.

When he smiled at someone he knew, everything about him lighted up. Smiling suited him, and he did so easily. He had a little gap between his front teeth that I found adorable. Once or twice I saw him explaining how one of the machines worked to someone else—usually women—and being patient and helpful. I always tried to interrupt, both to help the client but also to interact with him, however briefly.

I was pretty sure he was gay. For one, the suits he wore were impeccable, and for all that the metrosexual revolution muddied the waters, this guy oozed class and didn't have his hair slicked back or an overpriced watch. Also, the guy who'd called him Benny had more swish than a swizzle stick, and Bike Bunny Boy had responded with just a bit of an affected lisp in return.

The name on the screen that matched the swipe-in time was Reuben Wright.

I almost smacked myself in the forehead. I had a niggling familiarity with the name from searching the client lists, but until I saw it on the screen with the swipe-in time, it hadn't occurred to me that Benny could be short for Reuben.

I slid the new applications back into the in-basket where Mick would no doubt leave them for me and casually made my way out onto the floor, cleaning the elliptical and treadmill areas with more attention than they needed.

Soon enough, Bike Bunny Boy—Reuben—arrived. His usual workout uniform was the same, an old T-shirt and a pair of sweatpants, but he seemed different. I forced myself not to stare as he walked over to a nearby treadmill and punched in a program.

His hair was quite a bit shorter, no longer long enough to curl, and he had a neatly trimmed goatee that suited him but aged him a little. His skin was lighter, accentuating the dark smudges under his eyes. He looked exhausted. When he started running, I noticed he wasn't running a very challenging program compared to what I'd seen him do, and his gaze was less focused.

Barely five minutes later, he aborted the program and stopped. He'd broken out in a real sweat and was breathing heavily, and I saw him favouring his right leg when he stepped down and reached for the cleaning rag to wipe his sweat from the panel.

"I've got it," I said, stepping over. He glanced up at me, and for just a second, something on his face made me stop moving.

Fear.

"You shouldn't push it," I said, feeling awkward. The look of panic on his face had come and gone quickly, but it had definitely been there. I nodded at his left leg. "Accident?"

He met my gaze and nodded, still breathing heavy.

"Don't worry," I said. "I'll wipe it down. Maybe take some time in the steam room before you go."

He glanced at my shirt and then flicked his eyes back up at me. "Thanks," he said, and nodded again. He left the floor, and I wiped the machine down, trying hard not to dwell on the look he'd given me when I'd spoken to him. Having placed myself near the desk, I offered a friendly wave when I saw him swiping out. His smile was wan.

When he was gone, I opened up Firefox and held my hands over the keyboard for a long time just staring at the Google search page. This felt a little skeezy. I sighed, typed in "Reuben Wright" and our city, and hit the search button before Mick could come over to see what I was doing. My stomach clenched at the links that appeared.

Man Gay Bashed in Local Park, Hospitalized

Gay Bashing Victim Lay in Park for Two Hours

Homeless Man Calls Police After Finding Gay Bashing Victim in Park

I closed down the window and made myself breathe evenly.

Now I knew why the name had been vaguely familiar.

❖

"You ran the marathon last year?" I asked him three days later. He'd changed for his workout and was wearing the T-shirt all the entrants were given at the marathon finish line. I had the 5k version. I'd never tried even the half-marathon and had nothing but respect for the marathon runners. Cardio had never been my strongest point.

He glanced at me, then nodded. "Yeah."

"I did the 5K that year," I said. "I don't know how you guys do it."

He smiled faintly and said, "I loved running." The past tense fell awkwardly between us, and I forced myself to remain casual as I glanced at his leg. "Was it a break?"

He frowned a bit. "Yeah. And there was other stuff, too."

I nodded, working hard not to let my face show the anger I was feeling. Other stuff included a broken jaw, some missing teeth, more than one cracked rib, and a concussion, I knew. I'd read the articles at home. I'd surprised myself by becoming furious, actually having to stop myself from reading at a few points to take deep breaths. I'd wanted to pitch my laptop across the room.

No arrests had been made.

"Did you do physio?" I asked, struggling to maintain my client voice. I hoped I was coming across as professionally interested.

"I'm doing some on my own." Reuben paused. "I had one visit with a physiotherapist. He explained how to do some hydrotherapy for when I got the air cast off. I've done some swimming. I'm almost there." He shrugged. "I can't get my stride right. No marathon this year."

One physiotherapist visit? One? I felt my temper rising at whatever doctor hadn't bothered to help Reuben plan a recovery, but swallowed. The bitter edge to Reuben's voice made me want to punch the wall.

Or hold him.

"Well," I said, keeping my voice even, "if you'd like, I could help you with a workout plan. Nothing with major impact, but focus on some core strength recovery. And your range of motion—I think that's what's throwing you off. I'm not sure you should be on the treadmill."

He seemed surprised. "Uh. I don't know." He glanced at my shirt again, rereading my name tag, I figured, which was pinned on the front left of my chest. "I'm…I'm not working right now, I'm on leave, so hiring a trainer…"

I nodded, as if this was no big deal. "Did you use the five trainer days you got when you signed up?"

He blinked. "Five trainer days?"

I sighed and pointed at Mick across the room while his back was turned. "Did that guy sign you up?"

Reuben looked at Mick, who was chatting with a young woman doing free weights. No doubt he'd soon be offering to show her better posture techniques.

Reuben nodded. "Yeah."

I'd already known that from Reuben's file, but I shook my head as if slightly disgusted. "You were supposed to get five free trainer days with him. Don't worry about it—he's a bit of a jerk. I'll transfer them to me, and it won't cost a thing. And we'll break it up into bits, make it last." I smiled.

Reuben looked at me, hesitant. He exhaled. "That would be good. Thank you."

"You're welcome." I offered a hand. He waited a second, then took it and barely squeezed before letting go quickly.

"I'm Ben," he said.

"William."

"I knew that," he said and looked at my name tag again, then smiled.

Of course, we didn't offer five free trainer days for new members. I'd have to pay for it myself. But that smile was worth every penny.

"You're probably right about the treadmill," he admitted. "I really felt it after last time."

I wasn't surprised. "Let's go figure out a schedule. And next time, bring your trunks. We're going to start in the pool."

I put my hand at the small of his back to lead him to the front desk. He flinched, then tried to hide it by stepping to the side and gesturing for me to go first. I cursed myself. I knew better.

Two men had come upon him in the park, where he'd been going for an evening run.

No arrests.

"This way," I said.

❖

I'd suggested the mid-mornings on Mondays, Wednesdays, and Fridays because I knew the pool had no classes going then, and the mid-mornings were the quietest times at the gym. I wore one of the gym tank tops management had given us. I didn't like the way it stuck to me, but they preferred we wear a shirt of some kind when working with clients in the pool.

Reuben—Ben—kept his shirt on as well, which surprised me until it occurred to me he might have scars. He slipped into the water eagerly after I'd explained what I wanted him to do.

"This is a floater belt," I said, tying it around him, hyperconscious that I was close behind him and trying not to notice how tense he was about it. "It'll add to your buoyancy and help keep weight off your leg. You're going to run in place in the water."

I finished putting it on his waist and felt heat rising on my face as I walked around him. We moved deeper into the pool, and once he had clearance, he bobbed a bit in the water. His shirt clung to him, and I couldn't help but notice his left nipple was pierced. I forced myself to maintain eye contact.

He went at it like a trouper, awkward at first but getting his balance and getting the hang of what motions he was aiming for pretty quickly. I watched him, keeping an eye on his face for any grimaces or signs of trouble, and I gave what I hoped was gentle encouragement. He didn't tire as quickly as he had on the treadmill, and when I suggested we'd done enough, he seemed slightly disappointed it was over.

I focused on his range of motion, and as the sessions went by, Ben relaxed a little in my presence. I still avoided touching him beyond what was necessary, and he still rarely smiled. I tried to think of him as a client and ignored the way my chest tightened when he winced or got frustrated with himself if he had to stop earlier than he'd wanted to. He came in one morning having obviously not slept at all the night before, and I imagined the nightmares he was having. It took every bit of willpower I had not to grab him in a bear hug.

With my help, his leg was getting stronger. I only wished I could do the same for the rest of him.

❖

"No bike bunny boy today, Billy?" Mick asked when I came back in for my next afternoon shift.

"Mick, you need to shut up," I snapped.

Mick stepped back, surprised. "Whoa, dude."

"Seriously," I said, angry at him, and angry that I'd let him get me angry in the first place. "It's not funny, it's not charming. You have no idea what it's like, okay? The jokes aren't funny, the comments aren't funny. You, Mick, are not funny." I heard my voice rising, but I pulled myself back together and turned my back on him. I sat at the computer, pounding the keys as I entered the membership forms he'd once again not bothered to put in.

I did two forms before he spoke again. It surprised me; I thought he'd left.

"Sorry," Mick said. "I really didn't mean to piss you off."

I turned in my chair. "No," I said. "I'm sorry. I shouldn't have yelled."

"You're pretty freaking scary when you're mad."

I felt my bad mood dissipating. "Hell hath no fury like a fag scorned," I said.

Mick glanced around, then said. "Scorned, huh? Did that guy turn you down?"

I shrugged. "No. I didn't make a pass at him. Ben's…" I wasn't sure why I was telling Mick of all people about it. It occurred to me that I'd listened to his women woes on any number of occasions and never offered up anything myself. "It's not the right time," I said.

He sat on the other chair. "You were both hanging out in the pool, weren't you? On your own time?"

I was surprised he'd noticed, and I looked at him. Mick seemed a bit hesitant, but genuine.

"He thinks we owe him training sessions from when he signed up," I admitted.

Mick raised his eyebrows. "Dude. That's…Wow." He paused. "That's a pretty good idea, actually." He seemed to be considering it.

I rolled my eyes. "You're not going to use it on the next blond to walk through the door."

He looked chagrined. "So, why are you two doing all that pool work?"

"Broken leg," I said, skirting the hows and whys. "Four months ago or so. He's a runner, and wants to get back to it, but…" I shrugged.

Mick nodded. "Car accident?"

I shook my head and again found myself volunteering. "He was attacked. Bashed."

"Oh jeez." Mick grimaced. "That must suck."

"And not in the good way," I sighed. I finished the last membership sheet and pushed away from the computer.

"I'm really sorry," Mick said. For the first time ever, he wasn't annoying the crap out of me.

"When did you become a nice guy?"

Mick rolled his eyes. "Always have been. Just normally, it's the ladies who notice."

I laughed. "Right."

"He'll come around," Mick said. I'd heard him say that a dozen times about the ladies he'd dated who'd found him wanting.

"I doubt it. Even if he's interested, he'll be too ashamed and too timid," I said. "That's the worst part. You heal, and you don't look any different, but it takes something from you. Things you used to do? You don't do them any more. It's like…" I thought about it. Remembered. "It's like you lose your range of motion. Confidence, I guess. Takes a really long time to realize you're not to blame, that you couldn't have done anything different—and that you shouldn't have to—and a lot longer to believe it."

Mick stared. "William…" He'd never called me that before.

I smiled. "It was a long time ago, and nowhere near as bad. No broken bones, no broken teeth, but a lot of bruises, black eyes, and a bloody nose. And I gave as good as I got. But it's enough to understand what it must be like for him," I said. "Your friends and family all find out, and it's in the room all the time. I had to tell my parents why I'd had the crap kicked out of me by my best friends. I got caught with this other guy. Everyone found out. I had to quit football, had to try and disappear. But that was in high school. You get to leave high school."

I'd escaped to the city and had never looked back. It was different for me, I imagined, than for Ben. I couldn't imagine going through it now. Coworkers, neighbours, and friends; his life would be completely disrupted. Tainted. "I'm gonna go do rounds."

Mick let me go without comment. Who says miracles don't happen?

❖

"How does it feel?" I asked Ben. We were drying off after time in the pool.

"There's burn," he said. "But it's good burn." He smiled then, an actual open smile, and I noticed the gap between his front teeth was gone.

Something must have shown on my face, because his smile faltered. "Is something wrong?" he asked.

I shook my head. "No," I lied. I remembered the article had mentioned he'd lost teeth. One or both of his front teeth, I supposed, had been replaced. The gap had been fixed. "You go hit the sauna, get some heat. I'll see you next time?"

He handed me the belt. "Bright and early." He rubbed his chin. "Or maybe a little later?"

"There's a class at nine," I said.

Ben sighed. "No rest for the wicked."

I laughed. "Are you wicked?" I'd intended it to be light, but he met my gaze for a moment, dark eyes full of a rare mirth.

"I do have the beard for it."

"Goatees are wicked?" I asked.

"Just ask Spock."

I blinked.

"Wow, I just dorked out, didn't I?" he said.

"It suits you."

"Being a dork?" Ben smiled again, that dazzling smile. This time I didn't notice the missing gap.

"The goatee," I said, and I felt my face flushing.

His smile faded again. "Thanks. It hides a scar on my chin." He shivered. "Time for the sauna."

I watched him go, wishing I had an excuse to follow him.

I managed to convince him for three weeks, but on the last day of the third week, Ben got out of the water and said, "I can't possibly have any time left." He'd made real progress, and I was wondering if it might be time to try the treadmill—not a full-out run, but a good long walk—to see if he'd gotten past his slight limping.

I tried to brush off the comment. "We only spend an hour or so together. It doesn't add up to a full session."

Ben wiped his legs with the towel, then looked at me. "A session is two hours. I asked that other trainer. You've been comping me, haven't you?"

I felt my face heat up. "Maybe I've been stretching the rules a little," I admitted.

He put down the towel and shivered in his damp shirt and trunks. "Why?"

Because you used to smile all the time, and it's possible I have an insane crush on you. I hesitated. "I, uh, know about your accident," I said, my voice low.

His expression shut down. "What?"

I swallowed. "I read about it. Online." A line had appeared between his eyebrows, and I rushed on, realizing I'd made a huge mistake. "I just…It made me so angry. I thought I could help." He looked down at the deck, and his lips had narrowed.

"I have to go now," he said, his hands shaking.

"Have lunch with me," I said. It came out in a rush. I needed to explain.

He stared, dark eyes darting back up to meet mine. "What?"

"I'm sorry." I shook my head. "I'm doing this all wrong. Just… You're hungry, right?"

He nodded.

"Let me take you to lunch."

"Aren't you working?"

I winced. "Actually, no. I've been coming in, uh, on my own time whenever you and I…" At the look on his face, I trailed off.

He swallowed. "I don't think that's such a good idea."

My chest tightened. "Okay." The word burned in my throat.

Reuben Wright turned and left, leaving the pool room without the slightest limp.

❖

"Your guy hasn't been around," Mick said.

I grunted, punching in more of Mick's membership paperwork. "I pretty much fucked that up completely." We'd found a nice new balance, Mick and I. I was trying to consider it the consolation prize.

"You did?"

"I told him I'd read about his bashing on the net, and that I was comping him the sessions, coming in on my own time…I came off really stalkerish."

Mick shrugged, holding up his hands. "Dude. You pretty much did stalk him, right?"

I groaned. "Thanks, Mick, that makes me feel so much better."

"No." Mick shook his head. "But you had, like, good motives. Also, he's a hottie."

I blinked.

"What? Guys know when other guys are hot. They just pretend not to. He's hot. I'm secure in my masculinity."

"What have you done with Mick and how long can you stay?" I asked.

He swatted the back of my head. "What I mean is, go after him."

"Chasing a victim seems like a bad idea," I said.

Mick frowned. "You call him a victim?"

"No. No, I…" That stopped me. "Shit."

Mick sat down beside me. "Dude, call him."

"And say what?" I looked at him.

"I don't know. Tell him he's hot. Tell him you're sorry. Those two work on women all the time. Tell him you wanna make him feel like a lady."

I raised an eyebrow.

"Or…well, gay that up a little." He waved a hand.

I laughed. "Thanks, Mick, but it's okay. I screwed up. I scared him off."

"Pussy," he said.

"I prefer cock, actually."

He sat there for a while longer, but when I didn't speak, he pushed away with a grunt and left me alone at the computer.

❖

Ben was outside when I left work four days later. I saw him as I shrugged into my jacket—it was getting colder again—and stopped walking. He was leaning against the wall outside the gym and looking at me, his hands in the pockets of his coat and a small smile on his lips.

"Hi," he said.

"Hi." I felt awkward and wasn't sure what to say.

"You're right. That guy is a bit of a jerk," Ben said.

I wasn't following. "Pardon?"

"Mick," Ben said. "He called me. I'm pretty sure he's not supposed to look up my phone number."

I blinked. "Mick called you?"

"He said, and I quote: 'Billy went completely out of his way to help you, and you treated him like crap.'" Ben curled his lips in a crooked grin. "It took me a while to figure out who Billy was."

I grimaced. "You're kidding."

Ben shook his head. "I'm not. But he was sort of right. I'm sorry. You were very generous, and I was—"

"Blindsided," I said. "I really screwed that up."

Ben smiled, flashing his new smile with the perfect front teeth. "I missed that."

"Pardon?" Ben said.

"Your smiles," I said. "You have a great smile."

He blushed. "I kind of wondered if you were watching me when I used to come in."

"That obvious, was I?"

He smiled again. "A little."

I rocked on my heels. "I am really sorry for not being honest."

"If you'd been honest, I'd have walked out the door," Ben said, and then he frowned. "That sounded like permission to lie to me again. It wasn't."

"Got it," I said. I liked the sound of again.

Ben shifted. "Back then...before...if you'd have asked me out..."

"Yeah?" I said.

"I was hoping you would," Ben said. He blushed. "You've got great arms."

"And you've got great legs," I said.

"Had."

"Have," I stressed. I winked. "And an awesome ass."

Ben laughed. "Damn! You should have asked me out months ago."

I looked at him. "I'm asking now."

His smile faltered, and he blinked rapidly. "I'm a mess, William."

"You're allowed to be. Trust me, I've been there," I said. "Really."

Ben frowned, and I saw when he realized what I was saying. "Oh," he said.

I stepped toward him, and he didn't flinch when I opened my arms. He gave a shaky laugh then hugged me, rolling his eyes at his own hesitation. I gripped him.

"I've been wanting to do this for weeks," I said into his hair. It had a citrus smell. I breathed deep. The tension in his body relaxed in tiny increments, but it eventually faded. I looked around. We were alone; the street was empty. He felt me move and looked up at me. I leaned forward.

It was a gentle kiss, and I was surprised at how soft his goatee was. We lingered just a moment, and then I pulled back, though I still had my arms around him. I didn't want to let go, not just yet. I loved seeing him smile up at me like that.

"Get a room!"

Ben jumped, and we stepped apart. Mick took just enough time to grin at me before he zipped up his jacket and walked off the other way.

"Asshole!" I yelled.

"Pussy!" he yelled back, not turning.

"He's going to be insufferable now." I sighed.

Ben chuckled and put his hands back in his pockets. He looked shaky, but better. I'd take it.

"So," I said. "About that lunch."

"I'd love to," Ben said.

CREWMAN

Jerry Rabushka

Y ou're picture framing."
    "I'm not."
"Stand back, Crewman."
"Must be the brush."
"The brush is top of the line, must be the *you*."
I stood back to look at the wall. It's a color called Blueberry
Tropics. It's trendy, it's *this year*. He was right. Well, he always was.
And I didn't stand back so much as he grabbed my arm and yanked
me into the middle of the room. "It's a picture frame."
    It's a paint term. You roll out the wall as close as you can to the
edge, then you cut in with the brush. If it doesn't blend right, all four
edges of the wall look like you've painted a picture frame. Nobody
wants that to happen. We have lots of terms like that. We call "you
missed a spot" a holiday, but it means you have to work longer.
    Carl manhandled me in a way he rarely did with anyone else.
Crew members are all like, *why do you let him treat you like that?*
    "He's the boss."
    "I'd sock him one."
    Boss got the bid on a big job, and here we are finishing up in
this new-construction three-million=dollar mansion. Gotta travel an
hour to get there and get it ready for the owner. Pays pretty well. Of
course, we're the last crew in there. Painters have to wait till all the
trades are pretty much done, then we make up for lost time. So, a
picture frame? That was more time lost.

"I like ya, but if you wanna keep this job, you gotta learn to—"

"Why don't I roll and you cut?" I said. "We all got our strengths."

"My niece can cut in like a master," said a painter. "And she's five years old." He's so perfect it hurts to watch, blond jock hair, clean shaven, always smiling and courteous, and bangin' all the housewives when their husbands are at work. Good for him for being better than me.

I feel like a loser working a three-million-dollar home. My problem, I know. Once the owners move in, my welcome moves out. It's like those workers at the Chinese Olympics: *Hey, put up a stadium, now get out, you too ugly.*

❖

I like the boss. I like how he handles me, how he turns me around, how when I get all stupid, he sticks that brush or spray wand in my hand and curls my fingers over it. Yeah, I like all that. Truth is I know what I'm doing, but a rough touch is better than nothing at all.

But I'm not a damn Monet, and I can't always cut in so good. The light was bad, I couldn't see what I was doing, whatever my excuse, boss wasn't having it. "Now we gotta do that shit again."

"Okay, I'll try."

"Not you, Crewman. You screwed it up once." It was an odd term, Crewman, but boss liked it, and we all started using it.

We got all types here. Boss hired extra to get this job done. It's that or we work sixteen-hour days, and apparently that kind of labor agreement doesn't happen anymore. Sometimes they'll hire a bunch of illegals to do it for ten bucks an hour. Yep. I said illegal. So sue me. Tryin' to make a living.

I told you about blond stud, plus we got a couple smooth, cool black guys, and we got the college kid who sings Elvis all day and says he's gonna win *American Idol*, and I hope so because it'll get him off the crew. We got me—I'm the dark blond lanky guy with the hair on his face. Ain't seen my lip in a decade. My jaw's covered up too. Carl's always saying, *where's your damn lip?* I'm like, *boss, come find it.*

I think he likes me, he just doesn't know he does. Doesn't know how to say it, so he throws me around the jobsite like an oily rag. That rag of mineral spirits that you never know when it's going to burst into flames. I'm that rag, trying to stay oily, trying not to burst and burn, but damn I want to. I go home all lit up and have to put that fire out with that hand he curled over. These guys find out I like the boss, I might as well throw that rag down. You like guys, it's one thing. You like the boss, it's about ten things more.

Yeah, I'm the gay guy. Queer guy. Whatever they call it these days, I'm that. I don't know if they know or they don't, and I don't know if they care or they don't, so I don't talk it up. It's not like everyone on crew feels the same way about everything. I see some guys get all racial about painting with someone a little darker, Carl's like, *suck it, dude, he sweats just like you do.* I'm like, *oh no, he sweats better.*

Folks think you're a painter, so you have a problem with gay guys. Like we're all alike, all poured out of the same bucket. I watch 'em work, and I like who I like. I don't like who I don't. I want a guy who can cut in. Who can roll. Who can put in that time to do it just right. Who can bail me out of what I can't do while we're living in these Blueberry Tropics. I like the guy who can do it just right without having to be told. I wish it was me, but I'm just not that responsible. But boss wants to throw me up against a wall and find my lip, so I stay on.

For now, I tape up plastic sheeting on the counters below a row of fine-crafted cabinetry so someone can come by with an HVLP and spray up a stain. Someone shoulda sprayed them before they were installed, but whatever. I'm demoted to no-skill prep with a newfangled tape and plastic in one. Carl puts my hand over the taping machine and says go for it. If I learn to tape straight, maybe I can learn to paint straight. His hand stays on mine just a second or two longer than usual.

"What would you know about straight?" I asked him. Closed mouths don't get fed.

"What's that supposed to mean?"

"You got your hands all over me all day long." Our eyes met, and I felt like all those oily rags were gonna go up at once. "I ain't gonna file harassment, if you're worried." My lip trembled, not that he could see it. "I got this," I said. "Go babysit college boy."

❖

I don't wanna be that guy. The guy who likes the boss and everyone knows it. That I'm just there because I do more than paint. I don't wanna be that guy, but yeah I do. I like the boss and his tough love. I like how he calls me Crewman.

"My name's Noah," I reminded him once.

"I ain't all up in your grill like that," he said.

I wished he was. Damn, I wished more than I ever thought I could wish. Just had a bad day on the picture framing thing. This three-mil home pissed me off. Jealousy didn't look good on me, so I had to let it go somehow. I'm always being that guy I don't want to be. I'm lonely. I keep fucking up so he grabs me like a convict. It's all the sex I get.

❖

It's paint, dammit! All this starched white yes sir, no sir bullshit. We get a bad rap as drug addicted alcoholics. Well, it's the drug-addicted alcoholics that gave us that rap. Showing up as painters when they ain't.

That 'stache I got's longer than the hair on my head. I got dark blond fuzz on top. 'Stache curls over and covers my lip. Beard's about the same. It's clean, just thick. I'm a taller guy, have a bit of muscle, have a *Duck Dynasty* look to me, but I'm better lookin' and with more brain cells. I have a *don't fuck with me* kinda face, so I have to work extra to get someone to fuck with me.

Boss, he's dark haired, he's good looking but doesn't want to let that secret out. He can't do a beard like me, and it kills him.

That's why he wants to get close to mine. It's kinda like me and this three-mil house. I can't do it, and it kills me. In the summer, it gets hot and guys take off their shirts. We're still wearing goggles and all that safety stuff that covers up your looks, but Carl, I like to watch his arm move up and down when he actually paints something and doesn't just tell us what to do. On a hot day, he gets all rank smellin' and I get next to it.

"Y'all finish up," he says. "I need to take Crewman here and teach him how the hell to use a brush before I fire him."

I rode in with him to save gas, so we get in the company truck and head out. There's not much left to do but clean up anyway and come back the next day, except for college boy who's stuck fixing my picture frame. I'll never hear the end of that. Some young thing all up like, *I can paint better than the guy who's thirty-five.* I'm like *yeah, but boss don't like you, like he likes me.* He better not. I got a streak in me about that kinda thing.

❖

Carl takes me to his place. I've been there before. We've had staff BBQ and such there. I got sauce on my…oh, you're tired of hearing about that damn 'stache, aren't ya? I can't see the word *mustache* on a page without getting weak. The real thing on a man, it's worse.

"What's here needs painting so badly?" I ask.

"I wanna find your lip, Crewman."

I got it, finally. Saying *Crewman* worked him up. Working around guys like this and we're all a jack-off fantasy. You wanna say working with a queer guy isn't any different, then you're drilling your eyes right through his Dickies acting like you're just worried about picture framing.

"Find it," I tell him. "But you can't use your hand."

Carl's shorter than me. He's gotta step up, which takes the boss-crewman thing and puts me in the lead for once. He pins me up on a faux brick wall right next to that big screen TV—yeah, I painted my way through life so he could get that damn thing—he comes on up under my 'stache with his tongue and his top lip. He's all over that thing, and I'm pinned to the wall while he gets his fill.

I throb everywhere. "How long you been wantin' that?" I asked.

"How long you been workin' here?"

"That's too long to want that."

"Didn't want you to make a complaint."

"What you gonna curl my fingers on now?"

Kissin' the boss feels weird. He's the boss, he's not even supposed to be into guys, he's supposed to be the guy I hide from the most. Turns out he doesn't really care what we are, other than we can paint. For all my shootin' myself in the foot, I need thicker shoes.

He was all about me, though. He threw me into the bedroom, ripped off a couple buttons, and told me it was time for a new set of painter's whites. He knew when to call me Crewman and when to call me Noah and when to talk about forty-day floods and all that stuff. His eyes burned into my face watching me react to his hands. Some guys are jealous because I got chest hair thick like my 'stache. Carl got all into it, he got all into me like no one ever had. I didn't think I could ever feel this, much less deserve it. I'm just a crewman, after all.

I hate feelin' like that. Letting someone so far into my soul that they can see through my skull. I want to feel it, but I just can't. Part of me is like, *damn, no one's done that to me* and another part's like, *can't let him know*, so yeah, it was as good as it could be.

"We shoulda done it in that house," I said. "In the doctor's bedroom."

"Don't shit where you eat, Crewman," he said.

I look at his wall. I'm lying here naked and all full of his drool, every part of me's exposed to my boss, my heart most of all. He's pretty much sniffed and licked off whatever I smell like during whatever day it is. Paint doesn't smell like it used to. Some of it's so low odor, as they call it, that you gotta stick your head in the bucket to smell it at all, and this way we don't come out having to wash up with turpentine and mineral spirits. It's all water and soap, and we're clean. Your boss's tongue just scrapes off the rest.

"There's a picture frame up in the corner."

Boss looks at me like I'm crazy, then he looks at the wall too. It's slight, but you can see it if you pay attention. I like that angle of his face, the way his nose and jaw jut out, the stubble on his lip, fierce eyes. He's forty-five, and he's got it goin' on. I wanna say, *wow, your lips make me float on a cloud*, but I say, *there's a picture frame up in the corner*. I trained myself too well. Not to let it show even when I need to, when he just wants to hear, *you sure know how to take care of your crewman*. You are how you are, or you're not. So I am how I am in that way I shouldn't be at the biggest moment I shouldn't have been.

"I didn't paint it," said Carl. "And after painting all day I don't want to fix it."

"I'll fix it for ya," I offered. "Just dressed like this."

Picture frame thing kinda set him off. So did the doctor's bedroom thing. I shoulda known better than being this way I don't like myself to be. I don't got nothin', just a damn apartment they won't let me paint. Now I know why.

"You call everyone Crewman all day long," I said. "You're getting your rocks off on all of us calling us Crewman, and we don't even know what's hit us. How many other guys been your crewman after hours?"

"It's my company. So, yeah. You got me figured out. You can't paint for shit, Noah. But I love you, so I keep you on."

Can't remember the last time I heard that, and the words didn't fall right over me. I want to say it back, but I can't cut myself open like that. "I didn't think you even liked me that much."

"Y'ain't figured that out 'cuz you're an idiot. Too busy being tough. So, get it together. I don't want to have to tell you again."

"It did feel awfully good, boss."

"Well, if you're gonna be in here again, you'd best fix that wall. I can't be drivin' you *that* far into ecstasy if you're scoutin' around for paint problems while I'm tasting the goods."

❖

Carl overdoes it now at work. He'll toss me from room to room. I hate that he calls everyone Crewman. I get scared 'cuz he's starting to do the same shit to that college boy. I'm terrible at this. I'm used to everyone having everything I don't: love, friends, money, even those damn cabinets. I'm trying hard not to let him down and not to punch college boy right out of a singing career. Boy's growing a handlebar trying to outdo me. It's dripping with sex, big and black, and it curls up on the sides and fuck him. It makes me weak. It makes Carl drool. It's just a natural reaction. It is, right?

Carl calls him College Boy and everyone thinks it's an insult, a step below Crewman.

Maybe this love thing will work. It's got to. It's all I have.

American Master Bakers

Dale Cameron Lowry

Joey hated Terence. He hated his perfect puff pastries, his melt-in-your mouth mille-feuilles, the way he arranged lebkuchen on a platter, and his baritone voice barking "yes, chef," and "no, chef" loud enough to be heard over twelve roaring stand mixers. He hated Terence's salt-and-pepper hair, prettier than white buttercream dusted with silver sugar, and how Terence didn't seem to think anything was wrong with strolling naked between bedroom and bathroom at the contestants' dorm, his nuts hanging low beneath his meaty cock, swinging shling-shlong, shling-shlong with every stride.

Terence had become the bane of Joey's existence from that first day on the set of *American Master Bakers*. There'd been fifty contestants then, each presenting their signature bake for a chance at being on the full season. Within the four-hour time limit, Terence had somehow managed to bake and decorate a three-tier wedding cake with a different sponge in each layer, two custard fillings, and three jams from scratch. That alone would have made him a shoo-in, but then he'd decorated its flawless ganache with handcrafted fondant lovebirds that looked like the real thing.

"Well, Terence, we might as well skip the whole season and give you the bakers' crown now!" had been the judges' assessment.

Fucking show-off.

Joey's goal in life became getting Terence axed from the show. If he could eliminate Terence, he would win the season hands down, easy as pie. Joey had learned to bake rugelach by his grandmother's side at age four, made his first croquembouche wedding cake at age nine, and by sixth grade ran an unofficial catering business out of his parents' kitchen. He might be the youngest contestant at only twenty-six, but he had been born to own this kitchen.

The camera crew knew Joey hated Terence. The judges knew it. Hell, all of America knew it. Joey never tried to hide his contempt.

"Oh, look at Terence make marzipan for his stollen from scratch—and watch him run out of time." Joey smirked at the cameras as he kneaded his Swedish coffee ring dough. It was the first day taping episode twelve: forty-four contestants gone and six left.

But Terence beat the clock, and the judges gushed so much over the final product you could practically smell the cream in their undies from five stations away. Both of them had a permanent hard-on for Terence.

"Experience beats youth any day, motherfucker," Terence said on their way back to the dorm that afternoon, flipping Joey the double-bird.

On day three, they had to grind fifty pound bags of flour by hand, then make four different kinds of whole wheat bread. "Hey, old man, don't give yourself a hernia," Joey shouted across the studio as Terence pranced around with two bags on each shoulder, one for each remaining contestant save Joey.

"You're just jealous because I look twice as good as you at forty-four than you do at—how old are you, anyway? If I based it on your maturity level, I'd have to guess twelve."

Of course, Terence didn't get a hernia. Didn't come close. He might be almost twice Joey's age, but he had a muscular chest and big burly arms from years of pounding dough out by hand. His thighs wouldn't quit, and his muscular ass also managed to look soft and pliable like bread dough. Joey had an urge to poke it just to see how fast it sprang back up.

Damn that ass.

Now they were at the final challenge of the episode, the one that would determine who stayed and who went.

Joey walked into the studio pretty damn confident. He'd slayed the bread bake the day before, and even if the judges hadn't liked his Swedish tea ring as much as Terence's stollen, day two had brought a Linzer torte technical challenge that Joey had knocked out of the park. The judges had gone on and on about the perfection of Joey's red-currant jam while sighing about Terence's being on the runny side.

Joey knew he was safe from elimination.

The contestants lined up shoulder to shoulder at the front of the room, like bride and groom cake toppers at a triple wedding. Joey was between the grandmother of eight and the four-foot-ten, ninety-pound elf woman from Santa Clara. With long brown hair and golden skin, she looked like a chocolate éclair standing on end. The grandmother was more of a Catalonian xuixo pastry—plump in the middle and dusted sugar-white all over. On the other side of elf woman was the guy who'd lost one arm in Hurricane Katrina. His muffin-top stomach made Joey think of saffron buns.

Completing the lineup were the Korean lady DJ with a face as round as an English muffin, and Terence, who was any and every pastry Joey had ever tasted, good or bad. That morning, his reflection in the camera lens reminded Joey of a Runeberg torte, a delectable brown-sugar cake topped with white icing. Joey's mouth watered.

Chef Dharma stepped forward to greet them. "Chefs, we weren't able to agree on a single chef who has excelled above all others this week. Therefore, all six of you will compete in the elimination round."

Someone might as well have dropped a bowling ball on Joey's stomach. But he didn't flinch or frown. He kept his face frozen for the cameras.

"A good chef knows how to learn from others. So for today's elimination round, you'll be working in pairs. Members of the two best-performing teams will progress to the semifinal. For the members of the weakest team, today will be good-bye. So get ready to put your brains together. The teams are—" Chef Dharma began pulling names from a metal mixing bowl. Joey crossed his fingers behind his back and prayed to get paired up with elf woman, or maybe Hurricane Katrina guy, or even DJ lady, but please not—

"Joey and Terence, you're a team!" Chef Dharma smiled maniacally. Her eyeteeth looked like fangs.

"Christ! How am I supposed to work with that old geezer?" Joey pulled the tea towel from his belt and whacked it against the counter behind them. The camera crew loved those little flourishes.

Terence looked straight into the camera. "Joey is an entitled douche bag. But I won't let him be the end of me."

They glared at each other as they walked to their station. Three metal cloches sat on top of it.

Chef Riordan stepped forward to give the contestants their next set of instructions. "Under the cloches are mystery ingredients that will help us get to the root of your baking skills. Don't worry, you won't have to use all the ingredients—just the one under the first cloche you pick up. The three ingredients are the same at each table, but ordered at random. You may lift any cloche you choose. Zina and Sandra, begin."

Zina was the ninety-pound elf-éclair woman. She picked up her middle cloche to reveal a big hunk of ginger root. Pfft, thought Joey. Ginger wasn't a challenge. It was a dessert staple.

The next team got carrots. Not quite as easy as ginger, but carrots could work in cookies, cakes, and sweetbreads, or even in a custard filling—anywhere that pumpkin or yams would work, with a few tweaks.

Joey had been ouija board king back in high school and had even gotten into ghost-hunting for a while. He wasn't actively doing the psychic stuff anymore, but he still had a killer sixth sense, and he had an awesome feeling about the middle of his three cloches. It was either ginger or something better than ginger.

He nodded toward Terence but didn't look at his face. Terence's face was distracting, and Joey didn't need that now. "I'll pick our mystery ingredient. I don't trust you not to fuck it up."

"Whatever gets your rocks off, kid."

Joey lifted the cloche.

For the first few milliseconds, he didn't register what the thing in front of him was. It was reddish brown like a bleeding turd, round as a baseball, and smelled like dirt. Then Joey's brain caught up with the image. "Holy fucking shit! What the fuck are we supposed to do with a goddamn beet?"

Zina tittered. Hurricane Katrina guy smirked. Joey lost sight of what the other contestants were doing because he was too busy seeing red.

"Contestants, you have three hours to make three amazing desserts. Begin!"

Joey kicked whatever his feet could reach. He sent an empty compost bin skittering across the floor, dented a stainless steel oven door, and stubbed his toes on the maple flooring.

Someone touched his forearm. He instinctively did the wax-off move from *Karate Kid*, trying to fling the hand away, but it held. It was strong and calloused, and as warm as Joey's raging blood. "Calm your tits, kid. I got this."

Joey looked up. He saw steel-blue eyes offset by brown skin. He got muddled for a moment, lost in thoughts of candied violets and chicory blossoms atop chocolate petit fours.

Terence. It was Terence.

Terence smiled, baring teeth as sparkly as crystal sugar.

"The fuck you've got this," Joey said. "This is the end of the road for you and me both. Who wants to eat beets in dessert?"

"Old hippies and nouveau riche hipsters, and I've baked plenty for both of them." Terence radiated composure. It seeped from his hand into Joey's skin, and then into his capillaries. Within moments, it circulated through his whole body, this strange, odd sense of certainty that everything was going to be okay.

"I hate you," Joey said, but it lacked the usual venom.

"Yeah, you've said it a million times. You're a broken record." Terence turned away, leaning down into the under-counter fridge to pull out eggs, heavy cream, milk, butter, and limes. "God, you probably don't even know what a broken record sounds like. An infant, that's what you are. But you're going to have to grow up now."

"I know what a record is, geezer." Joey reached for the tub of pastry flour. Even if he had no idea what the plan of attack was, they would certainly need that.

"Only because you saw them in some nostalgic window display at Urban Outfitters, I bet."

That was close enough to the truth to make Joey's face go hot. Terence smirked. "You're red as a beet. Portends well for us, don't you think?"

"Not if we don't have any ideas."

"I've got plenty, beet-boy. You ready to listen to me?"

Damn those sugared-violet eyes. Joey couldn't bear their gaze. He looked at the floor. "I got nothing, old man."

"Right, then. Here's what we do." Their pièce de résistance was going to be an entremets—a classic French dessert with contrasting layers of cakes and creams. They would start with a beet-brownie base, topped by cocoa-nib praline for crunch, a pink beet-lime sponge cake, chocolate cremeux, beet panna cotta, and a pale green whipped lime mousse. They would encase it in dark chocolate ganache and top it with a beet-colored fondant rose.

Joey could picture it perfectly: precisely defined layers of brown, fuchsia, and green; the contrasting notes of bitter, zest, sweet, and earthy dancing into a unified whole. His cock went from down-in-the-dumps to half-mast. He glanced around to make sure no cameras were on him, then adjusted himself through his jeans. "But that's only one thing. We've got to make three."

"The other two will be a hell of a lot easier. You ever had gajar halwa?"

Carrot-and-cardamom pudding? Of course Joey knew it. His next-door neighbors growing up had been Indian and cooked it every year for Diwali. He nodded.

"Well, you can also make it with beets. So we do baklava layered with beet-carrot halwa and chopped pistachios."

Joey's cock scooted farther up the flagpole. He shifted his legs and tried to get it to go toward his left pocket so it wouldn't press against his zipper. A camera turned toward him. He squatted out of sight, fishing in the cupboard for cardamom, cocoa, and pistachios. "What else? If beets work in brownies, I guess we could do chocolate-beet donuts. But I'm not sure that's gonna cut it around here. Kind of simple, not really dessert."

Terence didn't laugh or sneer. He simply said, "You're right. No donuts. Let's do a Schichttorte with alternating layers of beet and white cake, glazed with pomegranate jelly and white chocolate."

Damn, Terence really was good. And Joey's dick was the size of a jumbo éclair. If only he had time to run to the bathroom and let its creamy filling spurt.

He closed his eyes and pictured Chef Riordan barking, *You call that bread? Your dough is raw!*

Joey's cock started to shrivel almost immediately.

"You down with the plan, kid?" Terence's voice came from above. The usual malice was gone. All that was left was authority and indefatigable calm. "We need to get cracking."

Joey looked up. Terence's eyes were on him, cool as two blueberries fresh from the fridge. "Yes, chef. I'm with you."

They started with the beets. Joey peeled them; Terence ran them through the food processors. Their station was huge, with three ovens, three mixers, six burners, and a large butcher-block counter. Still, they couldn't avoid incursions into each other's physical space. Their arms brushed as they reached for this or that, making the fine hairs on Joey's forearm stand on end—something they did whenever he was turned on or terrified.

"Now start the phyllo dough. You know how to make that, right?" Terence's sneer was back.

"I've been making phyllo since I was in diapers."

"So, that's been maybe two weeks?"

Joey snapped his tea towel across Terence's infuriatingly perky ass.

"I'm too old for spankings, kid." Terence started the food processor back up.

"Oh, yeah?" Joey tossed the tea towel on the counter and used his bare hand instead. Terence's ass did indeed spring back just like a perfectly proofed loaf of bread.

"You try that again, and you won't see what's coming to you."

Joey took it as a dare and was just about to smack that perky loaf again when Chef Dharma interrupted with an infuriated "What the hell is going on here? You guys want to fight or win?"

"Win, chef," they muttered in meek unison.

"Good. Now tell me your plan."

Terence sniggered. "Go on, tell her the brilliant ideas you came up with, Joey."

Joey swallowed his pride and went over the details of Terence's plan for Chef Dharma and the cameras as he started the phyllo dough.

"Sounds good, if you two manage not to kill each other first," she said when he was done.

The next few hours were a blur. Terence was the brains of the operation, and both were the brawn. Joey was on automatic pilot. Mixing. Kneading. Melting. Chopping. Tasting the beet-infused batters and discovering them to be pleasantly sweet and piquant, not like dirt at all. Opening the oven every five minutes to add another layer to the Schichttorte. Doing sprints back and forth between the station and the blast chiller.

Joey was surprised by how few occasions he had to send barbs in Terence's direction. The man seemed to read his thoughts and agree to the next step in their plan of attack before it was even fully formed in his mind. He'd gear up to shout at Terence for not starting the panna cotta yet, and Terence would be on it already, stirring gelatin into the slurry of beet juice and heavy cream. They developed a consistent rhythm, as smooth and well oiled as the perfect handjob.

Terence spoke a little more than Joey. "Don't skimp on the limes, kid. The acid is what preserves the pink color during the bake," he said when Joey was mixing the sponge cake. And later, "Chop the pistachios a little smaller."

Joey *yes, cheffed* him and did as he was told. He wasn't going to spit in his own eye. The only thing he hated more than Terence was losing.

Two hours in, Terence said the weirdest thing. "You should make the pomegranate jelly, kid. You're better at it than me."

Joey's heart pounded something crazy inside his chest, harder than it had all morning. "Excuse me, chef?"

"You heard me." Terence didn't look up from his fondant.

"Yeah, dude. But I want you to repeat it, just to make sure I'm not hallucinating. Because I'm pretty sure you just said—"

"Don't let it go to your head, kid. You do one thing in the kitchen better than me. I do ninety-nine better than you."

"Still, you admitted—"

"Make the fucking jelly already."

Joey's cock sprang up. He didn't even bother trying to hide its outline from the cameras. Let pervy home viewers find it through his apron and gif it all over the Internet. Joey was champion of the world. Terence F. Greene had just admitted Joey did something better than him.

The meltdown came fifteen minutes later. "I forgot to put the sugar in the jelly! What the fuck is wrong with me?" Joey dropped the hot saucepan into the sink. Pomegranate slurry sloshed over the rim. He collapsed against the counter. No point in continuing now.

Bang! Terence's fist came down next to Joey's head. "Stand straight, soldier!" Joey jolted up.

Terence's cheeks were beet red, his eyes steely. "Ever since I got here, kid, you've been prancing around like a goddamn peacock, going on about how much better you are than the rest of us. Well, now's your chance to prove it."

Blood surged to Joey's groin. God, not another boner. "Yes, chef."

Terence spun Joey back toward the sink and gave him a sharp slap on the ass. Joey's boner grew bigger. He ignored it, focusing instead on making pomegranate jelly properly this time.

"Ten minutes, chefs!" called Chef Riordan.

Joey poured the glaze over the Schichttorte while Terence drenched the baklava in syrup.

"Five, minutes, chefs!"

Joey cut out fondant petals while Terence rolled them into roses.

"One minute, chefs!"

Terence straightened and set out the entremets. Joey added a pomegranate icing swirl to the Schichttorte that catapulted it from awesome to superb.

"Time's up, chefs!"

Joey's hand brushed against Terence's as they jumped back from their station. Joey grabbed on to it, gave it a congratulatory squeeze, and didn't let go.

Couldn't let go.

Because what he saw in front of him was pastry perfection. The Schichttorte shone. The baklava was golden and crisp. The entremets looked like edible bits of rainbow.

Terence's hand was warm in Joey's. His callused thumb fit perfectly in the divots of Joey's knuckles. "We did it, kid."

Joey smiled so hard his face hurt. He turned to find Terence smiling just as broadly, the corners of his eyes crinkling like the surface of baked saragli.

Chef Riordan's voice broke through Joey's reverie. "The carrot team has only completed two desserts. Carrot team, would you like to explain?"

Hurricane Katrina guy stepped forward. "We couldn't agree on a third one, chef."

"You do understand that's an automatic disqualification, don't you?"

"Yes, chef."

Chef Riordan sighed. "Fine. Everybody back in three hours for your formal critiques. But I might as well tell you now, Chef Dan and Chef Charlotte, you'll be turning in your aprons."

Joey's reaction was instinctive. He let out a whoop and flung himself forward into Terence's arms. They closed around each other simultaneously—Joey squeezing Terence's shoulders, Terence clasping Joey around the waist with his broad hands.

"We did it! Holy hell!" Joey couldn't stop babbling or bouncing on his toes, and Terence couldn't stop laughing, his chest rumbling like a stand mixer against Joey's chest, his lips as tempting as caramel cream.

Joey's cock stiffened. Damn, he wanted to taste that mouth.

"Do you have the balls, kid?" Terence's eyes were warmer than

Joey had ever seen them, two lavender sugar cookies fresh from the oven. He pulled Joey closer, hip to hip, snug like icing on cake.

Terence was hard, too. "Bigger balls than you, old man."

"Prove it."

Joey collided into Terence's mouth. They both grunted at the impact but didn't flinch. Terence lowered one hand to Joey's ass as he tugged Joey's bottom lip between his teeth. "Didn't think you had it in you, kid."

Joey wound his fingers into Terence's silver-sugar hair. "I'm up to every challenge."

The next kiss was interrupted by an ear-piercing "Arah begorra!" from Chef Riordan. Joey spun away from Terence to find every camera in the room trained on them.

The sound of a lone person clapping started from the corner of the room. It spread like an oil fire until everybody was cheering, even the two contestants just kicked off the show. As Hurricane Katrina guy said in an interview recorded later, "Everybody knew those two were hot for each other from the beginning. Seeing them finally get the memo almost made it worth losing. Almost."

Joey saw his opportunity to own this. He looked straight into the lens of the nearest camera and shouted over the applause, "America, I think I've finally met my match!"

More whooping. The director called cut. Joey and Terence sprinted to the dorm.

"Still hate me, motherfucker?" Terence said as he tossed a shirtless Joey onto his bed.

"For as long as you keep your clothes on." Joey wriggled out of his pants and briefs in the same move. His own dick was as big as a hoagie roll.

Terence pulled off his shirt and jeans but left on his blue briefs. "Maybe I want you to hate me. Maybe I get off on it."

"You're gonna get off regardless. I'll make sure of that."

Terence's cock sprang free when Joey tugged the blue briefs down, precome flowing from the tip like glaze from a pastry tube. Joey licked his lips.

"You want that, kid?"

"Yeah."

"Then take it." Terence nudged the tip of his cock against Joey's lips, coaxing them open.

Joey hummed happily as he licked the salty glaze.

Terence chuckled. "Always thought you hated my cock, the way you glare at it in the hall."

"I hated it. I wanted it. What's the difference?"

"What's the difference, indeed?"

Terence sank into Joey's mouth, his shaft hard as toffee, his skin smooth as icing on a cruller. Joey swallowed greedily around him, taking more and more until Terence was in as far as he could go, salty glaze dripping on the back of Joey's tongue where things always tasted best.

"I hate to say it, but you're good at this, kid," Terence moaned. "Real good." But it wasn't long before he pulled out with a sudden sucking swoop.

"Hey, I wasn't done!"

"But I would've been done if you'd kept going."

"No harm in that." Joey tongued at Terence's juicy nuts. "My favorite part of eating cannoli is sucking out the cream."

"But I'm not cannoli. I'm bread. You can't rush the process."

"So if you're bread…" Joey flipped Terence onto his stomach and ran his fingers over his luscious ass, working his thumbs into the crease where each cheek joined its muscular thigh. "I should knead you until you're nice and springy, like this." Joey squeezed Terence's ass cheeks.

Terence moaned into the pillow. "Noticed you couldn't keep away from my ass in the kitchen, either."

"Can you blame me? It's perfect."

"You're admitting something about me is perfect?"

"Damn near everything about you is perfect. That's why I've hated you for so long." Joey parted the two round buns. Terence's pucker looked like the pinched hole of a mini-donut, sugary and tender. Joey gave it a tentative lick, and then a firmer one. The skin was buttery smooth as a croissant, silken as ganache, velvety as a Sachertorte. The taste was better than a choux pastry's.

Terence grunted his approval, squirming toward Joey's tongue as Joey feasted on him like a starving man at a patisserie. They shifted into a sixty-nine so both could have their just desserts. As Terence's tongue worked him open, shocks of arousal spread from Joey's asshole to his dick, then up his spine to his nipples, and further until Joey's scalp and toes tingled. He wrapped his hand around Terence's heavy cock, felt its breadth and weight, longed for it inside him.

"Fuck me," Joey panted. "Please."

"Did I hear that right?" Terence slid a finger into Joey's spit-slicked hole. "Did you just say 'please'?"

"I'll say anything you want if you put your dick inside my—yessss," Joey hissed as Terence stroked his prostate.

"Hmm. Then say I'm a better baker than you."

Joey bit his lip. What had he gotten himself into? Still, he really would do anything for that dick. He'd wanted it since he'd first laid eyes on Terence, that much was clear to him now. "You're a better baker," he grunted, "but only because you've got seventeen years on me."

"Good enough." Terence smirked as he worked another finger in.

Joey's mind flooded with images of long crullers sliding in and out of donut holes. He reached for the condoms and lube in his bedside drawer, jellying up Terence's dick like the inside of a Swiss roll, then flopping stomach-first onto the bed, his legs spread wide.

"Uh-uh." Terence's hands were warm on Joey's hips as he flipped him over. "Face-to-face. I need to kiss you." He crashed into Joey's mouth as hard as they'd done back in the studio, teeth making contact almost as soon as lips. Joey didn't know if he was being devoured or the one doing the devouring. He didn't care. He was happy to be both pastry and chef, dessert and diner.

Terence drove hot and thick inside him, stretching Joey just right. He fluttered his blue eyes as Joey clenched his ass. "Damn you, kid," he grunted, and kissed Joey even harder this time.

They fucked and fucked. Joey was dough, and Terence the hands that pounded and shaped it, working Joey at a relentless rhythm, pulling him apart and pushing him back together into something stronger than he was before.

Joey looked down between their bodies, watched the muscles of Terence's abs and arms ripple and his own hard cock bounce as Terence pivoted in and out of him, mortar and pestle. Joey ran his hands over Terence's nipples and the flame of silvery pubes that licked up his belly, wiry and translucent like spun isomalt sugar, and over his firm, perfect ass, the muscles in it quivering with each thrust.

"Jesus Christ, I'm gonna come." Joey tugged Terence down, felt the muscular weight of Terence's belly heavy on his cock, pulled Terence balls-deep inside him.

"You do that, kid."

Joey's orgasm roared through him, splattered onto his stomach like warm sugar-glaze, but he still didn't have everything he needed. He kissed up Terence's jaw, whispered into his ear, "C'mon, now. Drizzle me with your icing."

Terence bit Joey's shoulder as he pulled out and flung off the condom. He groaned, and then with one stroke, two, he coated Joey's chest.

Terence collapsed onto the bed. "Damn it, kid. No point in continuing with pastry now. I'm pretty sure you're the hottest cake I'll ever decorate."

Later, when Joey opened his eyes, Terence was leaning over him, tracing patterns through the semen on his skin. "Flowers?" Joey asked. "Spirals?"

Terence's smile was different from any Joey had ever seen before. It almost looked—well, shy. "Hearts," he said, and buried his face in Joey's shoulder.

Joey felt a strange warmth in his center and a giddiness similar to the terror and exhilaration of being in an airplane about to take off. He kissed Terence's hair. "I think I'm over hating you."

"Yeah?"

"In fact, I might be heading toward the opposite, you asshole."

Terence looked up at Joey, gave him a solid kiss on the lips. "We're screwed, Joey. We're so fucking screwed."

"We totally are."

They smiled themselves to sleep.

❖

Despite their newfound ability to cooperate in the bedroom, neither man let go of his competitiveness in the studio, and they both survived the next episode.

But in the end, *American Master Bakers* could have only one champion.

It wasn't either of them. It was Zina, the ninety-pound elf girl who shouldn't have the upper body strength to work a piece of dough, but somehow did. They both had to admit she deserved it. Her pièce montée in the final episode had two more layers and three more types of pastry and sugar-work than either of theirs and, embarrassingly, its components tasted the best, too.

Terence got second place, and Joey third. "Just wait until next year," Joey said. "I'll cream your ass."

Terence slipped an arm around Joey's waist and leaned into his ear. "I was hoping you'd do that tonight."

The rematch never took place. They were too busy with their new bakery in Manhattan's Chelsea neighborhood to bother with more reality TV. It offered the most phallic éclairs in the whole city, and was the only place to taste the original *American Master Bakers* beet entremets and Schichttorte.

To this day, orders for the pink pastries skyrocket each February, requiring Terence and Joey to put in long hours as Valentine's Day approaches. The work finally stops at three o'clock on the fourteenth with the locking of the front door.

That's when they go upstairs to their apartment for a private celebration that involves drizzling warm icing on each other's skin.

BATHHOUSE BACKSTABBER

Michael Bracken

I first met Joshua—Josh—at a cocktail party hosted by mutual friends. When I discovered we were the only two men attending without a partner, I realized we'd been set up, and I confronted Scott in the kitchen as he was pulling a tray of prosciutto-wrapped asparagus out of the oven.

"How could you?" I demanded. "I told you I'm not ready to date again, not after what Alex did to me."

Ever one to trot out a cliché when he thought it appropriate, Scott said, "It's been two months since you fell off that horse. Isn't it time to get back in the saddle?"

Alex and I had been together for nearly eighteen months when he dumped me for a grad student teaching in his department at the university. The sting of his rejection had hurt all the more because his parting shot had been to denigrate my writing as fit only for sub-literates who sounded out each word as they read, and I had not written a word since he dumped me.

As he moved the asparagus onto a serving tray, Scott said, "You know Alex was denied tenure last week."

"He was?" I hadn't heard, and the news brightened my outlook.

Scott handed me the tray. "Take these into the dining room and put them next to the seafood dip."

I did as requested, and then prepared myself a plate of appetizers from the dozens already crowding the dining room table. I had just made my last selection and was about to pop a cube of Swiss cheese into my mouth when I felt someone brush against my elbow. I turned and found myself facing Josh. He looked nothing like my ex. With closely cropped blond hair, sparkling blue eyes, and a square chin, he had the stunning good looks of a surfer.

"So, we meet again," he said with a smile.

"You realize we've been set up, don't you?"

"I figured it out a few minutes ago," he said. "Apparently you know more of these people than I do."

I admitted to knowing everyone else at the party, though some were only nodding acquaintances.

"I really only know Scott and Drew," Josh said. He put two stalks of the prosciutto-wrapped asparagus on his plate, added some Triscuits and a dollop of the seafood dip, and then we stepped away from the table to let other guests graze. "We met last week at a fundraiser for the symphony. When they discovered I was new in town, they invited me to this evening's get-together."

"How new?"

"A month," he said. "I'm still getting my bearings. It would be nice to have somebody show me around."

Without thinking, I said, "Maybe I could do that."

"Maybe you could." Josh smiled. "So, what do you do?"

"I'm a writer." He didn't ask if I'd ever been published, so I didn't tell him that I hadn't. "You?"

"Photographer."

Scott interrupted our conversation. "How's the asparagus?"

"Looks good," Josh told him. He had yet to try it.

"And how are you two getting along?"

"Fine, thank you," Josh replied, "but you could have let us know this was a set-up. I might have dressed differently."

Scott winked at me, laughed politely, and moved on to a cluster of four men standing at the other end of the dining room discussing politics.

"What was the wink for?" Josh asked.

"Scott knows I wouldn't have come if I'd known he was setting me up."

"Oh?" Josh finally picked one stalk of asparagus from his plate, and I found myself unexpectedly watching his lips as he drew the head into his mouth and bit.

"It's only been two months since my last relationship ended."

Josh placed his hand on my upper arm, an impromptu act of commiseration that sent a warm tingle coursing through my entire body. "I'm so sorry."

Something about Josh's demeanor convinced me of his sincerity, which I hadn't felt from some of my long-term friends when I'd told them about the end of my relationship with Alex. Those who didn't mention that they'd seen it coming for months were too wrapped up in their own personal dramas to care one way or the other. Only Scott and Drew made any effort to console me, taking me to an expensive new restaurant where Drew, a tenured professor in the English department where Alex taught, repeatedly apologized for introducing us, and Scott insisted, as if he had inside knowledge, that "Karma's a bitch."

At that moment, with Josh's hand on my arm and his sparkling blue eyes searching mine, I melted a bit. Maybe, just maybe, I was ready for a new relationship.

❖

I started writing again the morning following Scott and Drew's cocktail party. By Thursday evening, I had made good progress on a new short story and was writing the climactic scene where my private eye enters the bathhouse and confronts the killer, an English professor who had murdered his lover, a thinly veiled reference to Alex killing our relationship. I was interrupted when Josh phoned to ask if it was possible to tear me away from my keyboard for a few hours.

"What did you have in mind?"

"I have a photo shoot Saturday morning and was wondering if you'd like to join me," he said. "It'll mean getting up before dawn. I'm doing a 'day in the life' of the farmers market, so I need to be there when they start setting up."

"That's no problem."

I gave him my then-current address, confirmed what time I needed to be ready, and was standing on the front porch of the English Tudor I was housesitting that semester, already fortified with three cups of black coffee, when he arrived Saturday morning in a recent model SUV.

I didn't have much to do but follow Josh around as he took hundreds of photos that morning, but we ate breakfast burritos and cream cheese kolaches prepared on the spot and we talked between shots.

As the morning progressed, Josh explained that he earned much of his living shooting photos for magazines, but he did other photography as well, including advertising and some wedding photography for close friends.

The farmers market was only open until noon, and just before the booths closed, Josh asked, "What about lunch?"

I looked around. "It'd be a shame to leave here without shopping," I said. "Why don't you let me fix lunch?"

I purchased organic vegetables, free-range chicken, bread fresh from a wood-fired oven, and half a dozen blackberry kolaches for dessert while Josh photographed the vendors packing their unsold goods and taking down their displays.

Instead of returning me to the house where I was staying, Josh took me to his loft, the third floor of an old warehouse converted into living space. Except for the enclosed bedroom and bathroom suite behind the kitchen area at one end, the entire loft was open and divided into separate functional areas through judicious placement of furniture and area rugs.

The end closest to the freight elevator was his work area, with two computers attached to large high-resolution screens, two desks, and a worktable. That led to the living area, followed by the dining area, and then the kitchen. Several large-format prints of Josh's photographs hung from the walls, and I admired them as we walked the length of his loft to the kitchen. All were of men in their natural surroundings, none of them studio portraits—a craggy-faced cowboy in a sweat-stained Stetson, a hirsute biker in his leathers, a shirtless construction worker with his yellow hardhat tilted back, a drag queen channeling Marilyn Monroe, and half a dozen more. None of the men captured in the photos were classically handsome, but all were appealing for their obvious self-confidence.

"These are prints from my All-American Male show last fall," Josh said. "My first gallery showing ever."

"That was here," I said, surprised. I named the gallery, and he nodded. "I was invited to the opening but had a conflict of interest." Alex had taken me to a lecture at the university, where I had listened to a snooty poet who couldn't earn a dime from her writing denigrate the crass commercialization of publishing. I hadn't enjoyed myself.

"It's one of the reasons I moved here," Josh explained. "There's a thriving arts community I hope to connect with."

By then we'd made it to the kitchen, a well-appointed work area gleaming with stainless steel appliances, and he showed me where he kept everything. While I chopped the vegetables, boned the chicken, added spices, and slid the result into the oven, Josh uploaded that morning's photographs from his camera to his computer. While lunch baked, I joined him in the work area, and we viewed his photos on one of the large computer screens.

As we went through them, he made notes about some of the photos, winnowing down the number he planned to present to his client. By the time we finished, he had selected three dozen and lunch was ready to serve.

Josh set the table, poured two glasses of wine, and soon we were settled into place. Over lunch, which he raved about after only the first bite, he asked me, "So, where have you published?"

There it was, the question I dreaded because I had to admit I'd never been published. "I have several dozen short stories making the rounds," I said, "and I'm working on my first novel."

"You should let me read some of your stories."

"You like mysteries?"

"I love mysteries, especially the old stuff—Raymond Chandler, Dashiell Hammett, all the Gold Medal books."

I brightened. Alex had always dismissed genre writing as pabulum for the masses, not worthy of his time or attention, and his attitude had done more to destroy my fragile creative spirit during our relationship than I wanted to admit. "Really?"

"Absolutely," Josh said. "My father got me hooked on the hardboiled stuff when I was a kid, and I've even taken jacket flap photos of a few mystery writers."

We talked about our favorite hardboiled novels before Josh brought the conversation back around to the inevitable follow-up question. "So, if you don't support yourself with writing, what do you do?"

I told him I was a housesitter, taking care of people's homes and sometimes their pets while they were away for extended periods of time. I'd become a favorite among university faculty during sabbaticals, long research trips, and teaching assignments abroad. "That's how I know Scott and Drew," I told him. "I sat their house several years ago while they spent the summer in Europe."

Though I didn't earn much, I didn't need much, and housesitting afforded me tremendous amounts of uninterrupted time at the keyboard to write. As soon as I could, I turned the conversation around and asked how Josh had made a career of photography.

"I learned from my grandfather. He had a studio in the small town where I grew up, and he was the go-to guy for portraits, wedding photography, and the like," Josh said. "I wasn't interested in studio work, so I took photos for my high school yearbook, worked as a stringer for my town's weekly paper, was photo editor for my college newspaper, and double-majored in art and journalism, both with a concentration in photography. After a few years working for a city magazine, I realized I'd rather be my own boss. I've been freelancing ever since."

We finished lunch, filled the dishwasher, and ate blackberry kolaches while Josh showed me his bedroom, where three of the four walls were covered floor-to-ceiling with bookcases filled with paperback mysteries he'd collected over the years.

Late afternoon we divided the leftovers from lunch and Josh returned me to the English Tudor I was housesitting for a chemistry professor and her husband. He walked me to the door, told me how much he had enjoyed spending the day together, and made me promise to join him for dinner mid-week. I wondered if he would try to kiss me, but he didn't, and I watched from the living room window as he drove away.

As soon as his car was out of sight, I emailed five stories to Josh, including "Bathhouse Backstabber," the new short story I'd been working on when he invited me to accompany him on the farmers market photo shoot.

Over the years, I had shared my unpublished manuscripts with many friends and potential lovers who expressed interest in my writing, but those expressions of interest were often more polite than sincere, so Josh's failure to mention my stories Wednesday when we met for dinner didn't surprise me. After he still didn't mention them the following Saturday when we attended the symphony and had drinks with Scott and Drew, I suspected he never would. Though I was disappointed, Josh's silence was far superior to my ex-boyfriend's outright dismissal of my work, and by then I often caught myself daydreaming about Josh when I should have been writing.

❖

We'd been dating for a month, seeing each other two or three times a week, when Josh took me to an expensive restaurant I had once mentioned in passing as one of my favorites. I thought we were going to celebrate his most recent assignment, a photo spread featuring lesbian motorcyclists with the working title "Dykes on Bikes," but I soon learned otherwise.

After our drinks had been served but before the appetizers arrived, Josh said, "I hope you don't mind, but I forwarded your stories to a friend of mine." He named a well-known mystery writer. "He's editing an anthology of new noir—crime fiction in the tradition of *Black Mask* but with modern settings. He wants to use one of your stories, if it's still available. He was going to mail this directly to you, but I convinced him to let me present it." He slid an envelope across the table.

When I opened the envelope, I found both a letter of acceptance and a contract for "Bathhouse Backstabber." I almost leapt across the table to smother Josh in kisses, but I restrained myself.

Barely.

Josh lifted his wine glass and made a toast. "May this be the first step in a long and successful writing career."

That night I invited him into my room at the house I was sitting that semester, and I spent several hours demonstrating just how grateful I was for what he had done.

❖

Scott and Drew took me to lunch the next week after they learned of my first sale, and they congratulated me profusely. Scott trotted out yet another cliché, reminding me that success is only ten percent inspiration and ninety percent perspiration. Then he added, "And you've been sweating like a pig for years."

After we all laughed at Scott's comment, I explained how my inspiration for the story's villain had been my ex-boyfriend, and how I had ensured that Alex—named Alexis in the story—had died a slow, painful death when my private eye protagonist caught him in the bathhouse.

"It couldn't happen to a more deserving person," Drew said. Then he told me Alex's contract with the university would not be extended when the school year ended, standard policy when tenure-track professors failed to make tenure.

Before I could react, Scott asked me about Josh. "I hear you two are like peas in a pod."

We spent the rest of lunch talking about Josh and how well our relationship was developing.

❖

Almost a year passed before the anthology containing "Bathhouse Backstabber" was published, and by then *Ellery Queen's Mystery Magazine* had accepted a story, an anthology editor was holding another of my stories for further consideration, I had just finished writing my first novel, and Josh had asked me to move in with him.

Even though I had less than a month remaining on a one-semester housesitting assignment and no new assignments lined up, I had yet to give Josh a definitive answer. I was contemplating my response late one evening when my cell phone rang, and I answered it to find Alex on the other end of the call.

"I miss you," he said. I'd heard through the grapevine that he was teaching freshman composition at a community college across town, a serious step down from the upper-level British literature courses he had been teaching at the university, and he sounded as if he'd been drinking.

I couldn't resist being catty. "Did your grad student finally dump you?"

"He wasn't right for me," Alex said. "He never understood me the way you do."

"Well, you never understood me at all," I told him.

"Why don't you come over, and I'll make it up to you."

"I'm nobody's drunken booty call," I told him, wondering why I had been so distraught when Alex dumped me. But I was thankful he was providing me with the opportunity for much-needed closure. If I'd had more time to think, I might have come up with a great exit line, but I'd been spending too much time with Scott and resorted to a cliché. "You made your bed, Alex, now lie in it. Alone."

After I ended the call, I phoned Josh and told him I'd move in with him.

❖

Several months after publication of the anthology containing "Bathhouse Backstabber," my story won a Robert L. Fish Memorial Award for best first mystery story by a previously unpublished author. Josh and I celebrated at the Mystery Writers of America awards banquet in New York, where Josh introduced me to the anthology editor who had accepted the story and where we met several of the writers who'd provided us with years of reading pleasure.

I thought my life couldn't get any better than the moment I walked onstage to accept my award, but I was wrong. Late that night, Josh led me onto the balcony of our hotel suite where we had a spectacular view of the Statue of Liberty. He dropped to one knee, opened a ring box, and asked me to marry him.

Of course, I said yes.

WILDE

Erzabet Bishop

Justin felt eyes on him. That in itself was not unusual. The members of the troupe often came to watch each other practice both before and after performances. He glanced up, looking at the canopy overhead. The swings and tightrope were vacant, and the Big Top of the Myriad Carnival was still, save for him and his unknown guest.

His cat ran close to the surface tonight. The full moon was nearing, and he was restless. Even still, a fuckup like earlier tonight was intolerable. His brain burned with the startled look in Gabrielle's eyes as the blade kissed the soft flesh of her ear.

What had he been thinking?

That was the essence, really. He hadn't been.

He didn't want to admit that, even to himself. As a knife thrower, safety was always his primary concern. But tonight he'd let himself be distracted by a dark-haired stranger. The man had stayed just out of view, but Justin caught a whiff of sandalwood and spice and his throw had wavered.

Justin hadn't matched a face with the scent as of yet, but as he readied himself to throw, the stranger had revealed his presence as the new roustabout they'd picked up three towns over. Instead of protecting his sister, he'd come close to truly harming her.

The scent of cotton candy and half-stale buttered popcorn filtered past his nose and his stomach growled, reminding him of the time. Dinner would be over soon. He needed to get the lead out and go, but he wanted to practice while the heat of the performance still burned in his blood. One near miss, and he'd almost taken off

Gabrielle's ear. Was he that close to a shift that he could make such a mistake?

Not. Acceptable.

If he thought for one minute he was a danger to her, he'd hang up his blades for good. His sister deserved more. A low growl of self-loathing reverberated up his throat.

A voice broke through his revere. "Are you coming to eat?"

Speak of the devil herself, if the devil had curly red hair and the curves to match. Gabrielle was the light to his dark both in looks and temperament, as their parents had often pointed out. Lately she'd taken over for them in the soapbox department and wouldn't let up about him working too hard.

"Yes. I'll be there in a minute."

"Go on a date tonight. It won't kill you, you know."

"Mind your own business, Red."

"Nope." She'd grabbed his arm and swung herself up on her tiptoes for to kiss him on the cheek. "You're my big brother, and I'm worried about you. You don't have to hide what you are, Justin. The others will like you."

He'd looked at her like she'd lost whatever marbles she'd had.

"I'm serious. People already see we're different. Let it out. A coiled spring breaks sooner or later."

Hell if she wasn't right. He'd had everything under control until tonight. His edges were fraying, and he didn't even know why. Being gruff with her was their natural balance, but he really did love her. She was the only family he had left, and he'd be damned if he'd let anything or anyone harm her, including himself.

He knew she was genuinely worried, and that made it hard to be mad at her. It wasn't for lack of interest, but he didn't have that many options. And he was busy.

You're a liar. That new drifter is one hot looker, and you can't stop staring whenever you see him in the chow line. "I'll eat at least. Promise. Let me get this out of my system, okay?" He shifted his weight and met his sister's gaze. If he went now, God knew he'd weaken and make a play for the man. His way was safer. You don't go outside the box, you don't get hurt. Besides, he had to fix his throw.

"Jesus, Justin. It wasn't your fault. I moved." Her blue eyes were crinkled with worry and full of feline energy judging by the yellow glow. "You want to go for a run later?"

Maybe she had moved, he thought, but he had the reflexes to account for that. "Sure. It'll be our last chance before we pack up tomorrow."

"Okay." His sister opened her mouth but closed it again. She fidgeted with the knives on the table next to the fading canvas wall of the tent. "Good. I thought that's what you'd say."

Justin narrowed his eyes at the straw-filled target and let the blade fly. As he released the handle, a noise in the stands distracted him and the knife veered away from the target and hit the floor.

"*Fuck.*"

"Okay, okay. I'm out of here." Gabrielle glanced into the stands, a knowing smile on her face. "Just remember. You won't venture out...so you leave it up to me. Have fun." She sashayed back the way she'd come, the spring in her step promising mischief ahead. What had she done?

"What are you talking about, Gabe?" Damn, that girl was always up to no good. The only answer he got was the tent flap closing and a giggle on the way out.

There. A footfall in the stands and the faintest scent of sandalwood. He was supposed to be alone when he practiced. Everyone knew that. Red he could forgive, but anyone else...

"Whoever the fuck you are, do that again, and the next knife I throw is going straight at your head." Justin held the knife blade up as he searched the shadows. In the distance, he heard the lowing of the animals as they went about their evening rituals and the noise of the camp as the carnival performers settled into their downtime.

A solitary figure caught his attention, emerging from the shadows of the stands. Clad in jeans, a tight-fitting black T-shirt under an open button-front plaid shirt, and dusty cowboy boots, the roustabout edged into the light.

Holy Jesus on a cracker.

"I didn't mean to disturb you." The words were one thing, but the expression on the drifter's face was anything but contrite.

"Like hell you didn't."

"I'm Riley. The girl that was just here said you had an opening for the knife-throwing act. For an assistant, I mean."

"Did she now?" He picked up the blade from the straw and measured the weight in his hand. That explained the impish look on her face. Minx.

"She your sister?" Riley gestured with his head, a curl of his tousled black hair falling across his forehead.

The man was dangerous. To whom he hadn't figured out yet. "Yes. And she's off-limits. Got it?"

Riley gave a dark chuckle. "Thanks for the warning, but I don't think she's exactly my type."

Justin turned his gaze on the drifter. "What is that supposed to mean?"

"It means I don't date women." Riley shrugged and leaned back against the post where the target rested.

"Ah. Okay, then." His stomach fluttered, and he closed his eyes. He wasn't that transparent, was he? No. If he'd talked to Gabe, then she'd no doubt filled his ear with all kinds of rubbish. He kept to himself most of the time, but his sister was a talkative little flirt if ever there was one.

"So, is there an opening?"

"I didn't say that."

"I'm here. You're here. How's about I just stand still and you give me all you got?" His voice was smoky and curled around Justin like one too many fever dreams. His cat took notice, and the beast began to pace beneath his skin.

Want.

"What did you have in mind?" He turned around, adjusted the too-tight jeans, and swung around to face the young man, thinking he must have a death wish. Justin's claws begged to come to the surface and run along the stranger's skin. "You want to play target practice with the guy who almost took off his sister's ear?"

Riley shrugged and ran a hand through his hair. "You won't hit me."

"How the hell do you know that?"

"Because you won't." The reply was soft, but Justin heard it anyway. How much had he heard? Not everyone at the Myriad Carnival knew he and Gabe were shifters, but now that the stranger had eavesdropped, Justin guessed there was a better than average chance he knew. The question now was, what was the stranger going to do about it?

"Fuck." He didn't need his sister complicating his life. Justin stalked over to the table and picked up two of his throwing knives and tucked them into his belt. "You really are brave. Or stupid. I'm not sure which."

"Just throw it already." Riley settled against the target, his lips twisted up in a grin. The T-shirt hugged his six-pack abs and tapered in to cover the waist of his jeans. The open shirt only framed what Justin knew would be heaven to rake his claws over.

Soft skin. Hard muscle.

Hard.

Justin swallowed and closed his eyes to get the image burning behind his gaze out of his overactive imagination. After this, he was going to get out more. Obviously, he was about to lose his shit, and that he could not do. You didn't shit where you ate. It was a hard and fast rule, but he was seriously starting to question it.

His cat purred deep in his belly, and the hand holding the knife shook with an effort to control the slow burn trailing through his veins. Temptation like this he didn't need. Didn't want.

The man was daring him. Justin's cat chortled under his breath, and he couldn't resist smiling. So what if a little fang showed? The guy had asked for it. He rotated his shoulders and shook his arms out, pumping them back for good measure. If he wanted to tango, then the dance was on. You play with the monsters, sometimes you get burned. "Just remember. I warned you. My game's off tonight."

Riley watched him with hooded eyes and said nothing.

So be it. He would practice on the drifter. God help him if he moved. "Hold still." Justin narrowed his eyes, drew back his arm, and let the blade fly. It connected with the target half an inch from the drifter. "And whatever you do, don't run."

"Oh, I won't." The words hung in the space between them, and the drifter smiled again. He removed the open button-front plaid shirt and whipped the black tee over his head in one fluid motion.

Justin let out the breath he hadn't realized he was holding. "Nice throw."

"Mmm. Thanks." He ambled forward, leaning in close and tugging the knife from the target. The heady scent of musk and sandalwood came close to overwhelming his senses, and he had to fight the urge to bury his face in the other man's hair. Instead, he turned away, a flush creeping up the back of his neck. "One more."

"You got it, boss."

Justin didn't speak, only raised his arm and threw the blade, giving it all the force he could muster. The knife sang through the air, but as it neared its destination, a flurry of black wings exploded from the space formerly occupied by the drifter.

Justin fell back a step, his pulse pounding in his veins. The cat roared to attention, and he laughed. A feather drifted down settling on the straw floor. "What the…?"

Birds flew overhead, some settling on the tightrope while others rocked back and forth on the trapeze swings. The murder of crows cawed and cackled at him, following his every movement.

"You cheeky bugger," Justin whispered, his face breaking into an all-consuming grin. "Are you going to come back down here, or do I have to come up and get you?"

His only answer was a cry from above and the fluttering of wings. Justin crouched low and let the change come over him. If his new playmate wanted a game, cat and bird sounded right up his alley. He left the knives where they lay and crept up into the darkness where a pair of hooded eyes waited, willing and wild.

LOVE IN PORTOFINO

Thom Collins

Jack Conway crossed the deck of *The Crystal Sea*, the gleaming white state-of-the-art super-yacht that had been his home at sea for the past week. With just a small backpack and carry case, he looked more like a student exploring the continent than a recording star with the kind of wealth most men of thirty could only dream of.

Roman Di Pritzi stood at the gangplank in white shorts and a navy sweater. With his deep suntan and silver hair, he looked every inch the billionaire fashion designer and proud owner of *The Crystal Sea*. "Why are you being so crazy?" Roman said. His expensive white teeth were a startling contrast to his baked leather skin. "We have everything on board you could want. *Everything*. And you insist on spending time in this peasant village."

Jack laughed with good humour and patted the older man on the shoulder. Roman was Italian through and through, complete with an outrageous flair for exaggeration. "Three nights. That's all, my friend. It's what we agreed. You'll pick me up on your way back."

"I have a good mind to leave you here for good. It's no better than you deserve."

Jack hugged his friend good-bye and left the boat, shaking hands with the captain and first officer as they stood formally on the dock. The last week at sea had been a heavenly voyage, following the coast of the Mediterranean along the French and Italian Riviera. On board Roman's luxury yacht, he had wanted for nothing. Roman's hospitality was famous the whole world over, but Jack was more than ready to set his feet on dry land.

And he wanted to spend that time in Portofino. The small fishing village on the Italian coast was the main reason he accepted Roman's invitation. Jack hadn't enjoyed a proper vacation in three years. Following the launch of his last album and a huge international tour in support of it, his life had been nothing but work. He became friends with Roman, who had designed the costumes for the tour. Jack was looking forward to a well-earned rest and Roman wanted to show off his latest expensive toy. When Jack heard the proposed cruise itinerary, he couldn't say no.

His success as a singer was mainly confined to the English-speaking countries of Northern Europe, America, and Australia. He could go relatively unrecognised through Southern Europe, so Spain, Italy, and France had always been his favourite holiday destinations.

He had visited beautiful Portofino ten years earlier, but the old village had been calling him back lately in memories and dreams, even through his music. Throughout the later stages of his tour, before Roman's generous offer, he was already planning his return. And now, at last, he was here again.

So long ago and yet nothing had changed, except for him. Standing on the harbour, looking at the small town clustered on the hills that surrounding it on three sides, he couldn't help smiling. He'd been warned not to go back or expect too much. It was inevitable things wouldn't be as good as he remembered them. But the naysayers were wrong. He felt like he'd never been away.

The pretty painted buildings were exactly as he remembered; the small hotels, boutiques, and restaurants remained unspoiled by the scars of consumerism which marred so many other beautiful tourist destinations. Portofino had no burger chains or corporate coffee shops and was all the better for it.

It was early, not yet ten in the morning, and the small town had barely shrugged off the cowl of night. Only a handful of shops were open. It was early in the season too, late March. The tourists wouldn't arrive in earnest for another three or four weeks. Then the small harbour would be packed with powerboats and ferries, bringing so many day visitors. But now, the peace was complete.

He hoped it would remain so for the duration of his stay.

Jack gathered up his light baggage and set off around the promenade. A decade might have passed since his last visit, but it was as familiar as yesterday. The narrow streets and the piazza were exactly as he remembered and hoped he would find them. His apartment was only a few steps away.

His PA, Cheryl, had made the reservation. "What do you want an apartment for? You know, there are no facilities, barely any service. Just a maid coming in once a day. Why not go for one of the bigger hotels around the hill? They'll have everything you need."

"No," he insisted, "this is the place I want. I've spent two years living in hotels and eating room service. The apartment is all I need."

What he didn't tell Cheryl was that he'd already stayed here before. He knew exactly what to expect and was delighted to find nothing had changed here either.

A beautiful Italian girl with soulful eyes and ravishing black hair greeted him with the keys and showed him inside. "I come to clean at ten each day," she said. "Okay?"

"Perfect."

And it was. The apartment was characterised by exposed stone walls and arched doorways, antique furnishings and original décor. It was a mini homecoming. Jack felt a rush of emotion as memories of the past came crashing into the present. The ghost of his younger self haunted these ancient rooms: the happiness he felt here ten years earlier, the flush of first love experienced at the age of twenty. The sights, the smells, the feelings.

Jack wondered for the first time whether he had done the right thing in coming back.

❖

Stefano Dante was reversing his truck down a narrow alley when a figure caught his eye for one brief moment. In the space between two buildings, he glimpsed a man with golden skin and thick blond hair for no more than a second. Stefano stepped hard on the brake, but by that time the man was gone, walking in the direction of the Piazza. Stefano held the brake and continued to stare through the empty gap.

It couldn't be him. Could it? Surely not after all this time. No, it was nothing more than a passing stranger with a resemblance, seen too fast for the eye to discern the difference. Jack. How long had it been? Eight years? Nine? A long time. They might pass each other on the street these days and not know each other. Ten years, was it? Maybe more. A man can change a lot in that time.

But just for a moment, it had looked so much like him.

Stefano released the brake and continued to back up. He had no time for daydreaming or reminiscences. He had a truck full of supplies that the restaurant needed.

The head chef and two of his assistants were waiting as he backed up to the door. They started unloading the cases of fish, meat, and vegetables from the rear before he cut the engine. There was much to be done to prepare for the lunch orders. Even early in the season, Stefano prided himself on the freshness of the food in his restaurant, and he visited the market every morning to ensure they had the very best.

Leaving the kitchen staff to their work, he passed straight through the restaurant, where Lucia, his head waitress, and two of the waiters were laying the tables with linen cloths. He cast a careful eye over their work as he passed. His staff was excellent, and the keen attention of a manager ensured they stayed that way.

Stefano stepped out onto the small terrace that overlooked the bay. The mid-morning sun cast diamond ripples on the clear blue water. Stefano shielded his eyes against the glare and searched the waterfront for signs of the blond stranger. He knew it wasn't Jack. It couldn't be. And yet he looked for him just the same, scanning the harbour hopefully.

A small group of tourists made their way toward the Church of St Martin. The man was not among them. A young couple stood taking photographs of the spectacular white yacht slowly exiting the harbour. He wasn't there, either. Stefano searched the full curve of the bay and saw nothing. Whoever the man was, he wasn't here now.

He sighed softly. His heart felt unexpectedly heavy. This reaction was crazy, raising his hopes so high because a stranger he'd glimpsed for barely a second reminded him of a man from a long time ago. Not just any man, that was true. Consciously or unconsciously, Jack was the man he'd judged all men against since that distant summer. He had known many good men since, but no one quite like Jack.

"What's with the face?" Lucia came out onto the terrace with two cups of coffee, very black, very strong.

"Caught in a moment," Stefano said. They sat at a waterfront table, enjoying the warmth and tranquillity.

"Care to share it?" she asked.

"It's nothing," he said, summoning a smile. "Just a memory from a long time ago."

"A good memory?"

He nodded and smiled. "A little bittersweet, but a good one nonetheless."

❖

Jack restlessly paced the pavement in front of the restaurant. Most of the tables on the terrace were taken, though a couple remained empty in the shade toward the back. If he didn't make a move soon, those would go too. His heart was racing, and his mouth was dry.

This was ridiculous. He had performed onstage to thousands with less apprehension than this. His hands trembled, and he'd already wasted half an hour approaching the terrace before shying away to circle the harbour again.

Get a grip on yourself, Jack, this is what you came for.

But a small voice inside continued to nag him. *You should never go back. Things won't be the same.* He knew that already. Things couldn't be the same, not after so long. A town like Portofino didn't change much in ten years, but people did. He certainly had. So what was the problem?

Summoning the performance skills he used to get onstage, Jack took a deep breath and approached the restaurant terrace. This was it. He was doing it, no turning back.

A striking-looking waitress in her early forties greeted him with a smile.

"Could I get a table for one?" he asked, returning the smile.

"Of course."

She led him to the two remaining tables on the terrace and gave him the choice. Jack chose the round table with the best view of the sea. His insides were still in turmoil, but he hid it well.

"My name is Lucia," the waitress said in perfect English as she presented the leather-bound menu. "Would you like something to drink while you choose?"

"A glass of champagne."

With another perfect smile, Lucia left him to study the menu. Jack dry swallowed. He glanced at the words on the page, but didn't understand their meaning. This was crazy. He was thirty-one years old. He had travelled all over the world. This was no way to behave.

A waiter appeared and served a table to his left with two steaming plates of mussels. Jack turned instinctively to look. The waiter was darkly Italian with a handsome face and a tight physique. He had long legs and a great ass, but he wasn't who Jack was looking for. Jack exhaled slowly. Just because the restaurant's website stated the owner/manager was a man called Stefano Dante, that didn't mean he would be here today. Or that the information was even up to date, for God's sake. He'd been too excited to learn Stefano still lived and worked in Portofino to actually double-check the facts.

Finally, he read the menu properly.

A shadow fell across the table. "Your champagne, sir."

A man's voice. It was older but unforgettable.

Jack turned as the man set down the sparkling flute, condensation gently misting its sides. As the man turned to look at him, time stood still.

"*Stefano*," Jack whispered.

"Oh my God. It *is* you!"

Jack was on his feet, and they suddenly had their arms around each other. Stefano's trunk was fuller now, more muscular than the young man he used to know, but his embrace was comforting and familiar.

"I don't believe it," Stefano said as they finally broke their hold. "What are you doing here?"

"I'm on a small vacation," Jack said. "Only three days. I've been dying to come back here for years. Now it's finally happened."

He stood back to look at Stefano properly. He had hardly changed. He was slightly matured, broader, stronger. If anything, he was even sexier than he used to be. His youthful cuteness had transformed into something fuller and more handsome. The last time they met, Stefano was just a boy. He had grown up to be a real man.

They sat face-to-face. Jack looked deep into Stefano's dark eyes. Though he'd dreamed about them so many times, he'd forgotten just how powerfully hypnotic those eyes were. "You own this place now?"

He nodded eagerly. "For almost two years, yes."

"Have you been here all this time? In Portofino?"

"I spent some time away," he said. "Studying. But I always came back during the summer to work. I was never away for long. I couldn't bear it. My soul is here."

Jack laughed. "That's no surprise. I couldn't imagine you being anywhere but here. I'm so glad to see you are. It wouldn't be the same without you."

"How about you? Where do you call home?"

Jack shrugged. "I don't know where I would call home. I've never lived in one place long enough to set down roots. I have an apartment in New York, so you could say that's my home, but I really don't spend much time there."

"You have not changed," Stefano said warmly. "Always travelling. I remember how you used to talk about seeing the whole world."

Jack smiled, remembering that young, idealistic version of himself. He'd been to a vast number of places all over the world, but had seen so little of them besides airports, hotels, and studios. His twenty-year-old self would hardly believe it was possible. Those were innocent, untroubled times.

Stefano insisted they have lunch together, instructing Lucia to take over management of the shift. "And bring us a whole bottle of champagne. I haven't seen my friend in so long, we have a lot to celebrate."

And they did. Across a long lunch of steamed clams, then langoustines followed by a rich chocolate torte, they talked about the last ten years and the highs and lows it had brought them. Jack tried to play down his success as a singer. Neither Stefano nor his staff treated him like a superstar, and that was exactly how he liked it. He told Stefano he was an entertainer and left it at that.

"Do you still play your guitar?" Jack asked as the desserts were cleared away.

"Only for my own amusement," Stefano said. "No one here would want to hear the noise I make."

"You were a wonderful player."

Jack remembered the night the two of them climbed the cliff above the town and lit a small fire. They'd had a bottle of cheap red wine, a selection of cured meats, and a guitar. Stefano played while Jack serenaded him deep into the night. As the fire died, they came together and found warmth in each other's bodies. In all the years since and all the places he'd been to, Jack had never known a night of such carefree abandon.

An English couple in their late forties tentatively approached the table. "Excuse me, Jack," the woman said. "We hate to bother you when you're having lunch, but we're such big fans of yours. We've seen you in concert three times now. I know this is terribly rude, but could we possibly trouble you for an autograph?"

Stefano grinned while Jack signed his name on the back of a postcard and posed for selfies with the delighted couple. "So," he said, as Jack sat down again. "I'm thinking you did not tell me the whole story about your life since Portofino."

Jack raised both hands. "Okay. Guilty. Sorry. I didn't want to make a big deal of it." He still didn't. It was just bad luck being recognised like that. He thought he would be safe this early in the season. The world was becoming an increasingly small place. He should know that better than anyone.

"You should be proud of your success, not ashamed of it," Stefano said. "I always knew you would do something special. You were such an amazing singer. Even when it was just the two of us, you gave everything to every song you sang. You must be very famous now, if people ask for your autograph. It's such an honour that you came back to visit Portofino."

"Stefano, please, this is why I didn't tell you. I don't want things to change between us. Anyway, I didn't come back to visit Portofino. I came back to see you."

Stefano looked straight at him. His face was unreadable. The words lingered in the air between them.

Jack wondered if he had made a terrible mistake. Of all the things they'd discussed, the one they had avoided so far was their personal life. What if Stefano was with someone now? He might not want to remember the intimacy of their affair, thinking it better forgotten. He might be married now and have a family. *How could I have been so stupid as not to think of that before?*

"You came to see me?"

"Yes."

Stefano gave a beautiful smile, and suddenly he was twenty years old again. "Then we shouldn't waste a moment. Let me speak to Lucia, and I will take the rest of the day off. I can't believe this. It must be a dream."

"I feel the same, but it's no dream. This is very real."

"Where are you staying?"

Jack couldn't stop smiling. "Would you believe me if I said the same place as before?"

Stefano's dark eyes widened. "The apartment?"

"Couldn't come to Portofino and stay anywhere else."

❖

They made love under the same roof, in the same bed they had shared ten years earlier. Older now, both more experienced, but the act of coming together was not so different. It was a profound fusion of lust, excitement, and exploration, but they possessed a confidence missing from their youthful union. Jack had thought this moment might never happen. Even today, arriving at the harbour, he was doubtful of finding the thing he'd yearned for all this time.

He'd imagined this moment. Dreamed about it. Even written songs about it. One of them, "A Future Night of Love," was one of his biggest hits, top ten in eighteen countries. But no dream or song compared to this sweet reality.

They were naked on top of the king-sized bed in the sultry heat of late afternoon. Two perfect, strongly muscled bodies. Jack pressed his pale skin against Stefano's dark, coppery tones. Constantly moving, limbs sliding between each other, hard cocks duelling as their mouths locked.

Jack thrust his tongue into Stefano's mouth. Tasting him, wanting to experience his body with every sense. The warm, spicy scent of his skin, the firmness of his muscle, the magnificent curve of his ass.

Ever since he became famous, people had thrown themselves at Jack: groupies, models, actors, and serious hunks with amazing bodies, but none of them compared to Stefano. He lit a spark no other man could ignite for Jack.

Jack gripped Stefano's weighty cock. Even that was thicker, more mature than he remembered.

"I want this inside me," Jack said, squeezing his dick. "*Now*."

Stefano put on a condom and gave him what he wanted. Getting between Jack's legs, raising his ankles to his shoulders, he lubed his cock and Jack's tender hole and entered. Slowly, carefully, pushing deep.

They were lovers once again.

As darkness fell over the Mediterranean, the harbour of Portofino became a twinkling semicircle of light. Music and chatter drifted from the restaurants and cafés to the balcony of Jack's apartment, underscored by the bombastic crash of the waves against the rocky coastline.

"This is Heaven," Jack remarked softly. "Heaven on Earth."

They stood on the balcony in just their underpants. The sea air was refreshingly cool on Jack's bare skin, especially after the heat of the bedroom and the intensity of their lovemaking.

Stefano slipped a hand around Jack's waist and pulled him close. "It's Heaven because you're here. The rest of the time, it's just a pretty village by the sea."

Jack wrapped his arm around Stefano and leaned into him. It was perfect indeed—the night, the place, and the man. What a fool he'd been, waiting so long to come back.

He had two more days and nights until *The Crystal Sea* returned to take him away from here, from a place he loved. From the man he loved.

"This will be over so soon, and I don't want it to be."

"Let's enjoy what we have now," Stefano said, "and not spoil it by worrying about tomorrow or the next day."

But Jack couldn't help it. He was a worrier. It had taken him ten years to find his way back here. The prospect of another ten was unthinkable. They would both be forty then, and another decade would have been wasted. Stefano couldn't leave Portofino, and Jack would never ask him to. What the hell could he do about it?

"I can't be here all the time," Jack said. "I have to travel all over for work."

Stefano squeezed him tight. "I understand this."

"I don't think you do. What I'm trying to say is, I'll be back very soon. I have a few commitments to honour in America and England, and then I'll start work on my next album. I'm going to write that album here, Stefano. Right here. I'm going to rent this house for the whole summer and work on my songs."

Stefano turned to look at him, his eyes shining bright in the dark evening.

Jack grinned. The idea had only occurred to him in that moment, and it was already absolute. His manager would have a shit fit. The record company would expect him to work in New York like he always did. He didn't care.

"What inspiration," he said. "The sea, the village, you, your guitar. This will be the best thing I've ever done. I just know it."

They were kissing again, bodies yielding to each other.

And after the summer? Who knew? He didn't want to think beyond this night.

But he was certain Stefano and Portofino were part of his life now, and that's how it would stay.

No more wasted years.

WHAT A COINCIDENCE

Matthew Bright

O n their first date, Winston and Travis talked about time travel.
It was because of the card game, a daft suggestion by
Winston's roommate as Winston was heading out of the door. Perfect
first date material, the Wolfman claimed. Breaks the ice. Pick a card,
ask the question, and voila: instant chemistry. And if anyone knew
about chemistry, the Wolfman did.

Winston was first to arrive, and in a nervous spiral, pocketed
and unpocketed the box of cards four times before finally deciding
that he might as well let the geek flag fly from the offset and damn
the consequences. It was unusually decisive for him, but downing a
full glass of wine helped.

"Would you like the rest of the bottle, sir?" asked the waiter.

Winston mentally tallied up his bank account. Twenty-five
dollars—possibly—and five dollars in change jangling in his pocket.
He definitely could not afford a full bottle of wine. "Yes, please,"
he said.

The *sir* made him a bit uncomfortable. In fact, now that he
had settled a little, so did the entire restaurant. This place was
several steps above the three-for-ten-dollar pizza joint on the corner
Winston regularly frequented. For a start, there was a waiter, for
seconds, there was that *sir*. Winston was quite certain he wasn't old
or mature enough to be a "sir" yet. And for thirds, he was fairly
certain he recognised one of the customers in the private booth from
television.

His discomfort must have shown. When he glanced toward the

older couple at the next table—one short, one almost comically tall, and both with salt-and-pepper beards—the shorter of the two caught his eye and smiled reassuringly. "First date?" the man inquired. "You have the look. Sort of hunted, but horny."

Winston smiled politely. "That obvious, is it?" He indicated his clothes, which felt hideously shabby, though they were the smartest he had. "He chose the restaurant, as I'm sure you can guess."

"Not your kind of place?"

"I'm a drama student. I can barely afford to walk here, let alone eat here. But's he a scientist. I think."

The short one laughed. "You poor baby. Have you met this mystery man yet, or is this a blind date?"

"I've seen photographs."

"Ahhhh." The short one winked knowingly. "From an *app*, is he?"

"No! Worse. From my mother. You know how they are. Find out someone they know is gay, and it's all, 'You should meet my son!'"

"My commiserations—" The man broke off, looking over Winston's shoulder. "Actually, I take that back." He looked away and theatrically hid his face behind a slice of garlic bread.

"Hello. Sorry I'm late!"

Winston leapt up. Travis had appeared at the door without Winston noticing and was removing his coat and scarf. The pictures didn't do him justice. Astonishingly attractive, he was tall, blond, and boyish without seeming fey. Striding purposefully across the room, he put Winston in mind of a lion prowling majestically on the savannah, and then he smiled as he drew near, fussing prissily with his scarf and gloves, and Winston downgraded the comparison. A stuffed lion perhaps. Still a bit wild, but more huggable.

Suddenly, bankruptcy didn't seem all that bad.

An awkward handshake-hug-no-handshake-no-hug ensued, punctuated by the arrival of the waiter. "Your bottle, sir."

Winston froze. "Ah, yes. Sorry. That's for, er, both of us, actually. Not just me. Sorry, presumptuous…"

Travis took the bottle and inspected the label. "Good choice," he said. "That'll be fine."

Winston sank miserably into his chair. "I hope you like red."

"I do, actually. It's my favourite." Travis smiled, and Winston perked up.

"Good."

"Yes."

Neither of them could find anything much to say after that, and they took an excruciating minute to stare in opposite directions around the restaurant. Winston noticed a lot of male-male couples dining, which was no surprise given they were in the fashionably gay quarter of town, but they made him feel self-conscious. Judging by their clothes, wristwatches, and choice of drinks, most of the clientele were considerably more wealthy and sophisticated.

Travis, on the other hand, fitted right in.

"It's nice to meet you at last," said Winston, once he had closely inspected the specials boards, the curtain rails, and the light fittings. It had begun to rain outside, and he conceded that as an early escape would involve getting soaked, he might as well make some effort. "My mother has told me a lot about you."

"Wonderful!" said Travis brightly. A little too brightly, perhaps, or was Travis imagining it? "She's said a great deal about you, too."

"That," said Winston, "is almost literally the last thing a boy wants to hear on a date."

"Sorry!" Travis looked awkwardly at his menu.

They really were marvellous light fittings, on second inspection. Winston took a deep breath. "Okay, look, so, I'm not very good at small talk and date stuff, as my mother probably told you, so…"

"She did mention you were socially awkward. She said it was odd because you were great onstage, but terrible with real—"

"Yes, thank you. Remind me to thank her deeply and fully for that later. Anyway, the Wolfman gave me this card game ice-breaker type thing. Maybe…Do you fancy…?"

Travis looked slightly aghast, as if Winston had in fact stripped naked and climbed up on the table. Winston bit his lip. Of course, playing cards in a restaurant like this, it was stupid.

"The *Wolfman*?"

Winston shrugged. "Sorry, yes. Should've mentioned. He's my roommate."

"Ah, of course. Is he hairy?"

"Not particularly."

"Oh. Well, sure. Let's put this in the Wolfman's hands. Fire away."

Winston unpacked the cards, shuffled them. "Sorry, I know this is really cheesy." He carefully watched Travis, who just shrugged and smiled faintly. He looked noncommittal, but at least he hadn't laughed the cards off out of hand.

"You know," Travis said, "I was reading a journal a couple of months ago, and there was an article about a set of questions you can ask someone, and by answering them, it makes them fall in love with you. Or something. It's a bit more complicated than that. You have to look them directly in the eyes all the way through, I think."

Winston flipped over the first card and leaned forward, fixing his gaze directly on Travis's. "First question: 'If you could only eat pizza forever, or pie, which would you choose?'"

Travis thought for a second. "I don't think that's one of the 'fall in love' questions."

He's smirking, Winston thought. He thinks this is ridiculous. I wonder if *his* mother hounded him to go on a date, too? The pity date with the socially awkward, possibly alcoholic, drama student who brought a card game to a swanky restaurant. "It'd work on me," Winston said. "I *really* like pizza."

From the next table, Winston heard someone slapping their own forehead, hard. Winston glanced over at the short man who had spoken to him earlier, but the man was sitting, smiling innocently back at him.

"Well, I'd have to say pie. For reasons I'm sure are obvious," said Travis.

Winston had absolutely no idea what the obvious reasons were but didn't dare ask in case "idiot" was added to the list of words to describe Travis's awful date.

"Another card?"

Travis shrugged. "If you like."

Winston translated this as *please god, no more*, but he'd committed to the course now and found he couldn't really stop. "Okay, 'If you could time travel to anywhere and any time, where and when would you choose?'"

Travis delicately folded his napkin and spread it on his knee. "Well..."

"Excuse me, are you gentlemen ready to order?" The waiter hovered stork-like at Travis's elbow.

"Well, I am," Winston said. He had checked out the menu earlier and carefully worked out what he could afford to buy. "I'll have the seafood special, please," he said, handing the closed menu to the waiter in what he fondly imagined was the confident, familiar manner of a man who ate in these kinds of restaurant all the time.

"Oh, I'm sorry sir. I'm afraid the seafood special is from the lunch menu. We're serving the dinner menu now. Perhaps I gave you the wrong one by accident?"

Winston very carefully did not look at Travis across the table. He plucked the menu gingerly from the waiter's hands. "I'll just take that back, thank you."

He opened the menu and looked it up and down. The prices were different. Still, if he walked home, rather than got the bus...

"Er—I'll just have the plaice. Thank you."

Travis peered at him over his own menu. "No starter? The pâté here is incredible."

Winston bit his lip and shook his head. He had never eaten pâté, and suspected he would not like it. "I'm fine."

"Okay, then. Well, me neither. I'll have the same as my friend." Friend. Ouch.

The waiter removed their menus and faded away.

"Go on then," said Winston. The menu mix-up had stung him, and he blamed Travis for some reason. Sixty minutes—ninety, tops—of strained conversation, and then they could go their separate ways: Travis in a taxi to some penthouse where he would probably eat pâté, and Winston on foot back to his student pit where he would eat an entire pack of digestive biscuits and call his mother to tell her never to ever set him up on a date again. Sixty minutes, and the least Travis could do was play the game. "If you could time travel anywhere…"

Travis ran his hand through his hair thoughtfully. Winston wilted a little, feeling faintly guilty for his rancour. Travis really was very attractive. Whilst this was quite arousing, it also made Winston hideously aware of his own shortcomings: short, thickening round the middle, in an outfit that probably cost less than the price of Travis's scarf.

"I think I'd go to—"

He was cut off by a loud *ching-ching-ching* ringing through the restaurant. At the next table, the man who had talked to Winston earlier had climbed up on his chair and was holding a glass aloft. "Ladies, gentlemen, and undecided, if I could have your attention for one moment, please!"

His tall companion buried his face in his hands. "Oh god," he mumbled through his fingers. "He is such a drama queen."

"A momentous occasion! Today is the thirtieth anniversary of the day that I met this wonderful man right here. Yes, him. The one that's about to hide under the table. The love of my life, without whom I would be nothing. Ladies and gentlemen, to my husband!"

His companion peeked through his fingers, looking half-embarrassed, half-pleased. Around the restaurant, people clapped and raised their glasses.

"And furthermore—"

"Nope." His companion hauled him down and pinned him to his seat. "Quite enough, thank you." He kissed him firmly on the lips. "I love you, but shh."

Beneath the sound of applause, Winston saw him mouth, "I love you, too."

And then, spectacle over, everyone returned to their own meals and their own conversations. Once even the gawkiest had looked away, Winston leaned over and extended a hand. "Congratulations to you both," he said. "Thirty years is good going."

The man beamed at him. "Tell me about it," he said. "But thank you."

"I'm Winston. This is Travis."

"Lovely to meet the pair of you," said the man, and then to Travis, "We were just talking about you before you came in. His mother's a big fan of your homosexuality. This is, er, Trevor. And I'm W…Winifred."

His husband flinched. "Winifred?"

"Yes," he said. "Winifred."

Travis shook the man's hand. "That's an unusual name. I didn't know it was a, er…"

"A man's name? Yes. It is."

That seemed to settle things.

"So," Winifred continued without pause, "how's your first date going? Oh, don't look so surprised, Travis. I'm an old queen, I've seen things. Of course you're on a first date. I can smell the fear. Also, Winston told me before you arrived."

Travis remained open-mouthed, looking sidelong at Winston, clearly unsure how to respond to his short, erratic man. Winston, for his part, was starting to feel unexpectedly at home. The restaurant might be alien territory, but people like Winifred were in every nook and cranny of the drama school.

"Well, you know, our mothers colluded and now we're here. It's how all the great romances started."

This seemed to please Winifred. "Oh, delightful! Young love is so nice to see, y'know, in the wild. Trevor and I's first date was dis-asssss-trous. He thought I was uncouth. Uncouth and possibly an alcoholic, and I thought he was stuck-up and boring. Still, all worked out, didn't it?"

Winston chanced a glance at Travis, who caught his eye. He thought he caught a glimpse of that smirk again, only this time it was directed at Winston. Conspiratorial, almost. Perhaps there was hope yet.

Winifred prodded Trevor. "Didn't it?"

With an air of rehearsal, Trevor nodded. "Never happy, dear."

Winifred cupped an ear. "I'm sorry?"

"Never happier, dear."

"Quite right. Ooh, what's this?" Winifred plucked the card from the table. "'If you could time travel to anywhere and any time, where and when would you choose?'"

Trevor choked into his glass.

"It's an ice-breaker thing," Winston muttered, suddenly acutely embarrassed. "The Wolfman…"

"It's an interesting question. How about you, husband mine? Where would you go?" Winifred fixed Trevor with that half-smile, half-cocked-eyebrow look of someone sharing a private joke.

"You know that answer well," Trevor said. "I would go back to our very first date—"

"Aww, how sweet!"

"—and warn myself away." Trevor ducked a light slap. "No, of course not. But that's where I'd go. I'd like to see myself looking young and thin again, not to mention this old thing." He jerked a thumb at Winifred.

"Me, I'd go back to Shakespeare's London and watch *A Midsummer Night's Dream* at the Globe," said Winston.

"What a coincidence!" Winifred said. "Me too! Though you'd have a job, actually. The Globe wasn't built when *A Midsummer Night's Dream* was written."

Trevor laid a hand on his husband's arm. "*Winifred*, darling, I think we should leave these two to their date, don't you?"

"Of course. Sorry, sorry! No one's ever going to get laid with some old queen banging on at them, are they? Don't let me get in the way."

Forced back into each other's orbits, Winston and Travis were struck for a second time with a complete absence of anything to say.

"Another card?"

"Yes," said Travis, a little too quickly.

"'What would you like to be when you grow up?'"

They pondered.

"I'd settle for 'reasonably functional adult'," said Winston.

Travis bit his lip and reached for his wine.

"Sorry," Travis said. "I mean, go on. What about you?"

"Well, I guess I *am* a grown-up."

Beneath the tablecloth, Travis screwed the napkin into a tight knot around his hand. Above the level of the table, he smiled politely. "Of course. Yes. But are you doing what you want to do now? You're a scientist, right?"

"I'm a mathematician."

"That's…that's exciting, too."

From the next table, Winston heard the slap to the forehead again.

"No, I mean, it is, right?" said Winston. "I mean, if that's what you've always wanted to be?"

"It is, actually. Numbers are the answer to everything. If you understand mathematics, you understand the universe. Honestly, it's far less dull that it sounds." Clearly, Winston didn't look too convinced, because he carried on. "Okay, so say you had a pizza…"

"I really don't like pizza that much, if that's the impression I gave you, and oh my god, I've just got what you meant about pie now."

"Right, well, if you have a pizza that has a radius Z and height A, the pizza has a volume of Pi x Z x Z x A."

There was the sound again. Travis and Winston swivelled their heads in tandem, but as before, Winifred smiled back innocently at them, his forehead a livid red.

Travis sighed. "Maybe you have to write it down for it to be funny."

"So what you really mean," said Winston thoughtfully, "is that if you understand mathematics, you know the secrets of pizza."

"Something like that. More wine?"

Winston watched the bottle empty. "I read that in a room with more than twenty-three people, there is a fifty percent chance of someone else having the same birthday as you."

"I'm not a statistician."

"Oh."

"February 23rd, though."

"Right, okay. Should I—I mean, mine's October 31st."

"What a *coincidence!*" Winifred interjected himself back into their conversation, brandishing a breadstick. "Sorry, sorry—but that's my birthday too! What are the chances?"

"Fifty percent, apparently," said Travis.

"If I had to bet who had February 23rd, I'd say her," said Winston, pointing to a large woman with an extravagant ponytail that fell to her waist. He was glad Winifred had returned. Every time Winston spoke to him, he felt like a naughty schoolchild giggling in a corner. It was much easier than conversing with Travis, no matter how pretty he was. "I don't know why, she just looks like a February 23rd to me."

"Did you say February 23rd?" said Winifred. "What a *coincidence!* That's Trevor's."

Travis furrowed his brow. "The two of *you* have the same birthdays as the two of *us*? That seems…very unlikely."

Winifred leaned forward, eyebrows raised dramatically. "Does it?"

Winston joined him. "Yeah. You did say you weren't a statistician. I mean, can you be sure?"

"Plaice," said the waiter, inserting himself between the two tables.

"Thank you."

"I assume actor?" said Travis, when they had been eating for several minutes and the silence had graduated from acceptable-pause-to-chew to awkward-absence-of-conversation. "Your answer, I mean? You're studying drama, right? And you wanted to visit the Globe."

"Actually," Winston said, "I don't. Drama school just puts me in the right industry. What I really want to be is a set dresser."

A chair scraped. "What a *coincidence!*"

❖

When the main course was done, a communal affair despite Trevor's best efforts to distract his garrulous husband, Winifred excused himself to the bathroom. "Actually," Travis said, "I need to nip, too. Excuse me."

"Sorry about Winifred," said Trevor, when the two were left alone. "He's a wonderful husband but he can be rather intrusive. He says he was a quiet child, so he's making up for it now."

"Oh don't worry," said Winston. He bundled up his napkin and tossed it into the centre of the table, dejected. "If I'm totally honest about it, I'm quite glad of the pair of you. Not going to work out, this date, is it? Completely different people. It's his stuck-up restaurant—no offence—and he's older, richer, sophisticated...er. See. Sophisticated-er. Not even a word. Why are you laughing?"

"You youth are so adorable. And blind."

"What do you mean?"

"He's trying to impress you."

"Impress me?" Winston had begun to feel like he was in the middle of a very stressful audition. With Travis's lion-like beauty and detached confidence, it hadn't for one second occurred to Winston that Travis might be in any way seeking his approval.

"Yes. He's chosen a nice restaurant, dressed up smart, and he's acting all grown-up to impress the cute young student he thinks is out of his league."

"That," said Winston decisively, "is ridiculous."

"Trust me," said Trevor. "I've done this exact date. This exact date."

"I," said Winston, "have thirty dollars to my name. I cannot afford dessert if he suggests it. What on earth does he see in me?"

"Oh, this is brilliant," Trevor said. "I never get to do the 'wise old queen' thing. Brace yourself, darling. Firstly, thirty years have taught me money doesn't mean a damn thing if you love each other. And yes, I know, first date. Love is not a word to throw around, but we've all got to start somewhere. Secondly, he's a mathematician, so he has no more money than you do. He's just pretending. For a start, that wine is awful, and the pâté is famously average at this restaurant. He's making it up. I told you, he's trying to impress you."

"He's not rich?"

"He didn't have a starter either, did he? And he picked exactly the same thing as you, which I'm guessing is the cheapest on the menu? But really it's his shoes that give him away—scuffed, and there are holes in the bottom. Everything else is smart, because you don't need to replace them often. But he doesn't have the money for new shoes."

Winston sat back. "By any chance, are you a private investigator?"

Trevor scratched his head. "Actually, you're not going to believe it. I'm a mathematician."

Winston felt the urge to laugh, loudly and uncontrollably. "You're right. I'm not going to believe it."

"Never mind. But trust me, it's just an act to make you like him."

"It's terribly miscalculated."

"Yes, but he's locked into the course now. Can't back out."

"And you really think he's as broke as me?"

"I do. Shh, they're coming back."

Winston folded his arms. "I'm a fast runner," he said. "This will be fun."

❖

"Winifred was telling me that he did the set decoration for *Hellraiser 13*," said Travis as he took his seat.

"Thirteen?" said Winston. "I thought there were only eight."

"Straight to video," Trevor said. "*Hellraiser: Hellter Skellter.* And now we're the only one of our friends with an S&M coconut shy in our living room."

"Not the only one…"

"I think you two are remarkable, actually," said Travis. Winston looked at him, trying to tally up the signs that Trevor had pointed out, though he couldn't precisely stick his head under the table to check out his shoes. Was it possible that this absurdly handsome specimen was actually trying to win Winston over?

"Us, remarkable?" Winifred winked at Trevor. "Maybe just a little."

"I agree. Thirty years of happiness, all from one terrible date where you thought he was stuck-up and boring."

"Yes, well, he was just pretending. I soon saw through all of that."

"Thirty years, though! I think that deserves a drink—on us, of course. Don't you, Travis? I mean, thirty years!"

"Er, yes."

That look Winston recognised. It was the look of someone caught in a trap. Trevor really was observant, though Winston supposed it was always the quiet ones.

"Where's the waiter?"

"Can I help you, sir?"

"A whiskey each for my friends," Winston said. "And more wine? Not the house bottle this time."

Travis looked as if he had been run over. "Er, I'm okay, actually."

"Nonsense. We need something to drink with dessert."

"Dessert? Well, I wasn't going to—"

"A bottle of red and two chocolate fudge cakes. No, make that four."

"You're too kind," said Winifred.

"Yes," said Travis, "he is."

The waiter departed.

"How about another card?" said Winifred, flicking through the pack. "Ah, this is always a good one. 'Favourite sexual position?'"

All four spoke in unison.

"See," said Travis. "I told you numbers were the answer to everything."

❖

Three rounds of whiskey, coffee, and mints later, through which Travis grew paler and paler, Winifred and Trevor announced that it really was time for them to leave and thanked them effusively for their conversation and generosity.

"It was lovely to see the pair of you," said Winifred.

"Wonderful," said Trevor. "You're going to have many years of happiness before you, we're sure."

"Really," said Winifred, pulling on his coat. "We're sure."

In the vacuum of their absence, Winston raised a hand for the bill. "Quite a pair of characters, those two, weren't they?" he said.

"You can say that again," said Travis. "Especially that Winifred. Do you know what he was doing at the urinals? Looking me up and down, and going on about how skinny I am."

"Really?"

"Actually, his exact words were 'it's been years since I've seen you look this skinny'. Quite creepy, actually."

"There's definitely no *Hellraiser 13*, either. I looked it up on imdb. Just eight."

Winston pushed together the Wolfman's cards, turning them over so they all faced the same direction. "You dropped one," said Travis, bending down. He placed it on the top, face-up.

If you could time travel to anywhere and any time, where and when would you go?

"I know this sound ridiculous," said Travis carefully, "but you don't think they—"

"That would be impossible though, wouldn't it?"

"Yes. Yes it would."

"Unthinkable."

"Exactly."

The waiter arrived with the bill. Travis regarded it, looking worried.

"I have something to confess…"

"I think I know what it is."

"Oh?" Travis blushed. It was so transparently shamefaced, so vulnerable, that Winston wanted to reach over the table and give him a hug.

"Yes. I've suspected it since I first arrived. You're a fantastic runner, aren't you?"

"I'm a—no—what?"

"Me too. I'm really good at running."

"Oh." Travis's eyebrows shot up. "I see what you mean."

"Even better," said Winston, "it's only six blocks to my apartment. And the Wolfman is out. All night."

❖

"This is always my favourite bit," says the short one, watching the couple in the window. "The bit where they look at each other and say 'do you think?' and 'no, that would be ridiculous,' and then they both pretend that neither of them thinks it's true."

The tall one peers through the wet windscreen across the car park. "Have you considered the possibility that you're a sociopath?"

The short one tangles his fingers in the other's beard. "Yes, but that's why you love me."

The tall one leans down to kiss him. "Seems plausible. But please, no more Winifred."

"Oh come on, that was a tough one. How many names sound like Winston?"

"True. But the lord taketh, and the lord giveth. You couldn't ask for an easier opener than 'where and when would you time travel'."

"That one I'll grant you."

Across the car park, the front door of the restaurant opens, and two figures sprint away along the street, coats held over their heads to protect from the sluicing rain. "Ah," said the tall one, "I guess they didn't see our note."

On the corner, the couple pauses and leans in to each other to kiss.

"Young love," says the short one. He nestles against his companion. "Time to go home."

"Back to our S&M coconut shy?"

"That's the one."

The tall one starts the car. The short one lays his hand over his husband's on the gearstick. "Happy anniversary," says one to the other. "Happy anniversary," the other says in return. The car pulls away.

In the restaurant, a new couple are being ushered to the recently vacated table. The bill from the previous occupants is still there. One of them takes a peek.

> *To W&T,*
>> *We've paid the bill. Consider it paying it BACKWARD.*
>> *Here's to thirty years of happiness, for all of us.*
>>> *With love from W&T.*

FIREBRAND

Megan McFerren

Have you seen this new hacker show yet?

Nearly knocking over his coffee in his hurry to grab his phone, Keith stares for a moment at the message from Marie before answering. Never want to appear too eager, nor too available, right? Never want to answer too quickly. He sucks his lips between his teeth, holds his breath for a moment more, and sweeps open his phone.

No, is it terrible?

Terribly GREAT.

Keith snorts a laugh and taps quickly on the screen. Screw appearing unavailable. He is nothing if not entirely available.

Aren't you at work?

Compilinggggggzzzzz, she writes back. *Watching in the background.*

Don't spoiler me.

If you watch it before Saturday we can talk about it.

Keith sets his phone back to the desk, as her words and cheerful winking emoji tease a pleasant coil of heat through his chest and down through to his belly. He drums a muffled, broken rhythm with his fingertips against the paper cup of cooling coffee, and he waits for a coworker to pass behind him before he takes up his phone again, shoulders bent.

Okay, he answers, *but only because you recommended it. And the first time they do the TYPE REALLY FAST NONSENSE CODE thing, I'm out.*

She sends another emoji, the smiling face with blushing cheeks. Keith's cheeks warm, too. Does he dare? He takes a swig of lukewarm coffee. He does dare. He sends back an expression, winking, blowing a kiss.

A moment passes, enough to allow for Marie's phone to be unlocked. Another passes, if Marie was invested in the show she's watching while working. Another, and Keith holds his breath to keep back a curse.

Oh my, comes her message just as he's working up the nerve to apologize. *How saucy for so early in the day.*

It's not exactly sexting, Keith sends before he can stop himself, muffling a laugh as he rocks back in his chair. From daring to outright bold, he should feel prouder than he does, a nervous tremor jiggling his leg. He's at work. They both are. Surely they're not going to—

Too bad.

Keith's brow raises, and he reads her message again. And again and again and again until the stirring in his stomach gets to be too much and he forces a curt breath.

Saturday, he types back. *IRL.*

"Still at it, huh?"

Phone clattering to the desk, Keith is quick to turn it facedown. He knows he's blushing as he looks up at Sarah beside him, and he knows from the tilt of her brow that she can see it.

"Everyone does it," he tells her. "Dating, I mean. Online dating. Everyone does it."

Keith wishes he believed the words more, even as he says them. He's certainly heard them enough from well-intentioned friends and nosey acquaintances alike.

"You hate blind dates. You hate small talk," she says, with a nod to the phone beside him. He turns the phone over, screen down, and lasts only a heartbeat before turning it right side up again. Sarah grins, squinting, fingers folding around her mug of coffee. "You're the last person in this entire office I'd expect to be on Firebrand."

She's not wrong.

But since moving out of his hometown after college, Keith hasn't quite figured out how to make "meeting people" work in a big city. Meet-up groups have been a collection of the equally awkward, and classes give little time for socializing about anything but the work or lecture at hand. He'd contented himself with having a few close coworkers who could stave away the loneliness, until another acquaintance recommended Keith try Firebrand.

He'd heard of it, some new Silicon Valley darling that allowed the user to quickly scan through profiles with little obligation. If you and someone else agreed on liking the other, the app would connect you. Otherwise, you could just keep swiping. Unconvinced that even the most ornate algorithm could take the place of actual chemistry, Keith left the app untouched on his home screen for several weeks until beer and curiosity spurred him to finally fill in his profile.

Keith calculated his ratio of swiping *no* to *yes* as roughly twenty-to-one.

It hadn't gone well.

And then he found Marie, dark curls of hair spilling wild around a buck-toothed grin and laughing eyes. For a moment, Keith thought her profile was a fake. No one else he'd swiped by came anywhere close to holding his attention the way she did. But what her picture did for him paled in comparison to what he felt in reading her profile. She liked first-person shooters and baseball, and she wanted to spend less time in front of her screen and more time outdoors. She was prone to bingeing whole seasons of TV shows in one sitting, and she was a fan of Terry Pratchett. And she was an engineer, always laughing at his terrible coding jokes.

Or she types a laugh, anyway.

"How is it any different than being set up by someone else?" he asks Sarah. "Meeting someone who's a friend of a friend or...or my mom's neighbor's daughter."

"At least they're vouched for. You can't even be sure who you're speaking to. Oh!" she says, eyes widening. "What if you're being catfished?"

Keith's dry look pulls a laugh from her, before he shakes his head. "At least we've talked before we're going out. That's more than I can say for most dates where I've been set up."

"You've typed," she clarifies, "not talked. Don't you think that's weird?"

Keith finally slumps back with a sigh. "I don't like talking on phones. It makes me feel like I'm thirteen again."

"Fine, so it's weird, but it's your weird at least," she relents. "She must be pretty great to get you out of the house."

"She is great. She's incredible, actually. You know that I was up until three in the morning talking to her? Typing to her," Keith corrects, and Sarah nods sagely. "We argued about who should be the next Bond for like, half an hour straight. It came down to Hardy versus Elba."

"And she still wants to meet you? That is incredible."

"Tell me about it."

❖

Where are you?

By the window.

Keith surveys the little bistro. Only a dozen tables fill the small space, but two sides of the little corner restaurant are nothing but window, flashing bright with the lights of the cars passing on the busy street beyond. Every ticking second echoes in his chest. Five minutes going on ten too late, and each one exponentially increasing his desire to just go home and forget it. He sends another text before looking over the tables again:

Bluebird on 6th and Broadway right?

Young couple on a date. Old couple on a date. Guy sitting alone, tapping on his phone. Woman sitting alone, but definitely not Marie. A sudden snare jerks his stomach tight. Maybe this is all a bad joke. A really fucking bad joke. Maybe his shaggy dark hair is really just a mess and his body not lean but unattractively skinny. Maybe he is, as Sarah once informed him, crap at dressing himself beyond jeans and a hoodie. Maybe he should have never downloaded Firebrand, and maybe he should never have moved here at all. Maybe—

His phone blinks.

I'm here! I'll stand up.

A chair grinds against the floor a few feet away, and Keith looks up from the screen. Beside the window, a young man stands with expectant eyes turned toward the restaurant. He shoves a hand nervously through his ruddy hair and checks his phone, cradled in his palm.

Keith nearly drops his own when he sees another new message. *Do you see me?*

Or maybe Sarah was right about more than Keith's clothing choices, and he's actually been catfished.

Shit.

Their eyes meet. The man-who-isn't-Marie has freckles and a crooked smile. His collared shirt, beneath a woolen sweater, is recently pressed. They mirror each other's slack surprise as the restaurant seems to fade away. With a tilt of his head and amusement on his lips, the redhead taps against his phone again.

Hi.

"Fuck," Keith whispers, shoving a hand through his hair. "I mean, not fuck, I—"

"No, I agree," the man says with a weak laugh. "I thought you might look different from your picture, but I wasn't expecting this."

Keith's throat clicks, and he finally lets his phone slip heavy into his pocket. "Look," he manages, "I don't know what kind of game this is, but I'm not—"

"Cara."

"Cara?"

"You're not Cara."

"Who is Cara?"

"The woman I've been texting with for the last week and a half," the man says, raising a brow.

"And you're not Marie." Keith sucks his bottom lip between his teeth and holds it for a moment, releasing it with a failing laugh. "Are you?"

"Not last time I checked. Let's start over. Hi, I'm Alex," he says, extending his hand. "Who are you?"

"Keith," he says, allowing a brisk shake. When the room starts to swerve, he takes the chair across from Alex and sits on its edge. "So, you're not Marie."

"Is that who you've been texting?"

"I thought so. But you're not Marie."

"Still no, not even after the third time asking," Alex says, his nose wrinkling a little when he smiles. He settles back into his chair with his long arms draped across the back. Blowing a sigh toward the ceiling, he laughs, darkly delighted. "I see what's happened."

"Do you? Because it looks to me like you were faking a profile."

"Like I don't have better things to do," Alex replies. "You should read the news more, you wouldn't look so lost."

"I try to avoid it."

"I know, you've said. You should consider this the most extenuating of circumstances," Alex says, accepting a menu from the waiter.

Keith looks away, pressing the backs of his fingers to his cheeks to cool away the blush there. He's so hot, he's sure he must be scarlet.

"Pull up 'Firebrand hack'," Alex tells him. "I'm going to get a drink. Do you want one?"

"I think I need one," snorts Keith as he searches through his phone. "Whatever you're having." Keith hears Alex ordering a bottle of red wine as he searches the Internet. The spinning wheel on his screen disappears, replaced by bold headlines.

PRANKSTERS HACK FIREBRAND—FIREBRAND HACK PAIRED SAME-SEX USERS—DATING APP FIREBRAND MASKED USERS WITH OTHER PROFILES

"Fuck," Keith sighs again.

"You're much more eloquent in text. No wonder you weren't keen to use the phone."

"I thought you were someone else."

Alex's smile widens a little. "I am," he says with a grin, before lifting a hand to wave away the bad joke. "I'm exactly who I was then. I just don't look like whatever selfie they showed you."

"You're also a dude."

"Accurate," Alex says. "Is that a problem?"

Keith shakes his head before he can stop himself, and he can't help but wonder at the wisdom in immediate response. He meant to nod that yes—yes, this isn't what he was looking for. This isn't what he prefers. What he thinks he prefers. Because it should be a problem, shouldn't it?

Outside of a couple of awkward, quickly ended fumblings in college, he's had enough trouble trying to connect with one sex, let alone more than one. But the connection was there, over long nights and early morning meetings, flirtatious texts that weren't bound to any particular body. The connection is still here as Keith feels himself blush from the lingering look that Alex gives him.

"Did you get a chance to watch that show?" Alex asks suddenly, as the waiter puts a bottle of red wine and two glasses on the table.

"Did I—"

"The one I told you about," Alex says, tilting the wine into both their glasses.

"Yeah, I mean—yeah, it was great. How are you so calm right now?" he asks, his hands against the table and his voice dropping low. "Aren't you upset?"

"I think it's hilarious."

"Hilarious."

"I have to appreciate clever malware. They didn't grab any personal information, and they didn't compromise anything outside of our own presumptions. Besides, I've just spent a week and a half getting to know someone who, despite not looking quite like I expected, has had me attached to my phone like we were conjoined."

Keith sucks in a breath and holds it, as if he might at least find depth in his lungs when the rest of him feels so shallow. Alex hadn't deliberately deceived him. He wasn't pretending to be someone else. And Marie hadn't made Keith smile so hard his face ached.

It was Alex.

Alex who codes and binge-watches and loves a good argument. Alex with bright red hair and clever brown eyes and an easy smile. Alex who didn't laugh and walk away but takes even this surprise in stride, in favor of staying for drinks. For dinner. For maybe more.

Screw appearing unavailable. Keith is nothing if not entirely available. "I don't normally date," he says, taking up his wine for a bolstering sip.

"Men, or 'date' as verb?"

"Both. Never the former, rarely the latter. Do you?"

"Almost never, anyone," Alex answers. Keith watches as Alex rests his hand against his shoulder, fingers just beneath the pressed collar of his shirt, knuckles against his slender jaw. "It's a pain trying to find a person who clicks. I try not to be picky about what body they inhabit when I find someone worth leaving the apartment for."

Keith's chest aches, a curious bruising sensation, as if his heart is too big for his ribs and trying to press its way free. All his earlier thoughts about how the night might go suddenly shift. He isn't sure how the physical will play out, how it will feel to touch another body like his own rather than the soft curves he'd imagined. He isn't sure how it will feel to kiss someone with a bit of stubble, or how it will feel to run his hand over furry thighs instead of smooth.

He isn't sure, but his stomach tightens pleasurably all the same, and none of that changes the fact that he still wants to spend time curled on the couch with the person who has already made his life so much more enjoyable just by lighting up the screen on his phone.

"Okay. We're both engineers," Keith finally says, and Alex nods. "And when we write something new, we don't just release it out into the wild, right?"

"Right."

"We test it."

"Until we're sick of looking at it," agrees Alex with a grin.

"So before we commit," Keith suggests with a shrug and a small smile, "maybe we should test."

Alex glances around the bistro, and Keith does too, his tongue pressed between his lips. Small groups and couples speak low and laugh over the candles that provide pale light on each table. No one pays them any mind, all too busy making their own connections. Keith turns back to Alex, and when Alex leans forward, Keith does too.

Their mouths meet, almost chaste, as they hold a soft kiss above their glasses of wine. With the tang of red wine tannins sweet against their tongues, they deepen the kiss just enough to test their own coding, and when Alex breaks the kiss with a grin, Keith is smiling too.

"We should—"

Does he dare?

He does.

"Pay for the wine and ditch this place?" Keith offers.

Alex narrows his eyes, delighted. "Get take-out and watch a movie," he counters.

"Or a series."

"The entire thing," Alex agrees, extending a finger to stroke down Keith's fingers where they clasp the stem of his glass. "Or at least a season."

"At least."

"I already miss having emojis to reply with." Alex laughs.

"It's okay," he says, curling his finger over Alex's. "Now I can see you blush in person."

CONVERSATIONS WITH AN ANGEL

Kevin Klehr

He said your heart wants to protect the other person while your head tries to protect yourself." Farnham stared at me as if I'd farted. "What's the matter?"

"He said the same thing to me."

"I guess it's his token advice."

Even with this curious look, he still was the man I wanted to share my life with. For six months, I'd found sanctuary each time I visited his one-bedroom apartment. It was always messy when I showed up, and, like a dutiful husband, I'd whip out the rag and the cleaning products I bought for him and get to work.

But it went with the territory. It was him, and he truly had me under his spell. And even though at first his weekend sleep-ins, his habit of buying gadgets he didn't need, and his unbreakable pattern of always showing up an hour late to anything we'd planned irked me, in time they were the little quirks that made him who he was.

And let's face it, when you wake next to someone who is clutching your naked body with their hand on your chest while you cushion their waist with your ass, you know there's no use sweating the small stuff.

My phone rang. Farnham groaned, but not in a good way. "It's her, isn't it?" he asked.

I checked the screen. I nodded. "You know I have to answer."

"No, Jamal, you don't have to answer. Can't you put that thing on silent?"

"It doesn't matter. It stopped now."

"But we both know it will ring again. Just wait five minutes. She'll ring again!"

"Babe, do we have to?"

He stared through me as if I wasn't there. *Great start to the morning*, I thought. *Two people I love are going to be cross with me.* I wiggled my ass against him.

"That's not going to work, Jamal."

"Isn't it? It feels like it's working."

He grinned. "Smoke and mirrors. That's your weapon, smoke and mirrors."

I pushed back harder while I held my phone near his face, then with a master stroke of my thumb, switched it to silent mode. I placed it on the bedside table, turned to him, and planted the sloppiest kiss I could muster on his willing lips. He was mine, but more importantly, I had to show him I was his.

❖

"I dare you not to look at that phone," he said. His tone was half pleading, half demanding.

"Hun, I have to see what she wants."

He gritted his teeth. With only one shoe on, I checked my phone. She'd left three messages in the last half hour, one saying I had chores to do around the house, one saying she needed to tell me something private, and the last informing me my brother hadn't been home all night.

"I can already guess what your mother has texted," Farnham said. His expression resembled that of a soldier who was losing the battle.

"At least she's not claiming it's a medical emergency."

"She knows better than to try that trick again."

He was right. My mom even got my dad to ring an ambulance the last time. The medics weren't impressed when they were told to go back to their base because she suddenly felt better.

Farnham gazed at me, knowing I would soon leave. But I had to. Family was calling, and my job as the oldest son was to take responsibility for my siblings. Yes, I'd have a word to my brother when he got home. Yes, I'd turn the vacuum cleaner on or wash the bathtub or do whatever she expected me to do. And then I'd brew coffee so she could bitch about Dad like she always did.

"So what is it this time, Jamal? What excuse has she come up with to rip you from my arms?"

"I'll come back this afternoon. Now don't look at me like that. This afternoon, I promise!"

He sighed. "Is this a Jamal promise or a real promise?"

"Now don't be like that, babe."

"I'm serious. She'll keep you there. She's done it before. And I'll sit here waiting for you to come back, only to get a text message or a very quick phone call saying you won't be back, and you don't know when we'll see each other again. Come on, Jamal, it's been six months. I know the drill."

"Babe, it's my brother. He hasn't been home all night."

"That's because he's out doing what you're doing. But she's not texting him—" My phone chimed. "Like I said, she's not texting him ten times an hour because he's out sleeping with a woman." I glanced at my phone. He sighed again. "What does she say this time?"

"Same old, same old. Don't worry about it, babe. She wants attention."

"No, she wants *your* attention off *me*."

"I *have* to go."

"You don't *have* to do anything you don't want to do. You just feel obliged to go."

I wandered over, reached around, and caressed his back. I kissed his cheek several times as he kept his lips shut tight. So, I nestled my nose into his earlobe. He loosened up and half grinned. I brushed my lips against his. He kissed me, so I encouraged a longer embrace. Soon, he was rustling my hair and pressing his mouth to mine, and I was in a place where the world seemed normal.

❖

Again I was dressing myself. The phone had chimed several more times while Farnham and I made love, but I told myself not to look until I was outside his apartment.

"Darl, I won't be waiting for your return. I have things to do. Ring me if you're definitely on your way back, and I'll let you know where I am. And I mean ring me, don't text."

"I will be back, babe."

"Only ring me if you are on your way back. If you're not coming back, don't contact me."

"You're serious."

"Deadly serious. I'm learning not to wait for you."

"Ouch."

"Sorry, Jamal, that's just the way it is."

We still kissed good-bye, but his severity haunted me as I made the journey home. And with his cutting words repeating like a broken record on my mind came the punch. That feeling in my gut that came with no physical contact, but boy, was it twisting me in knots.

I parked to the side of the road. I had to think. In the past, only two other men came close to how I felt about Farnham. One was a two-month thing because we both realized I was more in love with his city views than with him. It still didn't stop us seeing each other from time to time. We had more fun after the breakup than before. The other broke my heart. He said I was a rebound. I said I loved him. He said he was sorry for believing he loved me.

And Mom had a field day with that one. She said you can never trust men and listed off Dad's faults for the umpteenth time. I replied that I thought we were talking about me. She answered that we were because she knew best.

With Farnham, I never expected more than just a bit of fun. But all he had to do was smile at me, and I'd slip into a daydream. Hearing his name by chance was better than a serenade from a thousand minstrels. And nights without him by my side hurt as if someone had cut off my conjoined twin in a botched operation.

A tear ran down my cheek. I didn't know why. I turned the key and started the engine. Soon, I was back home with my accuser. She was washing plates and handing them to my brother, who was busy with a dishcloth.

"Mama, you said he wasn't home!"

"He's home now," she replied. She gestured toward him like a prize on a quiz show. "He came home."

"I came home from where?" my brother asked.

"Apparently I had to come home because she was worried about where you were."

"You did? Sorry, bro. Were you with Farnham again?"

"Obviously. That's why I have fifteen messages from Mama."

"Don't mention that boy's name," she said. "That goes for both of you, don't mention his name."

"Whose name? Farnham's name? My boyfriend's name?"

"No. No. No. I told you not to use the devil's name."

"Oh, he's the devil now. What happened to the dirty temptress? At least that one was original."

"I liked 'the man who'll sell your soul'," my brother added. "That one was poetic, Ma."

"What would your father say if he knew, Jamal? Think about that."

"I'll have to tell him at one stage," I replied.

"And bring shame on this family! Who do you think you are?"

"He's a homosexual in love," my brother answered.

"Go to your room!"

My brother folded his arms.

"It's okay," I said. "I can handle this." He shared a cheeky smile, handed me the tea towel and ran off.

"Jamal," she continued in a lighter tone, "what is wrong with you? Don't you want children? Think about these things. How can you go out to a party with a man on your arm? What is he going to do, wear a dress?"

"Mama, his name is Farnham, and he's not that kind of gay man. Besides, he'd look like Aunt Rihanna in a dress." I shook my head. "Not a good look."

"Jamal!"

Our doorbell rang. My mom grinned as if her cheeks would burst. My brother answered the door and instantly I heard a woman's voice asking for me. He paraded her in. She stared at me like a sorceress with a spell to cast.

"Sweetheart, I'm taken," I declared. I stormed out, only to hear my brother inform my failed blind date that he was single. Our neighbor, Guy, was on his driveway washing his car. He took one look at me and told me to come inside.

"Do I look that frazzled?" I asked.

"Oh yeah," he replied, turning off the tap.

"This is what she wants," I began. I sat in what he called the counselling seat, the plushest armchair in his living room. "She wants me to be a good family member, marry some girl, any girl, and have kids while I screw men on the side. It's the honorable thing to do. Everyone will know what's going on, but they won't talk about it. That way, no shame is on the family."

"A medieval mentality in a twenty-first-century world," Guy replied. He filled my wine glass. "And somehow I can't see Farnham putting up with being the mistress."

"Some woman that Mom invited just showed up at our place. She's stunning, but my body doesn't work that way!"

"Calm down, Jamal. Trust me, this doesn't have to be complicated."

"But it is. It is complicated. That family next door raised me. They were proud of me when I came second in my third grade spelling bee. They told everyone about it. Then when I was a teenager, they kept bragging about how many female friends I had. I can see my dad's sly grin just thinking about it. And Mom's right. What will he say when he finds out?"

"Surely he already knows."

"I don't know."

"What would be the worst thing that could happen if he finds out?"

I thought, but the answer in my head rose like a toxic beast from a radioactive swamp. "I need more wine, Guy."

He took the glass from my hand. "I don't think you do. I think what you need now is to see Farnham."

"I need a sounding board."

"But your sounding board shouldn't be me."

I brushed my hair back with the palm of my hand, then stared in the direction of my parents' venomous house. "Mama thinks I'm screwing you as well as Farnham. It's the way her mind works."

"Well, she has seen both of you visit me. How does she feel having a gay neighbor?"

"She puts up with it. My dad doesn't seem to care. But he hasn't seen me visit you."

He sat back down, still with my empty wine glass in his hand. "You know, Jamal, the heart wants to protect those we love, while our head tries to protect ourselves."

"I know. You've said that before."

"Now think about those words as you drive to see the man that loves you."

❖

There's something about blue eyes. You gaze into them as that person talks to you, but you're really diving into their soul as their words float by. I caught him by surprise as for some reason he was home. He had no errands to run as he had claimed before I left him that morning. It was his way of protecting himself from my absence.

And even in his confident stance, I could see the small boy wanting more from his play friend. While here was I, the child who let everyone down. It's a lonely place inside my skin. Elders judge my every move unless I seek forgiveness and play the role I was born to play.

But while I keep the peace, a huge grate skims my heart, taking off slivers as if it were cheese. It whittles away the love I once had to share with the world. And somewhere inside my body I want to scream, but those screams get muffled. What does it matter? I'm not sure I'm ready for anyone to hear my screams.

Here in his arms, though, I'm the chameleon whose fears slowly melt away to find clarity. He struggles to hide the distrust in his blue eyes. And I want those eyes to care again. I want those eyes not to dismiss me. I need to follow through this time and not let him down.

"Let's dance," I said.

"But there's no music," he replied.

"There's a tune waiting to be written. It's titled 'Farnham and Jamal', and if we touch and sway a little, it will write itself."

"Are you on drugs?"

I didn't answer. I shuffled my right shoe forward, followed by my left. I was a doo-wop girl making my way to my lover. And he smiled a smile I hadn't seen in god knows how long.

I blew a puff of air on his face, which made him giggle, as I reached around his waist. We waltzed like amateurs. No one judged. No one minded. No one cared.

❖

"Imagine both of us living in this apartment," said Farnham.

"I can imagine that."

We lay on his bed naked, my back against his chest. A breeze had begun, sounding more like a gentle ocean outside than a gust of wind. Trees rustled as if they were waking from their stillness, and a few stars gathered in the night sky to peek into our world.

"I'm serious, Jamal. You're twenty-five, and you still live with your family. Imagine coming home to your own pad. We'd cook dinner together, fight over the bathroom sink, and complain about each other's snoring. It would be bliss."

"As long as you were near, I wouldn't care if cockroaches set up house in the kitchen."

"I could trim your beard hairs. With your beard and my nose hairs, we'd clog the sink like confirmed bachelors."

"Yeah, and we'd change the sheets only when visitors complain about the stench."

"Like I said, it would be bliss."

"Hmm, it would be."

"Then move in, darling. Move in with me."

"Babe, I might just do that."

On cue, my phone chimed. I ignored it. Thirty seconds later, it chimed again.

"I know you want to look, Jamal. I can sense it in your body."

"How?"

"You're tense now."

"Farnham, consider this. Your mom is so cool. She's had us over for dinner often, while your dad and your sister fuss over me. You have the life. Mine's more difficult. I could lose my family, you know that."

He coughed, more to clear his throat than as an involuntary action. "Can you stay here tonight?"

"You know I can't. It's a work day tomorrow. I promised my mom I'd be home on school nights."

"It's nice to know you keep some promises."

"Don't be like that, babe. That's our arrangement, and trust me, I had to negotiate long and hard so I could spend Saturday nights with you. That's our night."

"Hmm."

"What? That's all you have to say?"

"Hmm."

I wished we had a storm. We had only calm, but no storm. And there's always something eerie about the calm. Farnham and I would normally have argued so passionately, our protests would shake the neighborhood. But tonight he was lobotomized. His kind heart, misplaced.

❖

Although I parked in front of my parents', I couldn't go in. I wanted to know if Guy was still awake, so I snuck into his front yard like a spy and peered into his living room. His back was to me while candlelight accentuated his lanky outline. But that's not all that was accentuated. I looked closer.

He had wings. They towered above him a third the length of his body. I stepped back, not meaning to, and then I huddled closer to the glass. I definitely saw an angel praying with a candle in his hands.

I ran to his front door, but I stopped myself as I was about to knock. What would I say? What would I do? I turned toward my parents' place, but as I took the first step, his door opened.

"Why didn't you knock?" he asked. His wings were no longer there.

"It's late. I shouldn't have come to see you at this time of night."

"Nonsense. I want to know how your talk with Farnham went. Come in."

He opened the fly screen, and I stepped inside. The candle was still burning on a side table next to his counselling armchair. "Guy, I think we broke up."

"I find that hard to believe."

"No, I'm serious."

"That explains why you're acting shell shocked, Jamal."

"It's been a strange night for lots of reasons."

"Have you been home yet?"

"No, I needed a friend."

"So, tell me what happened."

I sat in the armchair as the angel crouched at my feet. A tear ran down my cheek, so I wiped it with the back of my hand. I heard fluttering, as if a bird had been startled. At the same time, the flame on the candle flickered.

"Guy, I think I fucked it up. He wanted me to move in but I acted cool and—" I wiped another tear away. "Oh, my stupid bravado."

"Go on, talk."

"Why am I scared to live my life? Why am I so scared of losing my family when all it's doing is making me unhappy? Why am I tearing myself and those I love apart?"

"Farnham must be worth it if you're putting yourself through this."

With blurred eyes, I saw his wings again. I swallowed hard. "But what if it doesn't work out and I lose both him and my family?"

He stood, jutting his wings out as a shield to protect me. "Jamal, let's look into the future."

As he folded his wings back into place, his living room and any hint of his house was gone. But I was still seated in the most comfortable armchair he owned. Behind him was the night sky as if we were floating in space, yet I felt the proper force of gravity.

As I peered into the darkness, two figures materialized. One was me without my beard while the other was Farnham, who'd grown a beard.

"What the —"

"Shh. Just sit and listen."

"Hey, Darl," said my boyfriend, "she'll come around. At least your dad knows about us now." In the vision, a kitchen appeared, and I realized the other me was peering into a pot on the stove. "Come on, stop moping. You're where the love is."

This image faded and in its place was a slightly older version of us. Historic buildings appeared in the background as we stepped onto cobbled streets. "If it wasn't for you, Farnham, I would have never made it to Europe."

"Oh come on, darling. It wasn't all my idea. The moment I mentioned it, you were listing off the cities you wanted to see."

"I didn't mean it like that."

"Well, what did you mean?"

"Never mind."

I knew the smile on my doppelgänger. It was a smile that said I was at peace. The vision changed again, but this time in more detail. Funky furniture littered this enchanted stage, and we were on a grand lounge suite. I rested my head in his lap as I held a book. He had his attention focused on the screen of a tablet. We were plumper. Both with no beards. And my peaceful smile still reigned.

Guy fluttered his wings, causing ripples which washed this scene away. A party appeared in its place. Old-fashioned streamers were tossed around someone's garden and about fifty people in various states of drunkenness were waiting. I knew some of them. Farnham's best friend, Pete, stood with a girl I didn't recognize. My brother drifted with his eyes half shut, until something caused him to clap. The rest of the party applauded instantly.

And out we came, a little thinner and definitely older. We kissed before Farnham stepped forward. He raised a glass of champagne.

"Thank you for all being here to celebrate our twentieth anniversary." The crowd cheered. "It means a lot to me and Jamal." He paused and breathed in. "You know, love doesn't always pop into our lives the way we expect it to. We have the ideal man in our mind, but the ideal man is never what we expect.

"The ideal man is always better than we could ever expect. We know his neuroses, and he knows ours. We know that if the outside world gets too dark, we just steal a glimpse at our man and light will fill the room. And we know that whatever age he gets, he will still be the most beautiful man in the world, hands down.

"Okay, I know that sounds corny, but it's the way I feel about this man. My man, Jamal."

More applause sounded as I lowered my head.

"Are you crying," the angel asked.

"No," I replied. "Damn it. Yes, Guy, I'm crying, just a little."

"Talk about it."

"We used to say things like that, Farnham and me. He used to call me the most beautiful man in the world, and—"

"And?"

"He was my ideal man. And when my family haunted my thoughts, I'd look at him and it didn't matter anymore, until Mama's concerns got louder."

Soon the starry sky returned, and Farnham and I were under it again. Tangled facial hair replaced the strands missing from our heads, and somehow between this image and the last, we'd lost more weight.

"Let's dance," said Farnham.

"But there's no music," the older me replied.

"There's a tune that's been written. It's titled 'Jamal and Farnham', and I bet if we sway a little, we'll hear it loud and clear."

So these men danced in synch, like a pair who'd spent a lifetime together. And I heard the music.

"Your heart wants to protect those you love," said Guy. "But who are you really protecting?"

"I've been protecting my family, to the detriment of the man I'm in love with."

My neighbor's living room reappeared as his wings faded away. "So who should you be protecting?"

"I know, Guy. I know. But what will my family say?" I stared at his far wall.

"You have a right to your own happiness, Jamal."

"Can you show me how my family will react in the future?"

"I can, but I won't. For nothing is written in stone. That is your challenge. You have to make amends as time moves on. But next door is your mother. A mother who believes she's doing what's best for her son."

"You know, Guy, I can't go home."

"Why?"

I stood. "Because it's not my home."

He gestured to his front door. I strode confidently, stopped, and then turned to thank him. When I swivelled back toward the exit, I noticed my suitcase at my feet. I shook my head, lifted the luggage, and continued my journey.

❖

I turned my key in the lock to Farnham's apartment. There he was, deep in slumber. I undressed and carefully slipped under his sheets. He stirred.

"Jamal, darling, it's a school night. What are you doing here?"

"Falling deeper in love with the man of my dreams."

"Are you on drugs?"

"I may as well be. My head is light. I'm deliriously happy. And I know at last what's best for me and those I love."

When the Sun Shines

Kassandra Lea

The sky couldn't have been any bluer that spring day, the white clouds floating across its surface. The world was still waking on the early May afternoon, a chill lingering in the gentle breeze. Birdsong filled the air, the robins and finches having returned to usher in the promise of warmer days. The trees were budding, early flowers blooming, and the water in the pond shimmered like a sapphire.

Lance Black took a step back, dusting off his hands, a faint smile on his lips as he admired his work. He wasn't entirely sure what had given birth to the idea, but once it started bouncing around in his skull, he couldn't ignore it. After all, it seemed like the perfect answer to the question plaguing him for the last week. His sweet beloved fiancé, the man who owned him heart and soul, had been caught in the waves of depression, some days barely managing to stay afloat. Seeing his suffering pained Lance, and he wanted to bring a smile to those lips he so loved to kiss.

A quick glance at his watch, a final check of the setup, and he was heading back across the yard. On his way, Lance thought for the umpteenth time how lucky they'd been to find the old Victorian with its couple of acres, complete with a pond and an old dilapidated greenhouse. For the last three years, it had been home. Lance had even popped the question under the birch tree by the glistening water on a cool October day.

They still hadn't set a date two years later, but Lance was okay. He never truly understood what it meant to be in love until they met.

If his betrothed wanted to take things slowly, he would happily wait. As his mama liked to tell him, all the best things in life are worth waiting for.

Lance slipped into the house, finding it quiet. Five feet in, he was greeted by their cat, a little ball of ginger fur. She meowed at him, weaving between his legs. Lance plucked her from the ground and headed for the stairs. Two flights later, he deposited the cat on the sofa in the tower room. The expansive window view allowed him an impressive sight of the prairie-forest mashup across the street. They'd spent so many winter nights in this room, void of any light source, watching it snow. He suspected, like the previous summers, they'd enjoy quite a few thunderstorms up here, too.

He leaned on the door frame, hands in the pockets of his jeans.

His fiancé, Jasper, sat in a chair curled up under a blanket, an open book on his lap. A neglected laptop sat on the coffee table. His short brown hair stuck up in an alluring just-got-out-of-bed way, which didn't seem like such a far-fetched idea since he was still technically wearing his pajamas.

"You look like you need a break," Lance said.

Pale green eyes shifted in his direction. "Hmm?"

Lance stepped into the room, offering him a hand. "Come on, I have something for you."

For a moment, Lance thought Jasper might pass, then he marked the page in his book and tossed it on the table beside the sleeping computer. By all rights he should have been writing, but Lance could tell the grip of depression had him good today. Jasper slipped his hand into Lance's, leaving the blanket draped over the chair's arm.

As was always the case when Jasper touched him, Lance experienced a heart-racing shock and a flutter in his stomach. No one else had ever elicited the same sensations. Entwining his fingers with Jasper's, he led his fiancé back through the house. By the time they reached the door leading out onto the deck, Lance was ready to burst, excitement bubbling up in him. Jasper, on the other hand, walked silently at his side, clearly lost in thought.

Wanting him in the moment, Lance halted and faced Jasper.

Without a word, he leaned in and placed a gentle, affectionate kiss on Jasper's lips. He lingered for a moment before drawing back, giving Jasper's hand a pleasant squeeze. He was delighted to see a glimmer of contentment in Jasper's eyes. They stepped off the deck together.

"Where are we going?"

Lance toyed with how much to tell him, not wanting to ruin the surprise. "You've been a little down lately," he started, "and I thought maybe a little spring air might help." He wanted to say more. He had all these sentiments running through his mind, but he opted to wait until the surprise had been sprung.

Only a few heartbeats later, they rounded the corner in the garden, and his little setup came into sight. Lance had put together a picnic, the perfect way to celebrate the arrival of spring as well as getting his beloved free of the gloomy rut. He'd spread a white blanket over the grass and added an open umbrella in case the sun became a touch too much, though he thought that highly unlikely. He'd also scattered three big pillows about to make things more comfortable. And of course, he'd filled the wicker picnic basket with a delicious assortment of goodies, all of which he managed to get together without raising suspicions.

They stopped at the blanket's edge. Jasper looked at him. "You did this…for me?"

"For us," Lance replied.

After a moment of hesitation, Jasper asked, "But why?"

"Why not?" Lance shrugged, sinking down onto the blanket and gesturing for Jasper to do the same. Lance hooked a finger under Jasper's chin, forcing his lover to look him in the eye. Oh, and how he so loved to get lost in them, their shade reminiscent of newly budded leaves. His heart fluttered and he was always amazed how he could still fall even more in love with Jasper. "I've noticed you've been caught up in a funk lately. Something is going on in that head of yours, and I know when you want to share, you will. Like always, I'll listen and do my best to help."

Jasper opened his mouth as though he meant to speak.

Lance held up a finger, wanting to say a bit more. "Now, I'm perfectly fine with sitting by and waiting you out. But, my love, it pains me so to see you suffering. I thought to myself perhaps I could find a way to help you get clear of the darkness, brighten your spirits. And what better answer than a picnic on such a wonderful spring day?"

"I don't know what to say." Jasper's words came out barely more than a whisper.

"You don't have to say anything."

Lance tasted green tea as he ran his tongue along Jasper's mouth. A wave of heat rushed over him as Jasper reached up and grasped hold of his shirt, his fingers curling into the fabric. For a moment, the world around them seemed to slow, then fade away altogether. Lance wanted nothing more than to pull Jasper close, to feel the rhythmic beat of his lover's heart, and to let his fingers wander over Jasper's muscles, but the timing for such things was all wrong. The absolute last thing he wanted to do was pressure Jasper when the poor man was mentally lost at sea.

When they broke the kiss, Lance was delighted to spot a twinkle in Jasper's eyes, the storm clouds that had been lingering there finally starting to break apart. Jasper gathered up the pillows, piled them at the base of the tree, then rested back against them, beckoning Lance to come join him. Lance settled at his side, slipping an arm around his shoulders and cuddling up close. He rested his head on Lance's shoulder, slowly rubbing his hand up and down Lance's thigh. Neither of them spoke for a while but sat enjoying each other's company.

After a few minutes, Lance found himself aroused, the constant touch of his lover's hand on his thigh more than enough to get the job done. He subtly shifted his position. "You know," he said, "if you keep doing that, I might have to have my way with you."

Jasper stopped moving his hand for a moment, then resumed his rubbing, bringing his hand a bit further north than previously, his knuckles brushing Lance's growing erection. "Maybe—" A loud growl from his stomach cut him off.

They were quiet a moment, then started laughing. The sound made Lance's heart swell. Oh, how he had missed it the whole week along with the light dancing in those pale green eyes and the smile curving those lush lips. The storm had died, the clouds breaking, Jasper finding the path out of the darkness. Lance couldn't help himself. He cupped Jasper's chin in his hands, kissing Jasper tenderly, lovingly, with the promise of something more.

"I love you, Jasper," he said when they broke apart. "More and more every day."

Instead of replying in kind, Jasper turned his focus to the picnic basket.

A touch uncertain, Lance waited for Jasper to say or do something. His mind was racing, going over every action and word, afraid he might have said or done the wrong thing. Then, much to his surprise, Jasper leaned forward and grasped the basket handle. In a flash, Jasper stood up and held his hand out to a somewhat confused Lance.

"I thought we were having a picnic," Lance said, his eyebrows raised.

Jasper smiled coyly. "We are."

"Then what are you doing?"

Jasper wiggled his fingers, clearly wanting Lance to take hold of his hand. "I say we have this picnic upstairs in our bedroom, where we can either have dessert first or right after. Or maybe in the middle even."

"Dessert…" Lance said, finally taking hold of Jasper's hand and getting to his feet. The impish look on Jasper's face was enough to put the final piece of the puzzle in place. Lance's heart fluttered, his stomach doing flip-flops. He knew that look, knew that Jasper had definitely managed to get free of depression's hold. "Are you implying, my beloved Jasper, that we indulge in some…play time?"

Jasper popped open the lid of the basket, peeking inside. "Well, well, I think we might have to go with the 'during' option." He pulled out a can of whipped cream, lightly shaking it side to side. "I mean, I guess this is for the strawberries and blueberries, but I can think of another use."

By now they were walking back toward the house, the denim of Lance's jeans rubbing uncomfortably against his erection. Lance pulled Jasper up short at the deck steps. "Can I just say, before we go in, that you have some of the absolute best ideas?"

"I do believe," Jasper said, "that you helped facilitate this adventure." He leaned in to whisper in Lance's ear. "Let me show you just how much I love you, Lance Black."

They spent the rest of the beautiful spring afternoon wrapped up in each other, the sun setting as their simple picnic became a feast of the heart.

PHOTO-LOVE AND SEVEN WAYS TO GET THE GUY

R. W. Clinger

G etting the guy. Good luck with that. It's not as easy at is seems. Then again, maybe it is…

❖

The number one way to get the guy: Jump when you are called on to jump. And jump high. Real high.

"Brody, I need you," Roarke said, his voice wavering with nervousness.

It was nice to be needed by a man. What gay guy didn't want that? "Where and when?"

"247 Mossdale Street. Two o'clock this afternoon."

"I'll be there. Count on it."

Before I ended our cell phone conversation, he hurriedly asked, "Do you have any lime green underwear?"

I chuckled, grinning from ear to ear. "I do."

"Wear those this afternoon. Can you do that?"

I could and would, excited to see him again.

❖

Springtime in the city. The time for lust, great sex, and love, if you're lucky. A colorful period between men who find other men attractive on various levels: physically, mentally, socially, and emotionally. Love happens to the best of us, when we least expect it, of course. I've heard if you don't look for it, it will happen within seconds, blowing you away. It happened to all my white collar friends: Ricky, James, Patrick, and Blaine. The winter thawed, the season changed, the sun came out to play, and men started to fall in love again, young and old. Even with me.

Love didn't happen to me until Roarke came along. Roarke Stephen McDixon with his ginger hair, muscular frame, fall-into green eyes, and chest covered in curly fur. Six-three Roarke with his *GQ* smile and charm, model-perfect and with a modern haircut, and a tight bottom that could have rocked the world off its axis. I could ramble about Roarke for the next four thousand two hundred and ninety-three pages but won't. Instead, I have some assistant work to accomplish, a "dog job," as I used to call it. Listen…

I was spoiled at twenty-eight, living in Los Angeles. My company was called Best Assets, a qualified agency that supplied business executives with competent assistants, not temporary positions at low scale paying jobs. My clients were professional men and women who were usually college graduates and experienced regarding work among white collars in the world, plus they had exceptional drives.

My company matched employable people with appropriate executives, concentrating on both parties' interests. For instance, Jude Barr was a curator at the Robindaux Gallery in West Hollywood. I paired him with Gregory Sander, a graduate from UCLA with a business degree and an interest/background in art. The pairing was just one success of many my staff and I had created. Best Assets processed approximately fourteen employees a week, matching those bright-eyed women and men to hardworking executives and established companies. All in all, my own company did well. I was living in a nice one-bedroom bungalow near Beverly Hills and wasn't starving like some people in the world.

April of last year was a little rocky, though. Bea LeCarre, my vice president and right arm in the company, needed a week because her older sister passed away in a horrible boating accident somewhere in the South of France. And Michael Chentar, my glue and everything-guy at Best Assets, went missing the same week, lost in the jungles of South America with a male tour guide named Juan Cinco. I honestly think the guy was his boyfriend, but it wasn't any of my business. Anyway, Michael and Bea were both out of the country and other staff members were doing their own jobs. I had some slack to pick up and...

Roarke McDixon rushed into my world, blowing me away. He entered my office unannounced and unscheduled. I usually didn't concentrate on what men wore, the complete opposite of a fashion diva, but Roarke looked attractive in his tight pair of beige jeans, burgundy Italian loafers, and white cotton dress shirt. The shirt was unbuttoned to the middle of his chest and showed off ginger fur and solid pecs. Some of the material pulled away from one of his pecs when he leaned over my desk, exposing one pink nipple. His chest wasn't bronze like most La Landers, but I knew that reds didn't tan easily because of their Irish genes, not that I minded or judged.

"Brody Neilson?" he asked, eyeing me up and down, taking all of me in: brown hair, muscular build with no fat, bright blue eyes, clean-shaven, five-eleven frame, and no earrings or tattoos.

I usually didn't have visitors, family, or clients in my office since it looked like a pigsty. Had Bea been working, Roarke never would have made it out of the foyer. "Yes, I'm Brody. Who are you?" I already knew who he was but wanted to humor him. Who didn't know Roarke McDixon and his bathroom photographs? He wasn't world-famous, but he was quite popular along California's coast.

"Roarke McDixon." He said his name, holding out his right hand for a shake. Then he told me what he did for a living.

What a weird name: Roarke McDixon. Strange. But I liked it. Hell, he could have been named Merlin Mudd for I all cared, into his red hair, freckles, and Popeye muscles. Damn, the guy was fucking hot, unbearable to look at.

❖

Number two: Know what the guy does, if you give a shit, of course.

Truth told, I was very familiar with Roarke's professional photographs of bathrooms. His work could be found in *Architectural Digest*, *Town and Country*, and in a heavily priced coffee table book titled *Bathroom Beauties*, which was oversized, comprised of two hundred and thirty colored plates of exquisite restrooms in Key West, New York City, Saddle Ridge, Malibu, and Houston. Roarke was not an amateur by any means and had made well over three hundred thousand dollars a year from his photography.

Some viewers didn't know about his edgier work in back alley basement bathrooms, subway latrines, public urinals in seedy bars. He was selective, of course, and good at what he did. A prodigy with his camera and subjects. For every high-end bathroom photograph he had been paid for, Roarke had twenty crud-infested ones that could have been considered disgusting but quite artsy, challenging to one's mind, and gasp-taking.

We had a drink together in my office because I needed one: whiskey sours. Then he told me he wanted an assistant with a background in photography. "My current assistant, Marcus Shore, decided to fall in love with a Saudi. Marcus moved to the Middle East. The two men look adorable together and will make the perfect couple, but their arrangement isn't going to help my career."

I wanted to tell him that I too was in a bind because Bea and Michael were not in the country, able to help me. Bad business entailed offering secrets of the trade, which I didn't want to share at the moment. Therefore, I kept my trap shut about my company's lack of help and asked, "How soon do you need an assistant?"

"Preferably tomorrow morning. I have a shoot to attend at a nearby mansion that overlooks the Pacific. Can you help me out?"

I couldn't help him out, but he didn't need to know that. But I would never turn down business and cash in my pocket, particularly from such a handsome and rock-solid red. "I can help you," I said, deciding to execute the job and position myself, since no one on my staff was currently available.

"Make sure the person has a background in photography, Brody. I want tomorrow to go smooth."

"Of course. And of course."

He winked at me, which melted my world and maybe caused me to fall for him on the spot. I didn't believe in love at first sight, but something strange rocked within my chest. And my blood pressure rose as my eyes met his, sealing together. Silence hung between us like an unresolved mystery until he finally reached for my hand, shook it, and clarified the address of tomorrow's bathroom shoot.

When Roarke left my office, he shifted his bulbous ass to the right and left, but not on purpose. Frankly, it was an ass I wanted to hold with both hands, rolling my palms against. And it was an ass that caused my dick to bounce with life, becoming semi-hard as he was leaving.

Over his left shoulder, he called, "Tomorrow morning. Ten."

I repeated what he had said and added, "I'll be there. No need to worry."

❖

Number three: Know the guy's issues, whether they are big or small.

There was one Herculean-sized problem about working for Roarke McDixon. I didn't know jack about photography. Of course, I was a member of Instagram and Pinterest, but those photographs had been stolen from the Internet. The only picture I had ever taken that could have been considered worthy was of Bea and Michael standing in my office, grinning and posing. The photograph looked cheesy and ridiculous as they shared a bogus hug, and lacked any sense of professionalism and art about it. In fact, it was somewhat blurred. The worst of the worst pictures ever taken by any man.

I hadn't slept at all the night before the bathroom shoot. Getting Roarke out of my head was next to impossible, I was so caught up in his handsomeness and charm. All I could recall throughout the night was his wink, maybe wooing me the way one man deserves to be wooed by another man, even a stranger.

My Roarke-invaded insomnia didn't stop there, though. Not in the least. I imagined him entering my bedroom in a pair of tight white briefs and nothing more, exposing his muscled and hairy chest. He leaned into my bedroom's door frame, tilted his head to the right, sort of chuckled, and said, "You don't know a damn thing about photography, do you, Brody?"

"Is it that obvious?"

"More than obvious. Not that it matters, though, since you're a fine-looking man. Plus you have some substance, which I like."

"What kind of substance?" I tested him, seeing if he had learned me as much as I had learned him.

"You like cats over dogs, you're obsessed with lottery tickets, and you enjoy the rain over sun."

"Nicely done," I said.

"And something tells me you like the company of men over women," he said, grabbing the junk between his legs and giving it a tug. "Plus you fall in love rather quickly."

"I can't deny any of those facts."

"I didn't think you would."

I was rolled over in the dream, facedown on my bed, and my underwear pulled away and off. Before I knew what was happening, Roarke had his nose and mouth against my bottom. His fingers and palms separated my behind and he darted his tongue inside me, pulled away, and darted inside again, teasing me. He growled behind me, hungry, and became relentless, continuing to pleasure me. When he eventually pulled his face away from my rear, he rolled two fingertips down and over my opening, growled again, and spanked one of my ass cheeks.

I became lost, kneeling with my legs ever so slightly spread apart. "Spank me again," I coached, practically begging for his play. "Don't be shy, Roarke. I'm all yours."

Again, his mouth met my bottom. As licks and laps ensued, I moaned with deep satisfaction and felt him wrap his right hand around my erection. He rolled his hand up and down on my dick, milking it. The action sent me into a spin of satisfaction. Hurriedly, his hand became chaotic motion on my cock, leaving me gasp for air, dizzy in front of him.

"I like you a little too much, Brody," he said, after pulling his face away from my bottom.

I thrust my dick inside his hand, and my ass against his face. After a string of minutes under his care, sent into a state of euphoria, I said, "You're making me come."

"Don't hold back. Show me what you have, man."

And so it was done. I felt a wave of enjoyment flood throughout my torso and between my legs. Vibrations of bliss blew me away, under the photographer's spell, which I didn't argue with or object to.

"Do it, Brody. Put on a show for me."

After his comment, white strings of semen blew out of my dick and coated my bed. One burst was followed by the next, leaving me exhausted on my knees and overcome with pleasure. The sticky explosion not only decorated the bed, but it also decorated his palm and fingers, leaving the man thrilled to be my sexual companion, getting me off and…

I woke from the dream with a gluey dick between my legs. "It was just a dream, Brody," I said to myself, staring into the dark room. "Roarke isn't interested in you that way. Whatever happens tomorrow should be professional. You can't cross that sexual line because you'll make a fool out of yourself. Even if you like the guy. Even if you've fallen in love with him at first sight."

My center was covered with ejaculate. Puddles lined my abs and pecs. Perspiration drenched my torso and thighs. Breathless, attempting to calm down, I whispered inside the room, "Roarke has you. And you want him too. It's more than lust you have for the guy. It's something more potent. You know it is."

❖

Number four: Expect the worst. Guys can be assholes, in and out. Don't ever think they are Prince Charming, because you're only letting yourself down. Don't bother. Keep your expectations low. If the guy just happens to blow you away, remember that with every good side comes a bad.

Before meeting with Roarke the next morning, I googled his work. Professionally speaking, he had photographed over one thousand bathrooms in the last four years. Oriental. Jungle-themed. Royal. College. Western. All gold. Outdoor. His photographs were stunning, in my opinion. He used light and shadows as vehicles for his observing eye. His colors were rich and refined. He had gone through five major thematic periods in his career: Tidal Wave Blue, Icelandic, Bamboo, and Granite. Shorter periods included marbles, sunflower yellow tiles, and Incan pitchers. No matter what theme he had taken on, sharing it with his clients, architectural firms, the media, and his fans in the art world, Roarke McDixon was always successful, never failing at anything—even landing me.

His last shoot was in an L.A. magazine called *Golden Gate Skyline*. The six-page spread depicted an eye-appealing bathroom from the Fritz Manker Estate. The bathroom was to die for, with black marble flooring, bronze hardware, a claw-foot bathtub, and triangular-shaped shower. The massive floor-to-ceiling bathroom windows looked over the Pacific.

I wanted to get to know Roarke better; the man's ins and out, everything about him. His soft edges and hard-boiled nature. His emotional likings and dispassionate moments. I wanted to get inside Roarke, beyond his physical appearance and the creation of his bathrooms. Who was behind the stunning bathrooms and their photographed brilliance? What was?

Number five: Sometimes it's necessary to play dumb with the guy you want. What do you have to lose, right? Games are important, particularly those that will bring you closer to the guy, and maybe even under him.

I couldn't be late if my life depended on it and arrived on time at 1683 Fairbanks Street. The house was massive, just as I expected:

Guggenheim-shaped, lots of windows, bamboo, granite, and all in light blue and white. The residence was three floors high and approximately six thousand square feet.

Roarke's Fusion sat in front of the place. Of course the man had a budget for a Jag, but he was environmentally cautious, which I respected about him. I parked my GMC truck by his car, climbed out, and made my way into the weirdly shaped mansion. "Hello?" I called out in the library-like foyer, but nobody answered.

The ceiling was too high, and there were too many books, most of which I believed were fakes. I walked out of the foyer and studied marble tile and Russian crystal everywhere, from floor to the high ceiling. The dining room could have easily sat twenty-four people. To the right of the dining room was a smoking room with a bar. All the walls were decorated with Van Goghs under glass, none of which were originals, of course: *The Orchard*, *The Zouve*, *The Chair and Pipe*, *Road with Cypresses*, *Old Man in Grief*, and *The Meadow*.

Thus far, Roarke was unaccounted for, so I decided to follow a spiral staircase to the second floor, which was comprised of massive bedrooms, a study, a private library, and four bathrooms. "Hello?" I called out again. "Roarke, are you here?"

Roarke was nearby, though. I heard a shower running and the familiar sound of a camera clicking. Flashes of bright-white light illuminated the hallway I was in, outside the bathroom where I believed Roarke was located. I walked down the hallway, passed two bedrooms the size of the Pentagon, and came to the third bedroom. When I walked inside, Roarke said, "Good morning, Mr. Neilson. You're right on time."

We shook hands and eyed each other up and down. Then he said, "I had the craziest dream about you last night."

"What kind of dream?" I asked.

He had a stainless-steel thermos and passed me a Styrofoam cup of coffee. As I took it, I looked around the exquisite bathroom for the first time. Bright yellows were mixed with gold and white, and it looked somewhat French with a Louis XIV settee, mirrors all around, and white marble flooring with swirls of gold. A spray of water streamed out of an elaborately designed S-shaped showerhead. I knew the water's temperature was warm, but not scalding, since the bathroom was steamy. Frankly, the room looked somewhat feminine and expensive. Anyone with taste would have gone mad over it.

"Never mind. We can maybe get into my dream later."

I studied the bathroom and asked, "Who owns this place?"

"Melinda Moretell."

"*The* Melinda Moretell?" She was one of Hollywood's highest-paid actresses and shot movies with only A-list actors like George Clooney, Brad Pitt, Matt Damon, and Bradley Cooper.

"She's the one. This is the smallest property she owns. She has a few around the United States."

I thought I was dreaming until Roarke asked, "Can you please run down to my Fusion and get the Quora."

I didn't know a Quora from a collie, and he knew it. "The lens. It's shaped like an oval."

I bolted to the Fusion in the front lot, zoomed back to his side, and passed him the oversized lens. He pointed to a black leather case and asked for a shutter release.

"A what?" I was bombing miserably. Shame on me for saying I was someone I wasn't. Damn.

He chuckled, though, playing my game. "You know nothing about photography, do you, Brody?"

"Listen, I thought I could help you. It's a little more complex than what I imagined." I sounded defensive but didn't mean to.

"Not to worry. Your company alone is enough to make me have a great day. I have this funny feeling we're going to spend some quality time together, for maybe a long time."

I felt flattered by his comment, warm and fuzzy. Being liked by a guy was one of the best feelings, even if it was a professional relationship.

He grabbed the shutter whatever it was from his equipment box and said, "Brody, I want to try something different today during this shoot."

"What kind of something?" I sounded naïve and ridiculous,

like someone who was twelve years old instead of someone in his late twenties.

"How would you feel about letting me take a few pictures of you in the shower?"

❖

Number six: Step out of your comfort zone for a change. Guys like this. Become unexpected. Get a little wild. Roar.

So what did I do? Something that wasn't in my job description. I stripped down to boxer-briefs in front of Roarke, showed off my chest, thighs, and my cotton-covered ass. It was sort of a slow striptease act for his pleasure and mine. Then I climbed into the shower and posed under the warm spray, grinned from ear to ear, flexed my muscles, and rolled my hands up and down my chest.

Roarke clicked, clicked, and clicked his digital camera. "If I didn't know any better, I'd say you've done this before."

"Never," I replied, and pulled the rim of my underwear down, showing off part of my right thigh and wet ass, which he didn't complain about.

"Take them off, but only if you want."

I didn't, and wouldn't...at least for a few weeks. Truth told, I fell for Roarke hard that day, head over heels for the man, and didn't want to come across as easy. I kept my underwear on during the bathroom shoot and for five more dates after that first photography gig. Thereafter, he ended up taking me on more shoots, and I teased him with my body, showing him a little more of my private parts each time, soaping my chest down with lather, sporting my bottom for him once, and making myself semi-hard for him, playing with my dick through my cotton underwear.

I admit, I treated our dates like a game, and maybe I shouldn't have. I should have taken him and his career a little more serious. I knew he didn't take men to his photography gigs on a regular basis, and he made me feel special because he did like to take me. Frankly, if I wanted the guy to like me more, and for keeps, I had to get serious.

But he enjoyed our game as much as I did. I knew that. And maybe he knew that, too, because he called me up last Saturday afternoon and said, "Brody, I need you." His voice wavered with nervousness.

It was nice to be needed by a man. What gay guy didn't want that? "Where and when?"

"247 Mossdale Street. Two o'clock this afternoon."

"I'll be there. Count on it."

Before I ended our cell phone conversation, he hurriedly asked, "Do you have any lime green underwear?"

I chuckled, grinning from ear to ear. "I do."

"Wear those this afternoon. Can you do that?"

I could and would, excited to see him again.

And then it happened, in West Hollywood, inside an artist's bathroom. A professional job between us had turned into an unprofessional job. To tell you the truth, I can't even remember what the bathroom looked like because Roarke kissed me and things got out of hand. He turned on the shower and stripped me, and then I stripped him, and we ended up under the spray together.

Once in the shower, we started kissing under the spray. The kissing we shared with each other was intense, potent, and passionate, the kind of kissing maybe only lovers shared, investing their lives, minds, and hearts into each other.

And while we kissed, he grabbed the bar of soap from the tiled shelf and rolled it up and over my back, then down my back and against my ass. By then I was as hard as granite, ready for whatever else was going to happen between us, which I had a funny feeling was going to be very exciting. Afterward, he pulled away from me ever so slightly and rolled the bar up and down my chest, over my swollen pecs and nipples, having the time of his life, judging by the adorable grin smeared over his handsome face. He decided to soap up one of my thighs, then the other, and said, "Rinse off. I have something planned for you."

On his knees with his palms clamped to my hips, he sucked me. He moved his head to and fro, causing euphoria to shift throughout my entire body. He slurped and sucked and banged his face off my center, moaned a few times, and pleasured the both of us for the next few minutes inside the shower.

When did he spin me and spread my cheeks with his fingers? I couldn't recall, although I wasn't complaining. He started tonguing my rear in slow and smooth strokes, causing me to become dizzy.

Roarke lodged his dick inside my ass. His latex-covered cock jostled me with its gliding. He fucked slowly, fervent and unstoppable. He clasped my hips, and I felt his touch through bone, flesh, and muscles.

"Jesus, Roarke," I said, "you mean business."

His business included relentless, smooth humping inside my rear, huffing and puffing behind me. He dug his fingertips into my hips, and he pressed me against the shower wall, arching my back and sliding my chest against the warm tiles. I felt him drive his cock inside me again and again, and he kept whispering my name while licking and kissing my back, busy with his labor.

He eventually came after his continuous and gentle thrusts to my bottom. Roarke pulled out of me, lost the latex in the shower, and doused my spine with his load, murmuring as he came. His warm ejaculate clung to my skin, but it rinsed away when he carefully reached for my right shoulder, spun me around, and whispered, "Let me make you come."

I wasn't disappointed by his right-hand action on my dick. He worked my cock up and down with his fist, squeezing my prick in his tight grip. In doing so, he locked eyes with me and coached, "Come, man. Don't be shy. I want to watch you blow your load." And he kissed me, pressing his lips against mine, caught up in our naked act in the shower.

Our chests and mouths locked together, he moaned while he slowly jacked me off. Together we moved like peach-colored silk against the bed's surface. His hand stayed busy on my cock, working it slow motion, tightening and loosening its grip during every upward and downward motion. And then he pulled his face away from mine and whispered, "Come for me, Brody. Don't hold it in."

I listened, locked to his face again, and grunted. I thrust my cock inside his fist, felt elation buzz throughout my pelvic area, and released a load of thick semen on his hand and between our chests. A half dozen moans exited my mouth as I came.

Roarke said, "That's my guy. Blow it all out."

We kissed again and again as I emptied my body of ejaculate. The load was a thick and gluey mass, which clung between us, sealing our bodies together. Sometime during that moment I think I whispered to him, "I love you." Maybe not. I can't remember. But, nevertheless, that's how I felt.

Number seven: Let him know you're crazy about him. It's a great start to any relationship. Tell him what you've just shared with him wasn't just sex between adult men. There was something more to it than that. Something almost unexplainable, real, and live. Magic between men who have a mutual interest in each other. Let him also know the two of you have a future together as boyfriends and lovers, make a good couple, and can be inseparable, locked together by your hearts.

We rinsed off together under the shower's warm spray, and he held me in his strong, muscular arms. His chest of wet red hair rubbed against my bare one as he kissed me. When he pulled away from me, he asked, "Does it sound crazy of me to admit that I really like you?"

"Spring is here. It's all about falling in love, isn't it?"

"Is that what you call it?"

"It is what it is," I replied, kissed him again, and knew that we would spend the next thirty, maybe even forty years together, coupled.

THE ESSENTIALS

Vinton Rafe McCabe

The Rains of Ranchipur is on TCM.

Garth eats tuna fish on brown rice cakes and watches, enthralled. On the wide, flat plain of the television set, everything is in jewel tones, most especially Lana Turner, a '50s rich American woman visiting India.

When the rains at last come, Richard Burton attempts to part the flood with the rumblings of his vocal cords, like Moses at the Red Sea. He plays the part of a native, his face having been slathered with Light Egyptian by Max Factor. His eyes glow a sullen blue.

Garth mouths Burton's lines. Repeats along with him out loud, his voice tethered to a thick mock-Welsh accent. "Quiet. Quiet now," Garth echoes when Burton saves Lana Turner from the shiny cobra. Then he slaps her to combat her hysteria. And the music swells as he purrs at her and she sobs in his arms. Later, the floodwaters rise and release, smashing everything in their path. This is accompanied by an earthquake, in CinemaScope.

Garth lies across the long, low couch, throw pillows stacked all around him, a vicuna throw on his lap. He puts Ugged feet up on the coffee table, balances the plate that, until just now, held the tuna crackers on his stomach.

Jonathan walks through the room, glances at the TV.

"Quick," says Garth, "what movie?"

Jonathan stops a moment and squints at the screen. *"Rains of Ranchipur."*

"Which version?"

"1952. The original one with Myrna Loy is better."

Garth nods. "*The Rains Came*, 1936."

"Everything with Myrna Loy is better."

Jonathan turns his attention from the screen. He continues his cross behind the couch, touching the top of Garth's head as he leans down across Garth's body and lifts the plate from his stomach. He walks into the kitchen beyond, taking the plate with him.

Their dog, Blind Kevin, is curled up on his little red bed next to the couch. Blind Kevin raises his head and turns it side to side as the men speak, scanning space to locate the source of the sounds.

It is a weekend afternoon.

Earlier, there were bagels and cream cheese, scrambled eggs, strong coffee, and the *New York Times* on each of their iPads. As they ate, sunlight filtered through the dusty leaves of the potted tree that stood between the south-facing windows. Garth Pandora-ed light jazz on his iPad.

As they ate, Blind Kevin stood off to the side in the warmth of a wide ray of sunshine. His cataracts glowed in reflection as he stared into the sun. Dust motes slanted down the sunbeam, enveloping him.

❖

Later, when the pizzas have arrived, Jonathan will join Garth on the couch for the next movie, *The Parent Trap*. He will lie with his head on Garth's ample stomach, resting his face in a nest of vicuna.

Both will agree more than once that the original with Hayley Mills is better than the remake, despite Lindsay Lohan playing the twins in that version. This is the one that has the song, "Let's Get Together (Yeah Yeah Yeah)." Both will note the tragedy of Brian Keith's passing many years after the film is made as a result of suicide, although Jonathan will only be able to refer to him as Uncle Bill, having misplaced the actor's name.

❖

But this is now, this moment, the moment in which a cloud has moved in front of the sun, and the only light in the room is from the television screen, and Blind Kevin, ancient, arthritic, diabetic, and sightless from fifteen years of willful and purposeful hard living, both snores (loudly) and wheezes (softly) on his bed. The sound comforts, if only as it stands as proof that Blind Kevin is still breathing, something that is a near-constant concern for both men.

❖

They got the dog—he was simply "Kevin" then—when he was just a pup. The dog had been abandoned and had lived for some weeks surviving on city streets before he was rescued. Jonathan and Garth saw him first at a house in the country where he had been fostered. He was little then, small enough to be lifted by a single finger. Kevin, instantly christened as such by Garth, drove home with them that very day, although they were so ill-prepared for a pet they had to stop at Burger King and feed the dog beef patties Garth tore into tiny bits. The hot meat burned and greased Garth's fingertips and he laid the bits of meat on his palm and then blew on them to cool them, all to coax the puppy to eat.

Blind Kevin's eyes were bright back then as he looked around his new world.

❖

Garth thinks that Richard Burton looks especially sexy in his blue turban.

Throughout the film, Burton wears a great deal of mascara in the way that actors in Hollywood movies tend to do when they are playing persons of color.

Disturbing as this perhaps racist trend may be, the mascara, like the robin's egg turban, sets off Richard Burton's eyes in a very fetching manner.

Garth notices the rain streaking down the windowpane. It is a calm and quiet rain, unlike the rains in Ranchipur.

❖

In the kitchen, Jonathan clears the detritus of their meal. He rinses the plates and places them in the dishwasher. He sets the carton of eggs, the butter, and the cream cheese back in the refrigerator. He puts the nonstick skillet in the sink and turns the water up full and hot, scrubbing the pan with the kitchen sponge.

He then crackles the eggshells up together in the paper towel on which they had been resting. He tosses the wad into the garbage bag from a distance of nearly ten feet and congratulates himself on his achievement.

Jonathan hums tunelessly. Then, hearing himself, he turns on the radio to a public station on which a woman is introducing the next blues song she will play. Giving background, she names the artist and adds, "He's playing his own harp," in a gravelly voice that itself seems filled with the blues.

Jonathan wonders, as he does whenever she says this, what a "harp" refers to. He wipes the counter. Cleans the sink with Soft Scrub.

He thinks then of the time, years ago, when he first met Garth at the Smith Club book sale in Greenwich, which was, that year, held in the small auditorium in an elementary school. He remembers that, at the time, he felt that the large tables on which the books had been stacked looked out of place with the tiny tables and chairs that had been pushed against the walls to make room.

He met Garth among the architecture books, large volumes with colored plates of finished houses and line drawings of interiors. They were introduced by a mutual friend, an author of YA fiction. And the three, each carrying a small stack of purchases, went off to lunch, during which Garth invited Jonathan over to see his apartment in the turret of an architecturally significant Queen Anne Victorian in Stamford.

He remembers the feel of Garth's hot breath on his bare stomach as they lay together on the frayed Oriental carpet that was nearly all he had at that time in his apartment. Except for the floor lamp that stood up erect from the carpet. "I'm not looking for a relationship," he'd said as Garth tugged gently on his zipper.

They laugh about that sometimes nowadays, thinking of how many years have passed.

Back then, Garth answered, "Make sure to let me know when you're ready." And he pulled open Jonathan's khaki pants.

❖

Back on the couch, Garth frets about his body. He pinches a huge mound of stomach fat.

"I'm a Peep," he says out loud. "A goddamned fucking gigantic Easter Peep."

"What?" calls Jonathan from the kitchen.

"Nothing. Just talking to Blind Kevin," Garth answers. "He needs to go for a walk."

The kitchen done, Jonathan fetches his ring from the place by the sink where he always leaves it while cleaning up, puts it back on his finger, and goes into the living room, where he lifts Blind Kevin from his little red bed and carries him outside into the yard. He puts him down in the garden near the statue of Buddha. The ground is wet; the rain has stopped.

Blind Kevin stands as still as Buddha for a long moment, the breeze ruffling his ears, before he sniffs the air and begins to patrol the garden in wide circles that tighten inward and inward as he walks, until the smaller and smaller circles bring him again to a full stop, at which point he pees, sniffs the air, and walks directly into the rhododendron. Jonathan carries him back inside. The relieved Blind Kevin curls back up on his bed when Jonathan gently lowers him down.

He looks over at the TV. "It's over?"

"Just ended."

Garth stretches without rising up from the couch. Then he leans back against the pillows once more and sighs. "But *The Parent Trap*'s on in a bit." He pats the inside of the couch next to his body.

"I ought to get some work done before Monday."

"Oh, not today." Says Garth.

Jonathan joins him on the couch. He places his head up against Garth's mighty stomach. "You're all gurgly," Jonathan says.

"Pizza! I need pizza," says Garth.

And, digging his head a bit into Garth's stomach as he pulls his phone out of the pocket of his jeans, Jonathan speed-dials the pizza place that delivers.

"The usual?" he asks.

❖

Before the food arrives and the movie starts: "So, did I ever tell you about the time Grand Theft Otto and I drove across Pennsylvania on the night of July Fourth?"

Garth is asking Jonathan, who, after putting his phone away, has flipped over on his back, his right leg up over the couch and kicking slightly in the air, his head now fully resting against Garth's warm body.

Garth had told him, of course. Jonathan had long before heard every story that Garth had to tell. Garth had informed him of his list of favorite films—*Annie Hall*, *The Apartment*, *Nashville*—and books—he was inordinately fond of *Great Expectations*—the names of old boyfriends, old addresses; he'd shared the whole timeline of his lifetime, bit by bit over the years, over meals, during car trips, and in bed, late, late at night, interrupting the litany of sighs that was the soundtrack of their sleeplessness, while they stared up at the stars through the skylight that would soon need replacing.

Garth always started in in the same way, "Did I ever tell you about the time...?" He continues his story: "By the Fourth, we'd driven so far already on the way here.

"But back on the first day out, we'd rented a U-Haul and had one of those ball joint things welded to the back of my Mustang.

Then they put the trailer on it and, I thought, chained it in place. But five miles out of town and suddenly, in the rearview mirror, I see the U-Haul disappearing in the distance.

"We're in the middle of nowhere, and it's lucky we were, because I had to back the car up on the highway to the place where the trailer is just sitting still in the middle of the road, held in place by the big metal tongue that sticks out the front.

"This is before cell phones, so if we wanted help, we'd have had to walk to a town and find a phone and I thought that someone was bound to have driven into the back of the U-Haul by then, so I figured that it was the best bet to just put the thing in place ourselves.

"So I backed up, and Otto and I knew we had to lift the damned thing and get it back on that little metal ball welded on the back of my car.

"And Otto gets this look on his face that suggests that, like Bartleby, he would prefer not to, and he places his right hand on the front of the U-Haul like the big metal arm was a teacup and cucumber sandwiches were sure to soon follow.

"So—"

The doorbell rings.

A deliveryman is holding two pizzas, one Spartan, with just olives, mushrooms, and onion, the other laden with toppings.

Jonathan answers the door, pays the man, stops in the kitchen for plates, napkins and beer, and returns to the living room.

"Blind Kevin…" Garth mouths, pointing.

Jonathan sets everything on the coffee table, turns on his heel, and returns to the kitchen. He returns a couple of minutes later with two bowls, one of food and the other water, which he places in front of the dog, who, smelling the pizza, stirs on his bed.

Jonathan taps the side of the food bowl with his index finger. The dog noodles over the bowl, sniffs it, eats. Jonathan sits on the floor next to the dog, watching as he eats. He picks pieces of chicken off the rug and hand-feeds Blind Kevin. Then he holds the water dish up for the dog to drink.

Blind Kevin slowly centers himself on the bed and lowers

himself down in stilted, achy motions. Jonathan lingers with Blind Kevin for a long minute, stroking his head and whispering softly to him as he listens to the story:

"—So, at the time I am not finding any of to be this funny. We're trapped there with the trailer in the middle of the road, and I'm furious. This is my car, after all, and the roadway can't stay empty forever. So, like those people who get all adrenalized and lift the car off their baby who happened somehow to get under there, I am just filled with rage and, all in a moment, I lift the damned thing up and drag the U-Haul a few feet to the back of my car and just drop it down on the ball thingy.

"And I see the back of my car sort of bounce and then accept the weight of the trailer, and I grab the chains and hook the front of them on the inside of my back bumper.

"And I'm sweaty, see, and I'm breathing hard, and it's about a hundred degrees, and I feel like I am going to pass out, and I must have glared hard at Otto, whose eyes get all big and moist like they always did, and he says to me, 'I was intending to help you...'

"And we get back in the car, and we begin to drive again, and I'm hauling a U-Haul, which I'd never done before, and, suddenly, in the side mirror I see an old blue car thundering down on us. Racing ahead, apparently totally unaware of the fact that we are traveling about five miles an hour.

"So I floor the gas pedal, and both Otto and I are sort of pumping our torsos, as if that would help the car and trailer move faster. But we are only very slowly picking up speed.

"At the very last moment, as the blue car gets bigger and bigger and bigger in the side mirror, the driver, who's wearing a baseball cap on backward and has one of those wispy beards, and a face full of pimples, which I can see clearly because he is getting so fucking close, notices what's happening and jumps over to the left lane, leaving a trail of dust and cigarette butts and the echo of 'My Sharona' in his wake.

"And I'm shaking, see?" He takes a bite of his pizza and continues talking before swallowing. "I mean, I don't think I can take any more. I lifted the fucking trailer. I raced with death.

"And Otto says to me, 'I think maybe this is when I should tell you that I forgot my glasses, so I don't think I can help you drive...'"

Jonathan laughs, picks up the bowls, and puts them on the coffee table next to the plates and food that Garth has arranged into a buffet of sorts. He has placed the bottles of beer on napkins to protect the coffee table.

"We should have gotten a salad as well."

They begin to eat and Garth again speaks:

"So, I'm driving," says Garth. "Five hundred miles. A thousand. God knows. And we're supposed to be in Connecticut on July fifth at noon. And the days are just flying off the calendar, like they do to simulate time passing in an old movie. And I'm driving.

"And, of course, Otto has to stop for food. He has to use the bathroom. He needs to stretch his legs. And while we're in the car, he sits and stares out his side window. He doesn't talk. He won't even attempt to change the radio station when the old one wears out. And I'm driving and driving, and we can't go too fast because of the U-Haul, which has become sort of normal to me by this time.

"And it's the Fourth of July, and I believe we can still hit our deadline, but only if we approach this last day like a death march. We get up early, and I all but shove Otto out of the motel room and into the car.

"And it's one of those days when the immediate surroundings still are a bit cool and there is a mist of dew on the flowers, but a day in which you can feel the heat gathering even then, even just after sunup. This day is going to crackle.

"And I'm driving and just snarling every time Otto wants to stop. And after a while he's sort of shell-shocked, sitting with his hands in his lap.

"And the radio station starts to fade and suddenly I'm yelling, 'Can't you at least find a new station—can't you at least do that?'

"And, truth to be told, he tries and he can't. He turns the dial so slowly with his moist hands. He leaves a damp mark on the dashboard with his right hand. And there doesn't seem to be another radio station to be found, as if we'd driven through a nuclear holocaust without realizing it and the rest of everyone had been wiped out.

"Suddenly, I suspect he is quietly sobbing. He's looking out the side window again, so I can't be sure, but there is a sort of tidal motion to his body. So I asked, 'Do you want to stretch your legs?' And, of course, he did.

"So, we get back in the car and begin to drive again. I put a cassette in the player, and we listen to Joni Mitchell, which I hope will make things better. But I've driven so far and I am fucking exhausted and he forgot his glasses."

Garth pours sarcasm into his. Garth is staring at the television. TCM shows clips of upcoming movies.

Jonathan splits his attention for a moment between the TV and Garth. He notices that *Brief Encounter* is on on Monday and makes a mental note.

Garth continues: "And night begins to fall, the long, slow onset of a hot summer night. And suddenly, off to the right side of the car—Otto's side—there is a flickering in the sky. Fireworks from some distant town.

"And we're up in the Laurel Highlands of Pennsylvania on Route 80, headed toward New York, so we can see forever across the valleys to towns all around us. And as we travel, as we make tracks, hauling the U-Haul, we hit town after town, just as the fireworks begin. Like a million jeweled fireflies all around us. It was like when you get lucky and hit a run of green lights that take you through miles of city streets, each on turning green just the instant before you arrive at it.

"Just as we approached a town, it lit up the sky for us. And the colors faded into the pop pop pop of the big finale just as we moved on past. Otto opened his window, letting in the hot night air, and stuck his head out like a dog, just watching the lights in the sky.

"Finally, it was late late late, and we were outside Wilkes Barrie or someplace and I had to stop. I'd planned to cut through New York City in the late night, when I hoped things would be kind of easy, since I'd never driven there before. But it was late, and I was too tired and too hot to even give a crap. So we stopped at some motel to sleep for a few hours.

"After a Pennsylvania Dutch breakfast special—scrambled eggs with chunks of ham cut up in them, I remember that—and several cups of very hot coffee, we set off. Once you hit the New Jersey line, you can no longer even pretend that New York City is going to be something you can just drive through, especially after days on the road, hauling a U-Haul in your wake.

"As New Jersey became more and more, I don't know, militarized around me, I tightened my grip harder and harder on the steering wheel, until all the blood had been forced out of my white white hands. And I can hear Otto sort of hyperventilating.

"To get on the bridge just as morning rush began involved starting and stopping, the likes of which I'd never experienced before or since. The U-Haul pushed hard against the bumper with every stop, fishtailed if I wasn't careful when starting up again. I began to swear, at first under my breath, and then louder and louder. We made the bridge. Then we were in the maze that followed. I kept asking Otto to look at the map and tell me which lane I should get in, when I should prepare to merge onto the next road, but, apparently, nearsighted as he was, having forgotten his glasses, he could neither drive nor read a map.

"Again, he went limp. And, as a huge truck attempted to run me off the road, I began to scream and scream like Lana Turner in *The Bad and the Beautiful* when she just lets go of the steering wheel and her car spins and spins and spins to a crashing halt.

"How we made it, I will never know. But I just kept merging with anything that seemed to be pointed to New England, and we finally found our way to Stamford.

"And it was like that trip was like the labors of Hercules or something. Like my whole stored-up karma sort of balled itself up and let me work through it all, all at once. It was only a few months after that that I went to the Smith Club book sale, and, ba-boom. Like after years of having misplaced my glasses, I finally found them."

He looks over at the television screen one last time. "Movie's starting." He watches the credits. "I never remember that Maureen O'Hara's in this…"

❖

Day shifts into night. The room is dark now, except for the light emanating from the screen. Garth reaches behind him to switch on the table lamp. *The Parent Trap* ends. The men look away from the screen, their eyes tired from staring at the flickering light. Neither stirs.

The remains of the pizzas are in their boxes on the coffee table in front of them, Jonathan conjures the scheduling grid on the television screen. Blind Kevin snores softly.

Garth lifts a partially eaten slice, takes the last bites of the sauced edge, and drops the naked crust onto his plate. He picks up a mushroom from his plate and eats it.

Jonathan says, "*Dark Passage* comes on at eight."

"Humphrey Bogart and Lauren Bacall, 1947." Garth taps the top of Jonathan's head as he announces the year the film was made. "It's one of the essentials. Robert Osborne says so."

"Of course it is."

"I love it when Agnes Moorehead jumps out the window, don't you? She sort of swirls up in the drapes and then crashes through."

"Why, yes, yes I do," says Jonathan.

They are quiet a moment. Jonathan removes the grid with the click of a button. He switches over to HGTV, in search of something to watch until the movie begins. Garth leans over with a kiss. And Jonathan turns his face upward to accommodate.

"Happy anniversary," Garth says.

THE SEVEN FORTY-FIVE

Richard Natale

At first, Donald saw the man intermittently, glimpsing him through droopy morning eyes like a flicker in the margins of a dream. He was a smart dresser, the same gabardine suit in two shades of taupe during the warmer months, one lighter, one darker. Fall and winter, he switched to twill, navy and midnight blue. The ensembles were more tailored, less baggy than the current fashion, and with a lower waist. European, Donald surmised. They tended to be dandies.

Or "show-offy," as his wife, Helga, might say. "Isn't he full of himself?" she would snort at some indeterminate foreigner combing back the sides of his brilliantined hair in public or chewing on a toothpick from the side of his mouth and grinning as if he had figured out the secret of existence.

Except for his clothes, though, Donald was too distracted to get a good fix on the man. He usually had to run from the bus to make the seven forty-five ferry, heart pounding and sweaty, or he'd be late for work at the bank. He was a problem sleeper, his insomnia exacerbated by Helga's "little talks."

"We need to have a little talk," his wife would say. Nothing little followed, and she did all the talking. Donald would nod dumbly throughout the harangue after which he promised to "think about it." To which she would rejoin, "Don't just think about it. Do it."

From their very first date, when she disparaged the service at Nino's restaurant in Port Richmond, Helga seemed to have a permanent burr under her skin. A shame, since she was otherwise sweet and certainly pretty. Donald fell for her cherry lips, which were so naturally plumped and ripe, they required no more than a splash of lipstick. She was lithe, with a wonderful bosom, ample without being ostentatious, highlighted by ice-cream-colored angora sweaters. And she had flowing Anita Eckberg dirty-blonde hair. No beehive or Jackie Kennedy flip for Helga. He admired the way she tossed it when she spoke. To his mind, it epitomized femininity.

Putting up with her petty dissatisfactions was the price he paid for having a wife other men admired. "You dog, Donald," several of his coworkers said when he announced his engagement. "How the hell did you land a doll like Helga Guilfoyle?"

"I have my charms," he replied with a wink. Not much truth to his boast, however. During their courtship, the farthest he got was some under-the-sweater action. And once, she magnanimously gave him a peek. Donald, she remarked, was different from the other men at the Miami Club where they first met. "They always get a little too close when they talk. You keep a respectful distance, even when we're dancing. I like that."

Gliding across the floor with Helga was exciting. All eyes in the club were focused on them. But he never lost control, and she rewarded him for his gentlemanly demeanor with the occasional hand job, either in the front seat of his DeSoto or under a newspaper while they were watching a movie at the Victory Theater. She complained about that too. "You take too long."

When they'd been dating for six months, Helga's mother, Gert, gave him an ultimatum. Either he proposed or he moved on. Their neighbor, John Capodano, who owned a chain of dry cleaners, was waiting in the wings to give her "plenty of grandchildren."

His grandmother loaned him the money for the ring, and he worked at his uncle Pete's tire store on weekends to pay her back and save up for the honeymoon. Niagara Falls. Someone's idea of romantic. Helga found it damp and hair-frizzing.

At weekly Sunday dinners, Gert reminded him that he needed to "get busy." Two years and Helga was not yet inseminated. "I'm trying," he explained. And indeed, he stepped up on the appropriate days when he wasn't too tired, provided Helga was "in the mood."

"Leave it be, Ma," Helga said through a haze of cigarette smoke. "If it's going to happen, it's going to happen. I'm in no rush to lose my figure. Hell, I'm only twenty-two."

Donald was a year older, but if he didn't get a good night's sleep soon, he'd look fifty before long.

❖

Then the man appeared more regularly. The same boat in the morning and, sometimes, even the four forty-five coming home. Once or twice, Donald could have sworn he was loitering in the ferry terminal anticipating his arrival. He always brushed past with his attaché, the *Times* under one arm, and raced to the front of the boat with never so much as a sidelong glance. Slowly, Donald filled in the details. He wasn't a foreigner at all, more than likely of Scots-Irish stock. Probably played football in college. Had the shoulders for it. And the heft. Fordham was his guess. Strong jaw too and a manly stance from behind. Feet planted wide apart. He didn't need to brace himself when the ferry bumped against the pylons as it docked.

At night, in mid-toss and turn, he found himself wondering where the man got his suits made. Bespoke or off-the-rack and specially tailored? Went to an awful lot of trouble, that's for sure. Donald scoped out the left hand for a wedding band. Sure enough. Wide, gold, etched. Probably had a wife out of a TV ad—perfectly coiffed, wearing pearls and an apron, with two kids and another on the way. Definitely a man with purpose. Donald fervently hoped that in a few years, when he was more seasoned, someone would make a similar observation about him. The thought pleased him.

Perhaps his first step should be to emulate the man by riding up front. This way he'd get a jump on the crowd. When he did so, Donald discovered that the extra five minutes he gained from being closer to the double exit doors made a difference. No more over-the-glasses glares from his supervisor.

Also, the man was now in his line of sight for the entire twenty-minute ride, usually positioned diagonally across, features obscured by the *Times*, folded neatly, one column wide. How did he get it to do that without making a mess? He read with full concentration, only looking up if someone knocked over the attaché by accident. Then, without remark, he righted it and went back to the newspaper.

For their anniversary, Donald took Helga to the Copa. Xavier Cugat. They danced and drank. One too many, and he was unable to perform later. "That's okay," Helga sighed. "Take two aspirins and drink plenty of water, or you're going to have a bitch of a headache in the morning."

He did as he was told and was up half the night peeing. Add to the mix the two cups of coffee he drank in the morning to get his motor running, and Donald had to make a beeline for the downstairs men's room on the seven forty-five. Got there just in the nick of time, too.

A sigh of relief as the trail began, matched almost exactly by that of the man less than two feet away, the one with the *Times* under his arm. Donald looked away and then back and down. The man took no notice of his inquisitiveness as he tapped off several times.

As the man reached for a paper towel after rinsing his hands, the *Times* cascaded from under his armpit and splayed on the ground. Donald picked it up. The man nodded a curt thanks and with one or two flips, the paper fell back into place. "Impressive," Donald observed.

"All in the wrist." The man chuckled and made a quick exit.

Donald stood there half-open-mouthed, the way he did when his favorite team scored.

"You look as beat as I feel," the man said, depositing himself heavily next to Donald on the four forty-five back to Staten Island.

"Tough day," Donald said as the fine gabardine fabric briefly grazed his thigh.

"George, by the way," he said, extending a hand. His palm was clammy, belying the declarative exterior.

"Donald. Pleased to meet you," he replied, rubbing the sweat off on his trousers.

"So what do you do, Donald?" George asked. Hardly a leading question, so why did it sound insinuating?

"Branch management, lower Broadway," Donald replied, trying to pump up his starter job. "You?"

"Architect, commercial mostly, though I have a little side business remodeling Victorians in St. George," he said, raising his chin as if they were standing at the bottom of the hill looking up.

"George of St. George," Donald said, a lame attempt at a joke that seemed to bolster Helga's claim that he lacked a sense of humor.

"I'm no saint, believe me," George said, rolling his eyes. Then he opened his briefcase and took out a sheaf of papers and was silent for the rest of the trip.

When George got up, Donald followed him outside. "They should have a bar on these boats, especially for the ride home," George said as they stood shoulder to shoulder. "I could go for a stiff one right about now. You?"

"It would certainly take the edge off," Donald said. "But I shouldn't. Have to drive out to Grasmere. Wife's waiting on dinner."

"C'mon. Just one," George suggested, though he did not implore. "There's a bar not far from the bus stop, the one right across from the library. You know it?"

❖

George had the salesman gene, a rah-rah attitude softened by an easy tongue. Donald had attended New Dorp High with any number of these "there's no problem I can't solve" jock types. Like them, George appeared unflappable, except for the noticeable jitter in his hands, which made the ice cubes in his whiskey clink against the side of the glass.

"I tell you, I fix up these Victorians," he said, "but I'd never live in one. They're dark, and the rooms are small. Not for me. Got myself a nice modern ranch on Todt Hill, double lot. How about yourself?"

"New development out by Willowbrook, with a mother-in-law apartment downstairs. Nothing special, except the mortgage," he said, glancing at his watch. "I should be on my way in a few—" He stopped short, recalling that Helga and her mother had bingo tonight at St. John's Lutheran. She'd left "something on the stove" for him. When he relayed this to George, he said, "Excellent. How about you and me grab a bite, then? Let me call the missus and tell her I'll be late."

"She's probably cooked for you," Donald said.

"Karen? Cook? That'll be the day." George laughed. "Kidding, of course. She makes a mean mac-cheese. Just follows the instructions on the box. Foolproof. Be right back."

Donald had few friends and was flattered that such a self-possessed man wanted to have dinner with him. The guy's energy was a kick. Made his pulse race.

When he returned, George tossed some bills onto the bar. Donald offered to contribute, but he said "next time," which pleased him. He was already looking forward to a next time and made a note to ask for George's work number before the end of the meal.

"Hey, want to take a scoot up around the corner and have a look at my handiwork, see what you think?" George asked. The request sounded clumsy, a well-thought-out invitation that had become muddled on its way from brain to tongue.

"Okay," he said, a shade tentatively.

❖

"Careful now," George said as he tripped gingerly over the debris in the front hallway of the empty Victorian house and started climbing the stairs. He looked briefly over his shoulder, indicating for Donald to follow.

He flicked on the light in one of the bedrooms, which was papered in an olive drab damask. "See what I mean? Dark, even with the lights on," he asserted.

"Sure is," Donald said, standing just inside the door.

As he reached over Donald's shoulder to flick the off switch, George thrust his body forward and groped him in the darkness. Donald's physical response contradicted the helpless terror he felt. Then he allowed George to gyrate his body and offered himself up without the slightest struggle, almost as if it had been agreed upon beforehand.

Hitching up his trousers afterward, Donald heard George's footsteps descending to the first floor and out the door, which slammed shut. Alone and shaken, he relived the intrusion as well as the discomfort and elation that had ensued. As he lumbered down the hill, a frightening thought crossed his mind and he was unable to dislodge it.

On the bus ride home, trembling and afraid, he fell into a dark torpor that, to the casual observer, resembled sleep, and missed his stop. He had to walk a mile back to the house, the same preoccupation dogging him the entire way, and again, he passed out the moment his head hit the pillow.

This swoon-like sleep became his refuge, kept him from dwelling on the disturbing ruminations. He would awaken no more rested than after an insomnia-plagued night, but at least his senses were dulled and too thick for reflection. He no longer searched for George on the morning ride, during which he dozed until the boat slammed against the pylons. Then he would start as if George was looming over his shoulder, forcing him to confront his acquiescence.

At home, he was absent, filtering out Helga's nattering and begging off his husbandly duties. When word got back to Gert, his mother-in-law upbraided him for his lassitude. Donald offered no defense. He patiently counted the minutes until he could go back upstairs and get into bed.

He was awoken abruptly from his trance-like state by the

appearance of a two-toned Buick Skylark across the street from his home. A man was sitting behind the wheel looking down into himself.

Donald threw on a jacket, went into the garage, and backed the DeSoto down the driveway. The Skylark followed him up to a dirt road in a local nature reserve. He got out of the car and walked a half mile into the woods. He could hear the leaves crackling behind him, crushed by the weight of heavy footsteps.

He stopped suddenly and waited, but not for long. George shoved him to the ground, fell on top of him, and Donald was consumed. When he awoke on the damp earth the following morning, his clothes in disarray, he brushed himself off and trekked back to his car. He waited around the corner until Helga and her mother left for their weekly hairdresser appointment. Entering the house, he climbed the stairs and emptied out his closet and dresser drawers, tossing as much as he could carry into two cardboard suitcases. He got back into the car and drove off.

❖

Growing up in rural West Virginia, Donald had enjoyed few social interactions with anyone outside his immediate family. When his parents divorced, he was sent to live with his maternal grandmother on Staten Island. And while the neighbors kept pretty much to themselves, life in the outer borough was nonetheless a major adjustment for a solitary fifteen-year-old. Now he was living in the heart of Manhattan and inexplicably found himself in the thrall of its chaos. A favorite pastime was sitting in the second-story window of his apartment on Perry Street and being entertained by the cacophony of street noises and passersby, day and night almost without cease.

The first time he glanced out the window and saw George standing on the sidewalk, he retreated back into the apartment filled with dread and excitement. George was bound to find him eventually, he reasoned, if he looked hard enough. When he peered out again, George was still there, staring blankly into the near distance. His exhaustion at trying to keep away from Donald—and failing—was tangible. When he called out to him, George turned and looked up, a scowl of defeat creasing his face. He pulled himself up to the second floor and sloped into the apartment. Donald helped undress him and hung his suit in the closet.

He offered George a key, which he refused. Rather than argue, Donald dropped it into his jacket pocket. Whenever he came home and found him sitting in a straight back kitchen chair looking completely undone, Donald would retreat to the bedroom and wait quietly. Then he'd hear a dish break or the chair being overturned, and George's shadow would descend on him.

Donald couldn't determine exactly when he started believing that George was in love with him, but his conclusion was based on more than conjecture. George had almost let the words slip a few times when they were in the throes, and he'd demonstrated it in the moments of heartfelt affection that began to infiltrate the necessary roughness Donald demanded. Any attempt on his part to address those feelings, however, might cause a seismic rupture, and not only in George. It would force Donald to confront his own complex yearnings. Instead he chose to classify their desires as some twisted need. Otherwise he might break apart when, after falling asleep on his chest, George slipped out from under him and headed out the door back to his real life.

They didn't talk much at first because it didn't seem to fit into their agreed-upon ritual. But soon, they began a casual exchange. George particularly enjoyed discussing his children, DeeDee and Jonathan, detailing the incidentals of the children's daily lives, mundane activities only a dedicated parent could fully appreciate. When George was particularly low, Donald prompted him with leading questions about the kids and he would immediately pep up and transform into the confident, well-tailored man he'd first seen striding to the front of the Staten Island ferry each morning.

Any talk of the "missus," however, was off-limits. If George could not be faithful to Karen physically, he'd carved out a chunk only the two of them shared. And Donald respected that boundary, depended upon it almost.

During their breaks, the days and sometimes weeks during which George beat back his dependency on Donald, he was forced to seek temporary asylum. He did not actively pursue other men. He stumbled upon them on a springtime stroll or while shopping at a local market. The men would look, then quickly look away, then back again. Donald viewed the non-flirtation flirtations as bizarrely comical and marveled that whiplash wasn't more common.

Ostensibly, these men were better acclimated to their needs than Donald, though he discovered them to be no less fractious. While Donald was willing to endure George's dourness and his own, he had little stomach for their irritability. He was having enough trouble coping with self-recrimination without having to listen to his inner voice coming out of someone else's mouth.

From among these disconsolate souls, Donald did manage to make a few friends whom he occasionally welcomed to his bed. Reynaldo was his age and masked all his anxieties behind a macho façade. Sexually, he was fierce and boasted he could satisfy women as well as men. He opted for men, he said, because women were more trouble, and he already had one bastard in the Bronx.

Terry was older, a veteran with a peripatetic nature. He was also a total charmer, down to earth and soulful, particularly when he talked about his "good buddy" Monty. Terry lit up at the mention of Monty in the same way George did when he spoke of his children. Donald became Terry's last chance saloon after a fruitless evening on the prowl. But he didn't mind. The void created by George's self-imposed exiles required many such compromises.

These stopgap measures, however, were not enough to obviate the sticky patches of loneliness and longing. And in moments of claustrophobic distress he took solace in the babble of the noisy stream outside his window. And if that was not enough, he would head out and become part of the flow, roving the busy streets until his legs gave out.

One night, after another wanderlustful evening, Terry rang the doorbell at two a.m. While they were at it in the bedroom, they heard the lock turn. Suspecting a burglar, Terry rolled off him and searched for a weapon. George was already on him by the time

Terry's hand fell on a metal teapot atop the kitchen stove. Terry was thrown to the floor, his nose cracking under George's hammy fist. He might have done more serious damage if Donald hadn't yanked him away.

"Get out!" George screamed as Donald struggled to hold him back. Terry gathered his clothes, limped off, and dressed in the stairwell.

"I'm sorry, Terry. I'm so sorry," Donald called after him.

Pointing a finger at him accusingly, George cried, "Who was that? What was he doing here? You're mine. Don't you know that by now?"

Donald stared at him and quietly shook his head. Of course he was George's, but hearing it out loud forced him into denial. He'd promised himself never to complain, no matter how long it took for George to return. He would not act the part of the abandoned wife, even if George now insisted on behaving like a possessive husband. Later, after he left, Donald would lock himself in the bathroom and expel his bile. But not in front of George; never in front of George. If he did, he would lose him for sure.

"What do you mean no?" George pleaded.

"You have your life, George, and so do I," he said calmly. "You're always welcome. But if you react this way again, I'm changing the locks."

He could hardly believe he'd made such an empty threat. But while he might be inured to George's impotent tirades, he saw no reason anyone else should be subjected to them.

"Do you think changing the locks would keep me out?"

"Then I'll move," Donald said with a flint of defiance.

"I'll find you, I always do," he countered.

"Then I'll move again. Someplace far away."

"I don't understand what you want from me."

A list? Was that what George wanted, a list? How much time did he have? Instead, he merely said, "Come to bed."

"Not until you clean yourself and change the sheets," George scowled.

"It's the only set I have. I'll take a shower and throw a coverlet over the couch."

His sangfroid manner only served to rankle George further. "Why do you let me treat you like a whore?" he yelled.

"I like being your whore," he said and was shocked by his own words. But why should he be shocked, he reasoned. That seed had been planted the first time he noticed George's impeccable suits ("A tailor on Delancey fits them for me. Guy's a genius," he once explained).

"Don't you hate yourself for that?"

"A little," Donald admitted.

"Well, I hate you. Every day I pray I'll open the paper and read your obituary."

Donald wanted to laugh. How much more proof did he need that George loved him, loved him so hopelessly that he wished him dead? "That's one way out," he said. "As long as you don't die. I couldn't bear that."

Donald wrapped his arms around George's waist. "Don't. You smell like..." he complained, but didn't push him away.

"I know," Donald said, squeezing him tighter. "I know."

They kissed, and he could almost feel the anger and hurt drain from George's body.

Rechanneled, those emotions proved potent and Donald was transported—another glorious moment to store in the bank vault and reflect upon during George's unbearable absences. Half a loaf, half a loaf, half a loaf onward.

Later, Donald gazed at the ceiling so he wouldn't have to watch George get dressed. Affecting a cheery lilt, he said, "So tell me; what are you and the kids up to this weekend?"

"They're away. Karen's folks have a summer place in the Poconos."

"Then feel free to stop by again," he said, adding, "I'll plan to be alone."

"I had considered sleeping over but—"

"You can't sleep with your whore," Donald said, finishing the sentence for him.

"You're not my whore. I've never thought of you that way. Never. That's why I got so crazy when I saw you with… Why do you we have to talk about this? If I sleep here, next thing you'll want is for me to…"

"No. I won't. I would never jeopardize what you have. Your devotion to them is part of what makes you so special to me."

"Stop doing that to yourself," George cried. "You are…you are…you are…" He choked as he repeatedly tapped his chest with the flat of his palm; and Donald reveled in the swallowed words. "Now ask me to stay," he beseeched. "Please. I want to do this for you."

"Stay the night, George, would you? But only this one time, hear? I wouldn't want you to make a habit of it."

The Second Time Around

Maryn Blackburn

"Thanks, Karen, but I got it. Really, I've been dressing myself for a while now. Jeff hardly has to help me at all."

My sister does not laugh. She's as stressed out as I am by having too many people around and too little time to herself.

"What you could do is talk to Reverend Cole until it's time. When I peeked out she was standing alone, which has got to be awkward. I'd really appreciate it if you could make her feel welcome. Maybe introduce her to Mom? And Jeff's parents."

"Sure, I can do that."

"Thanks. Jeff's mom is Donna, and his dad is Jeff, too, in case you forgot."

"I didn't. See you in a bit."

Once Karen closes the door to the bedroom, I'm alone for what feels like the first time in a week. Even in the bathroom, people have come in to pee while I was in the shower. "It's me, Matt. Lindsey. Sorry, but I couldn't wait," she called. "Just stay in there a second, until I'm done." It's not easy hosting guests in a one-bathroom house.

I showered first today. My shave is close, my haircut recent and a little too short, my shoes shined, my new suit pressed. It's identical to my first navy suit except a larger size to accommodate the last twenty-five years. The tie still fits, though.

Jeff, the healthy bastard, is wearing his original suit, purchased for a commitment ceremony with no legal standing, also navy but double breasted. The trousers are snug against his hard thighs. "That's what thirty years of running will do," he announced when he tried it on.

"Now aren't you sorry you don't sleep in like me?"

"Spoken like a true couch potato."

"Your couch potato."

"Exactly." He examined the brass buttons, which were tarnished. "Which is the whole reason we're doing this."

This meant a real wedding like we should have had the first go-round. We hunted down the guests who'd attended our first ceremony, praise God for Facebook and LinkedIn. Time and the job market scattered people, but we found nearly everybody and agreed to a days-long sleepover for those who couldn't afford hotels, although now I wish we'd thought that through. The invitation list grew with current friends and more family than we'd had then.

We held the original commitment ceremony in our friends' backyard, but Pat and Lydia's place is too small for the expanded crowd even without the deck taking up a third of it.

At least our jobs are stable and let us stay local. We bought this house nearly a decade ago, and our standard joke is that we hope to have it fully renovated within another three or four. The yard isn't especially nice, but it's big and flat, which is really all you need for an outdoor wedding. I check my tie in the mirror, which is tilted wrong for me. It would be easy enough to adjust it so we can both use it, but that's the kind of job that can always wait. I can't see most of my head, but the knotted silk at my throat looks good. A postcard from Jeff's brother is tucked into the frame of the mirror. A beach at sunset. I can't remember where they went, but our disagreement about our "real" honeymoon after today's wedding is still painful.

Jeff wants to go someplace fabulous. "Aruba? No, Tahiti. Or Paris! How many times are we going to get married, ya big lug? Let's splurge."

"Let's gut the bathroom instead. We could get years of pleasure from a new one, instead of a week."

"Redoing the bathroom isn't exactly romantic."

"But it's what we were saving up for when the legislature saw the light."

I finally wore him down, but I still feel bad that I can't take him to Paris and Tahiti. Maybe if I can keep my truck running for two more years. Maybe.

A fast peek out the gap between the curtains, and I see nearly all our guests have arrived. I'd been grateful for the sunshine and warm temperatures earlier, but despite the white tent keeping direct sunlight at bay, Mom is fanning herself and leaning on Donna a little. The chemo is kicking her butt.

In a perfect world, Dad would be here for her if not for me. Karen reports he's really great about doing every little thing for her, anticipating her needs, making light of lifting her into their high bed, announcing he can't tell her wig from her hair, which is a flat-out lie. But Dad made it clear when I came out of the closet that he no longer had a son. Unlike most people, his stance has not softened with passing years and changing public opinion. Mom and I phone and email, arranging to see one another pretty often, but even when she felt like shit on toast, Mom made sure Dad and I wouldn't run into each other at the hospital.

If she doesn't beat this damned cancer, fuck him. I'm sitting right in front at the funeral, my husband Jeff at my side. If Dad can't breathe the same air as his queer son, let him be the one who stays away.

The thought makes me both sad and angry. Karen and I agree Mom falls way short of being forthcoming about her health, and there's only one reason she'd do that. This makes us worry more. I haven't said it to Karen or Jeff, but I think we're going to lose her.

My vision blurs at the thought of putting my mom, who loves me no matter what, into the ground. It's going to happen. Maybe not from this goddamned cancer, maybe not for years to come, but someday. An invisible fist grabs my upper belly and twists from the inside. Fuck, I can't be thinking about that today. If I go out there and ask her to be honest about how she's doing, I know what she'd say so well I can hear it in my head. "Matt, honey, we can talk about me some other time. Today is your day, yours and Jeff's, and all I want in this world is for you two to be happy."

I pick up the framed picture from our first ceremony. It seems almost funny now, especially our hair and Jeff's looking like a very serious twelve-year-old. But the memories swirl.

❖

"Pat says there aren't any more chairs." Lydia pronounced the shortage as she might a death sentence.

"Don't worry about it," I said. "Anybody who comes a little late can stand over by the fence."

"The neighbors play bridge. I bet they have at least four chairs. Maybe eight or twelve."

"It's fine. We read through it, and it's short. People can stand that long."

"And if anybody can't," Jeff added, "I'm sure someone with a seat will give it up. You ready?"

"I've been ready for the last four years."

Jeff beamed. "Me, too, big guy. Me, too."

The late afternoon sun sprinkled golden coins on our guests seated in rows and sparkled off the legs of the folding chairs as they sank into the grass a bit.

"At least the rain stopped for us," I said.

"It sounds sappy," Jeff said, "but may the sun always shine for us, huh?"

"I'm good with sappy."

We stepped onto the concrete patio. Everyone lifted their heads and stopped talking. My big sister Karen, in the front row, was first to stand, giving me a thumbs-up and a huge smile. Her support eased my nerves a little, but it also reminded me my parents had chosen not to be here. Or Dad had, anyway, and he'd swayed Mom. Donna and Jeff Senior sat beside Karen, ghastly smiles frozen on their faces. What were they thinking? His father openly disapproved of Jeff's "choice," by which he meant being gay, although I guess he probably didn't approve of me, either, being a big fat queer and all.

Our friend Mara took the bus all the way from Boston to officiate. Since our commitment ceremony was for us, not for the government, it didn't matter that she was not an ordained minister but ran an underground bookstore-cum-coffeehouse that clung to the hippie spirit of its original owner, who'd sold it for next to nothing and left for Nepal.

She wore a flowing blue dress belted with shiny gold ropes, and a crown of flowers nested among her curls. I grinned when I saw her bare feet step onto the little platform Jeff and I had built the previous weekend.

"Good thing we sanded before we painted," I whispered to Jeff. We'd given it two coats of white paint after work during the week. The lattice behind it came whitewashed. We should have painted it, but Lydia made it her project to thread the holes with greenery and artificial flowers in every shade of blue. The effect of Mara framed in flowers was pretty cool.

Jeff and I locked elbows, although I had to bend a little. We agreed we were each our own man, that nobody could or should give us away, although both families wanted to be rid of us. We walked up the aisle between the folding chairs slowly, giving everyone a chance to check us out in our finery. Most of these people had never seen either of us in a suit.

We'd had to nix the idea of flower girl or ring bearer, but white petals lay scattered on the grass aisle. Up close, I could see them under Mara's bare feet, too. She had one orange toenail.

We stepped onto the platform in unison, just like we'd practiced. Mara's big smile was genuine.

"Jeff and Matt," she said, loud enough to be heard, "today you are surrounded by people who hold you dear. We come together to celebrate you, to witness your vows, and to rejoice at your union."

We'd struggled with the wording when we wrote the ceremony together. It started as *all the people you hold dear*, but as it became clear my parents would not attend, and that Jeff's folks could not bring his teenage brother or Karen her kids, that phrasing wasn't going to work. We held those people dear even if it wasn't always mutual.

"On this day and all the days to come, we will all remember your love is unique. Yet like all love, it changes and grows. There will come days of a love so much richer and deeper than what you feel today that its strength and size will cause awe. You will be so awash in love that you take it for granted, never doubting one another. We who love you wish you a lifetime of such days together.

"Yet we must acknowledge that love can also dwindle. Because we are humans, because we face pressures and difficulties every single day, because we forget our great love and speak sharply or fail to show our appreciation, one or both of you may fear that the light of your love for one another has gone out. Yet those of us who know you also know it remains, solid and enduring, awaiting its rekindling. A single spark can ignite it. I charge each of you, singly and together, to be the flint."

We didn't write that, but I liked it. We'd mailed Mara our first draft, expressing our horror at its quality and asking her to patch the holes and shore it up. Apparently she'd taken that as license to rewrite the whole thing.

"Please take one another's hands."

I turned toward Jeff, who gave me an impish smile. He hated being reminded of it, but he was small and cute like an elf, or maybe a hobbit from Houston, as he liked to add with an exaggeration of his slight Texas accent. The contrast with my oafish clumsy self made his compact size all the more noticeable. Despite the sunshine, his hands were cold. I put them both inside my grasp to warm them.

"Do you, Jeffrey, commit your love and life to Matthew, in times of powerful love and in times of weak? Do you promise to respect and cherish him for the man he is, when he is at his best and when he is not? Do you promise to place his happiness on a level equal to your own or greater?"

Again the elfin grin. "I do." He wriggled his cold hands inside my big paws. "I really do," he whispered.

"And do you, Matthew, commit your love and life to Jeffrey, in times of powerful love and in times of weak? Do you promise to respect and cherish him for the man he is, when he is at his best and when he is not? Do you promise to place his happiness on a level equal to your own or greater?"

Oh, shit. Shit! I looked upward, willing my eyes not to overflow, but the sun made the tearing worse. The right eye lost it first, quickly followed by the left, and of course the top part of my nose started stinging inside, indicating there was lots more where those two came from.

Tears streaming now, my nose clogged with them, my voice hoarse, I said, "I do."

Jeffrey pulled his hands from my grasp and clasped them around mine, as much as he could. His voice was soft. "Every person here wishes their man cried at the wedding. Commitment ceremony. I'm going to treasure this, Matt."

Mara placed one hand on my shoulder, like I was a skittish animal she might soothe. The steadiness of her touch, the strength of her friendship, and her maternal warmth helped. "It's fine, sweetie. I have a hankie if you need one."

I sniffled. "I'm good."

"You're better than good, and you know it, too," Jeff said.

"Ready to go on?"

We nodded. Jeff's smile wasn't the cute one I knew so well, but from some deeper store of happiness that radiated from his entire face.

Mara raised her voice again. "I now ask that you seal the vows you made to one another by the giving and receiving of rings. Their circle is as eternal as your love. Their metal is as strong as your love. Their gemstones are as beautiful as your love. Jeffrey?"

Now came the scary part, and the reason no children were here. I unzipped the trousers of my new suit and lifted my cock, exposing my balls. Jeff knelt in front of me, crushing petals with the knees of his suit, adding faint perfume to my fear sweat.

A few gasps came from the folding chairs behind us. I was glad neither one of us could see whose they were, although I'd have happily bet on Karen, Donna, and Jeff Senior.

My piercing had fully healed, and it was easy for Jeff to slip the surgical steel post from its position on the bottom of my sac and thread the silvery ring through, then screw tight the metal bead with its small sapphire that held the ring in place.

"Repeat after me," Mara said. "I, Matthew, commit my life and love to thee, Jeffrey."

I said the words in a daze. Although it wasn't heavy, I was overly aware of the ring dangling, the bead and its blue stone at its lowest point. The sensation did not stop when I zipped up and helped Jeff to his feet.

I didn't have his grace as I got to my knees in front of Jeff. His zipper was stubborn for a moment, but at least no one gasped when it opened audibly. His piercing was simpler and healed earlier than mine. I unscrewed the ball at one end and slipped the steel barbell from the base of his cock, directly before my eyes and just below his pubic curls.

The ring didn't want to go in, and I was so afraid of hurting him. Finally, he helped by pulling the skin to make the opening in his flesh just a little wider to get me started, then tugging down to make the tunnel through his flesh impossible to miss. I nearly dropped the ball that threaded onto its ends, making the ring a complete circle that twinkled with his emerald, and I was sweating by the time Mara asked Jeff to repeat her words.

They both helped me up. The knees of my new suit were damp, crushed flower petals clinging to the fabric. I was still crying. And committed, for life.

❖

"Matt, did you die in there?" Karen again. Shit, we were supposed to walk down the aisle two minutes ago.

"It's this tie," I lie, undoing my perfect Windsor knot. "Can you give me a hand?"

She is happy to tie it for me, not as well as I'd had it but with love, which is better. I hurry toward the family room and its French doors leading to the yard, where Jeff and I will meet. We put those doors in ourselves, two years ago, with much swearing and some heated words that required dinner out, a few tears, and an evening of lovemaking to cool.

After so many years together, it often takes something like that to get us started. We talk about our diminishing frequency now and then, agreeing that if we're both okay with how things are, then it isn't a problem. "What we have isn't even about sex," I remind him. "It's about love. About us as a unit."

"What, you want to see my unit?" He leered at me, ending it with a wink.

"Ha-ha. You know what I mean."

"I do. I just worry that you're not really okay with it. That you need what I'm not giving you often enough, and that you might get it somewhere else."

"Oh, right. Like they're lining up for me." He doesn't need to know how every so often some young guy will come on to me, seeking a bear type. I try to be nice while I reject them. I remember perfectly well how scary it is to approach a stranger because you're so strongly attracted you can't not approach him. "You're a nice-looking guy, for sure, but I'm in a committed relationship," I say, then make conversation for a while, ensuring they know about the places they might meet guys like me, or like themselves.

"You're woolgathering again," Karen says.

"Don't I know it. Every little thing is setting off some memory, you know?"

"Save it for later. Jeff's waiting."

"Got it. Go sit with Mom and the kids."

Her kids aren't kids anymore, of course, but she still inquired whether there'd be anything piercing-related. I assured her there would not.

Jeff stands at the glass, outwardly calm as always. "Thought you might've changed your mind."

"Thought about changing this tie. It's okay?"

"It's fine. You look good. We should dress up once in a while."

"I'm free most Fridays after six or six thirty."

This time we walk down the aisle to music from a string

quartet in the shade of our willows, which I trimmed high enough to keep the dangling leaves out of their hair. The aisle is real, made of circular pavers we'll use for a patio. The guests' chairs and high heels sink into the ground, just like last time.

Reverend Cole leads us through the traditional wedding ceremony, which we'd practiced at the rehearsal because this is really important to Jeff. When his parents' church officiates gay marriages, when their own pastor Reverend Cole marries me and their son, they have to let go of their bias. Or at least try to.

This time, when we exchange rings, they're gold bands each with a small stone, the same sapphire and emerald as on those earlier rings many of these guests don't know about, which we still wear. Right on schedule, I tear up. The guests make that "Aww!" sound people do at baby animals, and I laugh a little right through the tears. Jeff hands me a handkerchief, bought new for the occasion and kind of hard to find in stores.

We're married, at last, in the eyes of the law, in front of our mothers and his father, our coworkers, our friends and family. As married as anybody. I hadn't thought it would feel any different, but it does. It feels right, like it's about fucking time.

❖

We feed our guests and give them a little too much to drink. Jeff Senior, Donna, and Karen arrange rides for the people who really shouldn't be driving, then it's literally fucking time, and I'm as nervous as a bride as I get into the car, a pristine vintage Lincoln manufactured the year we held our first ceremony, on loan from a friend of Pat and Lydia's.

I park it with great care in the hotel's lot and check us in. Do the clerks at the desk, the other guests being waited on or lounging in the lobby, realize we're just married? Or do they think we're two businessmen saving our company money by sharing a room?

Upstairs, I lead Jeff to the double doors. The corridor is empty. I unlock the door, blocking him a little, then scoop him in both arms, carrying him across the threshold.

"Oh, my!" Jeff gushes while laughing. "Look at this place!"

I did, before I reserved the suite. It's perfect, and the management did everything I asked and more. "There's champagne on ice," I show him, sweeping my arm at the tray with pearl-draped goblets.

"Crystal flutes!" Jeff says.

Right, flutes. "There's canapés and fresh fruit. Bubble bath."

"Seriously?"

"Sure. Don't you want to take a bubble bath with your new husband?"

"Of course I do. But first I want to fuck his brains out."

That tells me he's had a bit much to drink already; he's not usually that direct. Which is fine, and why I drove. It's our wedding night. "Right this way."

The bed is turned down, the sheets sprinkled with a few yellow rose petals.

It's Jeff's turn to tear up. "For me?"

"You're the yellow rose of Texas."

"I love you so much. Come here." We kiss, and it only starts out the pure love kind before mutating into the horny kind, with some tongue and bodies pressing through navy suits.

It's been a while since we did it. Planning a wedding and doing as much of the work yourselves as you can takes all your spare time, for months and months.

"I did something for you, too." Jeff sounds almost shy.

"What?"

"I've been thinking a lot about the first time, the commitment ceremony. God, it was so long ago. And we were so out-there, with our piercings. Nobody straight had them back then."

"Yeah, probably not. I still love looking at your ring when I give you head."

"That's why I put it there, for you to have something beautiful, literally and as a symbol, to look at."

"Are you trying to make me cry again? Because that handkerchief is already a mess."

"No. I'm trying to make you happy. Look at what I did for you this time," he says. His zipper is loud in the stillness.

Oh. My. God! "What is that?"

"It's called a magic cross. An ampallang piercing—that's the side to side one—and an apadravya going up and down. With little barbells in each."

I'm sinking to my knees already. What will all that metal taste like? What will it feel like?

"You be careful," Jeff says. "The piercer said it's easy to break a tooth."

"I bet." The stupid fucking insurer says I can't be added to Jeff's dental plan until after the wedding. I told Jeff he'd better call from Vegas, honeymoon or not. "I'll be careful."

"So will I," he says, "when I put it up your ass."

The thought of that does something to me. I fold up inside, my needs and desires forgotten in exchange for his. This is my man, my husband, and I am his. I truly want nothing more than whatever my husband wants to give me, including a magic cross I'm not entirely sure I can take. I'll learn, I know I will.

I wait until morning to tell him about my wedding gift. The things we packed for Vegas will do, so we don't even need to stop at home. It's not Tahiti but a full week at a beach resort in Hawaii, and I got a package that includes everything, even tips.

By the time we fly home, we're lightly tanned, happy, and by-God married. Jeff has bought me so many Hawaiian shirts we had to get a cheap backpack to add to our luggage. I got him a bracelet made of silver and koa wood, a carved bone pendant on a leather cord, and a short necklace that's tiny disks of pale pink shell, which makes his skin glow bronze. I wanted to get him a rosewood watch, but he got a little snippy about overspending ourselves, soothing me by swearing he'd wear at least one of my gifts all the time.

In Hawaii, I came to love the magic cross. We agree we need an annual beach vacation because we have never been so relaxed, or so sexual, and that when retirement comes around, it will be in a beach community. "A little house someplace warm. Not necessarily a tourist destination or anything. We don't need that."

"Or the higher prices. Simple is good," Jeff says. "Two

bedrooms, one for guests. Morning sun in the kitchen. A patio. Tile everywhere. Hey, speaking of tile…"

The bathroom is gorgeous, with a terrazzo tile floor, walk-in shower with two heads instead of a tub, double sinks, and lots of cabinets.

"I had them mount one showerhead high enough for you," Jeff says.

Naturally, I have to cry again, but there's Kleenex in a holder that matches the tile. When we undress, he's wearing all the jewelry.

6TH & E

Gregg Shapiro

It began with a whistle. Two notes. One high, one low. The kind of whistle construction workers at a construction site blow at passing women showing even the most negligible amount of skin. The kind of whistle an amateur bird-watcher might attempt to get the attention of a bird high up in a tree. All I know is that it got my attention.

At the time, I was living on Capitol Hill. On E Street, between 6th & 7th, Northeast. The townhouse, which was in the middle of the block, was owned by two friends of my lover Matt. Bob was a former teacher of Matt's, Jack a former classmate. I rented the only finished room, second floor, center of the house, to the right at the top of the stairs.

Bob and Jack had bought the house in 1986, a year before the summer I moved in. They were in the process of slowly remodeling it. Bob had a booming interior design firm in the neighborhood, walking distance from the house. Jack taught at one of the local universities. I moved in with them when the house I had been living in in Mount Pleasant became uninhabitable.

In August, when Matt and some of our friends helped me move in, we had been dating for a little over a year. During that time, we never actually lived together, although the subject arose many times. While he was working and residing in Washington, Matt lived six blocks from Jack and Bob's house. By the time I moved in, he had already left town. Matt had moved to Baltimore in June, to go to graduate school at Johns Hopkins, in a program not offered in any of Washington D.C.'s fine institutions of higher learning.

At the time, we had talked about me moving to Baltimore with him. It reminded me of Boston, where I grew up, before my family moved to Bethesda, Maryland. It was on the water, it had history. But I was in the process of quitting graduate school. I had a job that I hated as much as I loved. My parents were begging me to move back home, stop paying high rent in Mount Pleasant, where I had been living with a neurotic woman, her sister, and their three cats.

I wanted to write. To be with Matt, and to write. I was working as a receptionist at the hippest hair salon in Dupont Circle. I sat in the window, looking bored, making appointments for boring people from all over the Washington metropolitan area. I thought I would have plenty to write about after spending my days looking out onto Connecticut Avenue, watching the parade of pathos. But I longed to be in school.

When I got to class and listened to another endless lecture on the importance of neo-formalism in late twentieth century poetry, I wished I was back at Bouffant Circle, filling in the appointment book with a #2 pencil and gossiping with the clients and stylists.

Matt and I talked on the phone every day. I loved him more than I'd ever loved anyone else. He was very supportive of my writing and encouraged me all the time. Whenever I had a poem published in some small college literary journal, he would buy three or four copies and give them as gifts. He would subscribe to them, to "keep them alive" as he said, so I could publish in them again and again.

Matt believed in me more than I had ever believed in myself. We had complete trust in each other. I believed in absolute monogamy, total commitment to one person, and he said he felt the same way. Neither of us had been promiscuous before we met, and with the health crisis being what it was, we vowed to be true to each other. And we were.

Until the man in the first floor apartment on the corner of 6th & E, NE, whistled at me.

I was walking home from the Metro stop at Union Station and was waiting for the stoplight on the corner to turn green. The batteries on my Walkman had died on the subway, but I left the headphones on anyway. It discouraged strangers from talking to me, asking for money or directions to the Smithsonian.

Traffic was unusually heavy, and I actually had to wait for the green light. While I was standing there, I heard someone whistle. It was coming from behind me, and I considered turning around to look at the source. But then I remembered I was still wearing the headphones, and in keeping with my policy of ignoring the world around me, I stared straight ahead.

When the light turned green and I could cross, I stood on the corner, not moving for about ten seconds, to see if anyone had come up behind me who looked like a whistler or a whistlee. I was the only one there, on that corner, at 6:00 that Tuesday evening. I crossed the street as the Don't Walk sign started to blink.

He whistled again on Wednesday, Thursday, and Friday. I say he, because I saw him, or part of him. Nearing the end of a summer I spent working full time at Bouffant Circle, I pondered what to do about my future. My schedule almost never varied. I was on the corner of 6th and E by six every weeknight. The salon was closed on Mondays, and I started earlier on Saturday and was home by three thirty. Neither of us was around much on weekends, but you could set a clock by him Tuesday through Friday.

The whistler lived on the first floor of a three-story apartment building on the northeast corner of 6th & E. From the street, I could see most of the rooms and corresponding windows. Facing onto E Street was a small, high-up kitchen window, the closest to the apartment building entrance. Next to that was his living room. His windows were always open, although he kept the mini-blinds half-drawn when he was at home. A sofa or love seat was flush against that windowed wall. Directly opposite the window was a fireplace with a large mantel, painted white. I could see the blue lights on his receiver, a CD player and cassette deck. I could tell from the glow that it cast that the TV was on some kind of stand in front of the fireplace.

As one week bled into the next, I grew to anticipate his evening salutation. I would make sure my flat-top was standing evenly, that the laces on my black leather Chuck Taylor high-tops were tied. I wore baggy shorts and oversized printed T-shirts to work. That mid-80's summer Tammy Faye Bakker, Pee-wee Herman, dinosaurs, and a punk rock Ronald Reagan, among other images were silk-screened across my chest. I had just quit smoking at the beginning of the summer and was conscious of a slight weight gain on my usually thin frame. I thought the walk to and from the Metro station was good exercise.

By the end of the second week, I was in a quandary. Matt had been in summer school since the beginning of summer. When he wasn't doing research or writing a paper, he drove down to D.C. to spend time with me. On most Saturday nights, however, I would take Amtrak to Baltimore. It was convenient, since Union Station serviced Amtrak as well as Metro.

I'd stay with him in the graduate dorm, where we had wildly safe sex and ordered pizzas and Chinese food. Occasionally, we'd head out and go dancing at the Hippo or meet friends at a seedy bar in Fells Point or have dinner at his favorite crab house in the Inner Harbor. He had arranged his schedule so that he didn't have classes on Monday, my day off, so we could have a full weekend together. Once in a while, he'd call me at work on Saturday and tell me he was too bogged down for a visit. I'd leave work, carrying my weekend bag, filled with condoms, water-based lube, and other accoutrements, back to the house, where it would sit in a corner of my room, still packed until Monday night. I was always afraid that if I unpacked it on Saturday, I'd end up crying myself to sleep.

The weekends with Matt were something to look forward to, a reward for getting through the week in one piece. Having a man whistling at me from his apartment window didn't make life any easier. In fact, the complications that existed, coupled with my growing curiosity, were a potentially lethal combination.

When it all began, I considered telling my housemate Jack. To me, he was older and wise beyond his years. He had been out almost as long as I'd been alive. He was a well-known figure in gay Washington. An outspoken activist, he was a well-respected educator, cherished as a friend and confidant, and I felt very close to him. He opened the doors of his house to me at a time when I thought I'd never find a place to live. But as close as he was to me, he was that much closer to Matt. I couldn't risk telling him for fear he would misunderstand and confuse matters even more.

I added the whistler to my growing list of traumas. My advisor at school advised me to make up my mind about my plans for the fall term, and be quick about it. There were a few too many incoming grad students, and if I didn't want to return to classes, I had to let him know soon. Time was running out. In addition to that, just as I'd gotten settled into Jack and Bob's house, my parents started in again about me moving back home. My room was as I left it, they reminded me. No rules this time, they insisted, I could come and go as I pleased. How, I wondered, could I come and go as I pleased, if either action involved asking my parents for the keys to the car. Their house was nowhere near a Metro station, and a ridiculously long walk to the closest bus stop.

❖

Then there was Matt. If I moved to Baltimore and we got a place together, how long would it last? Neither of us had lived with a lover before, and we were both apprehensive. Matt was something of a slob. When he was still living on Capitol Hill, he and his gay Republican roommate lived in what we all comically referred to as the "slaughterhouse." They both worked long hours and were busy with social activities outside of the house. Patrick went to his political rallies, which I insisted were Hitler Youth meetings. Matt and I plunged into a very concentrated romance. Love at first sight and all that other nonsense. We alternated between his house and mine, although we ended up at my place on 16th Street more often than not.

Matt had a car, so we spent a lot of time outside of the city, including weekends at the Eastern Shore, Rehoboth, or Virginia Beach. We drove to his grandmother's house in West Virginia for our first 4th of July together. His grandmother was more open-minded than I would have expected for a woman of eighty-eight and made us feel comfortable and loved. But these were only weekends. During the week, we'd talk on the phone, see each other for dinner, return to one of our houses for a full-body massage and hours of mutual masturbation. One or the other would leave and we'd sleep alone during the week.

Now, not five hundred paces from my house was a man who whistled at me every time I passed his window. Two and a half weeks after his first whistle, I acknowledged him. His persistence won hands down over what I considered one of my greatest talents: an iron will and the tendency to be incredibly stubborn.

He had, at some point, established a pattern, a mating dance, if you will. As I approached the apartment building, I could see him, or at least the back of his head, in the window. He would be sitting on the couch, watching the news or some reruns. Just as I got to the building entrance, he would look over his shoulder, out the window. He would stand up, lean on the windowsill, and watch me walk, as slowly and innocently as I could, to the corner. By then, he was standing in the bay window, a swag lamp glowing dimly behind him. Then he would whistle.

August in Washington is like turning on the oven and leaving the door open. It's like having big kettles of boiling water on all four burners of the stove, all going at once. And then someone holds a magnifying glass between you and the sun. Someone once told me that diplomats and ambassadors used to get hardship pay for their stays in Washington in August. Clothing becomes an obstruction to comfort.

The whistler wore red running shorts or blue and white vertically striped running shorts or black running shorts, and nothing else. His shoulders looked wide enough to carry the world. His arms were muscular and defined; I could see the veins from my vantage point on the street corner. There was a chiseled separation between his pectorals. I wasn't sure, but I thought I detected a small patch of hair in the crevice. He seemed to be tan, and his nipples were as dark as Godiva chocolate. The window ledge began mid-thigh, where his shorts ended.

He was cute, too. Short, brown hair, combed back. Big blue

eyes that always seemed to be on the verge of winking. And he smiled so much, I wondered how he found time to whistle. I smiled back, finally. After all, there was no harm in smiling. I smiled and then a few days later, I nodded. He smiled, he nodded, he touched himself.

I closed up like one of those underwater flowers, like a Venus flytrap. Suddenly, the whistler-smiler-nodder wanted more than I could offer. Sinless flirtation came dangerously close to the jagged, erotic line I could never cross. I had a lover. Who lived in Baltimore. That I saw on weekends. Well, most weekends.

He touched himself, and I could make out the outline of something bigger than both of us. I crossed the street quicker than usual and didn't bother looking back, as I had begun to do. I just kept walking, moving both arms as if to propel me safely to my front gate. Watching my feet, the sidewalk. Trying not to be conscious of George Michael singing "I Want Your Sex" blasting from my Walkman, the car parked across the street, the window of Bob's bedroom.

I called Matt that night. We talked about our plans for the weekend. He would drive down to Washington on Friday. My boss, Gigi, was going to cut his hair. While I was at work Saturday, he would help Bob and Jack paint and wallpaper the kitchen. We had tickets for a concert at Lisner Auditorium that night. We had dinner reservations at our favorite restaurant on M Street. He was going to spend the whole weekend, Sunday included. As we talked, I waited for him to tell me that something had come up, that he was going to have to cancel, again. I waited, anticipating every vowel. I realized I had drifted off, that I wasn't paying attention to what he was saying.

So, when he said that he'd see me at Bouffant Circle at four on Friday, I had to ask him to repeat himself. He laughed that hypnotic laugh of his, and said he loved me more than frozen grapes, and he couldn't wait to see me and kiss me and taste me and sleep and sweat with me on Friday. And Saturday and Sunday, I added. He agreed. We hung up, and I wondered how I would make it, on a Tuesday night, until Friday, without changing my route home or relocating altogether.

On Wednesday, I walked up F Street to 7th. I took the long way home. I couldn't help it. I couldn't risk losing control, now that I seemed to be back on track with Matt. This weekend would be a new beginning. Maybe I would leave Washington entirely. Start fresh in a new city with the man I loved. Everything looked brighter, as if I'd been viewing things through a dirty lint screen, and now it was clean.

Wednesday night, I got a craving for a bowl of Life cereal. I went downstairs in my grey sweatpants and Silence=Death T-shirt. I got my favorite big bowl down from the cabinet above the microwave oven and found a recently washed soup spoon in the strainer. I poured the cereal into the bowl until it was almost even with the lip. Then I discovered we were out of milk.

I left the bowl of dry cereal on the kitchen counter and ran upstairs. Sometimes at night it got cool, so I grabbed my Levi jacket and slipped my bare feet into a pair of old Nike running shoes. I knocked on Bob's door, but Jack called out from his room that he'd gone out for the night with some friends to a movie. I stood in the doorway of Jack's room, which was next to the bathroom, and asked him if he needed anything from the convenience store on Maryland Avenue. He was sitting up in bed, eating a bag of Utz crab-seasoned potato chips and watching a video of *The Way We Were*. He had a box of Kleenex on his lap. He smacked his lips and sniffled and said he was fine, thanked me for asking. I told him I'd be back in a few minutes.

It was an almost perfect summer night. People were sitting on their porches, on their stoops, talking and drinking and laughing. The air smelled like bar-b-q and flowers. Every car that drove by had its windows down, and no two cars had the same song coming from their radios. Children darted in and out of each other's front yards, playing Freeze Tag or Statue. A constant breeze carried sounds and smells around the corner and out of reach. I crossed against the lights at Maryland and 8th.

Once inside the convenience store, I realized I'd left my money at home. Luckily, I found my ATM card in my jacket pocket. I got in line behind two women who were arguing about what kind of beer to buy after they got their money. I recognized one of them as a waitress from Mr. Henry's on Pennsylvania Avenue, a restaurant Matt and I went to for Sunday brunch when he still lived in the neighborhood.

When I got to the head of the line, I inserted my card and punched in my secret code. I took out two mutilated tens. I walked up and down the narrow aisles, looking at the shelves jammed full of overpriced food. Even though milk was the only thing I ever bought at this store, I always walked around as if I was going on a shopping spree. The stock was a constant, dusty and unchanged. I doubted that they ever rotated the merchandise.

At the counter, I admired the displays of beef jerky and chewing gum especially for denture wearers. One of the clerks, in a logoed smock, was refilling the pornography rack behind the counter, occasionally flipping through one or two magazines that caught his interest.

The clerk at the cash register was voiding the purchases of the man in front of me because the convenience store didn't accept traveler's checks. The man kept saying, I thought these things were honored everywhere, I've never heard of such a thing, wait till I get back to Springfield. I wondered if it was in Missouri, Illinois, or Massachusetts, but I decided against asking him.

Instead of walking down 8th Street to E Street, I decided to walk down Maryland to 6th Street. I wanted to walk past Daniel and Tom's house and see if they were home. A man walking two Dalmatians came toward me. He had shoulder-length blond hair and a few days' growth of beard. He seemed to be younger than me from what I could tell by the street lamps. He was very thin, but in a healthy way. As we got closer to each other, he opened his mouth to speak, but a car blew its horn as it drove past, which made the dogs bark madly. He had to calm them down and untangle their leashes. I didn't look back; I kept on walking.

All the lights were off at Daniel and Tom's house. I'd left my watch at home, so I didn't know what time it was. I crossed Maryland where D Street cuts in and walked down D Street to 6th. Just a few blocks in from the busy street, a sudden hush fell through the air. Even my footsteps sounded muffled, as if I was walking on the sidewalk in my bare feet. Air conditioners and fans pulsed in the windows of some of the houses. Others just had their windows thrown open all the way, screens between the outside and the inside.

Before I knew it, I was at the corner of 6th and E. Every light was on in the whistler's apartment. All the windows glowed like a landing strip, a beacon in a lighthouse. As I stood like an insect attracted to the heat of a candle, he came into the living room in a pair of white Jockey shorts. He didn't stop and sit down on the couch, he didn't crouch to look out the window below the blinds. He walked straight to the bay window on the corner and looked out. If my mouth weren't so dry, I would have whistled.

He put his hands on his hips. I imagined he was tapping his foot slowly, patiently, beating out a rhythm that matched my heartbeat. The Don't Walk sign blinked in syncopation, without a moving car in sight. I crossed the street on a diagonal.

Come on up, he said, and he walked back into the living room. I stayed where I was. No, I said. Yes, he said, come inside, and he kneeled on the couch and raised the mini-blind a hair. He opened the window a little wider. I watched the muscles in his arms move.

I have to go home, I said. No you don't, he said and stood up and walked out of the living room. My heart seemed to stop. I couldn't see him. Where had he gone? And then I heard him say, I'll buzz you in. I looked up at the small kitchen window to the right of the apartment building entrance. What if I don't want to come in, I said. I don't want to come in. Oh yes, you do, he said, and I want you to come in. I clutched the half-gallon carton of 2% milk to my chest. It felt cool through the jacket and T-shirt.

I have to put the milk in the refrigerator, I said. I have a refrigerator, he said, come on, come in.

The security door buzzed loudly, and I was afraid the neighbors would run to their windows if I didn't go to the door and open it so he would stop pressing the button. I opened the door, walked up four steps. The buzzing echoed in my head, rang like an unanswered phone. He was waiting for me in the doorway of his apartment.

When I stand straight, I'm probably five foot nine and one half, although my driver's license says five foot ten. Matt and I see eye to eye, but I may be a fraction taller. The whistler was at least six foot one. I leaned my head back a little to meet his eyes, and he pressed his open mouth on mine. He had a tongue with a mind of its own that moved slowly across all of my teeth and then probed almost to the back of my throat. He wrapped his arms around me so tightly, I was afraid he'd crush the milk carton, so I pushed him away, our mouths still attached.

We bent slightly, together, so I could put the bag on the floor. On the way back up, he removed my jacket in one swift tug and began to lift my T-shirt over my head. Since we were joined at the mouth, I was certain he was going to rip the T-shirt off. Just as suddenly as he'd started, he stopped kissing me. Take it off, he said, now. The T-shirt was off me and on the floor in record time. He pulled me to him, and the hairs on our chests met. He half carried, half swept me into his bedroom at the end of a short corridor that also led to the kitchen, living room, and bathroom.

I fell on top of him on the king-size bed. He managed to work the Jockey shorts off and his huge, hard cock throbbed between us. He struggled with a knot in my sweatpants while licking my chin, my Adam's apple, and the rest of my neck. The string was untied and he slipped his hand into the sweatpants and gripped my hard-on. With the other hand, he tugged on one of my nipples. Ouch, I said, not really meaning it, and he let go. He wrapped his legs around mine. He held both of our cocks in one hand, each curving up and away from the other as he moved the skin back and forth. We were kissing again, our tongues slopping around inside each other's mouths. Both of our eyes wide open and staring wildly into the others. His eyes were not as blue as Matt's.

Suddenly, I closed my mouth around both of our tongues. I gently spat his tongue back into his mouth. I put my hands on his immense shoulders and pushed myself up, off the bed, into a standing position. My stiff dick was pointing at him like some kind of an indicator. What's wrong, he asked, the look on his face a combination of arousal and confusion. I have to go, I said. Go, he repeated, go where, you just got here. I have to go home, I said. Please don't go, he said. I'll put the milk in the refrigerator if you're worried about it, he said, just don't go.

I have to go, I said and began to pull the sweatpants up from around my ankles. He sat up, resting on his elbows. He watched me stuff my still erect cock into the sweatpants. It was pointing at him. I felt like a compass. He was a porno magazine dreamboy come to life. It was obvious, looking at him, that he'd worked out long and hard for that body. I tied the string and adjusted myself. He sat up quickly and untied it, pressing his face into my crotch. He brought his arms up behind me, around me. No, I said, please. And he let go.

Why are you leaving, he asked, what's wrong with me? Nothing, I said. I just have to go. Can't you at least tell me why, he asked. I looked at him. I was in his apartment, in his bedroom. I wanted to stay. I have a lover, I said. A lover, he repeated. Yes, I said. Where is he, he asked, where is your lover? In Baltimore, I said. In Baltimore, he said like the world's sexiest echo. Yes, I said, in Baltimore. I have to go.

If your lover is in Baltimore, he asked, what are you doing here? I wasn't sure if he meant here in his apartment or here in Washington. What do you mean? I asked. Why aren't you with him, he asked, doesn't he know how lucky he is to have you? Isn't he afraid someone might come along and steal you away? Someone like me? He believes in me, I said, in us. And you, he said, do you believe? Yes, I said, I believe.

As I walked around the bed to the door of the bedroom, he fell back on the bed, his head hanging over the end so he could see upside down, out the door, down the short corridor to where I stood, putting on my T-shirt. I meant what I said, he said, about your lover being lucky. I know, I said, I meant what I said, too. I put my jacket on, and he got out of bed and walked toward me with his cock still semi-erect. His cock was as beautiful as the rest of him. I wanted you to fuck me, he said, I wanted to feel you all the way inside me. He held my face in his hands and kissed me in a way that made me instantly hard again.

We bent slightly so that I could I pick up the brown paper bag with the carton of milk in it. Let me know if it doesn't work out, he said. You know where to find me, I said. All you have to do is whistle, I said. You know how to whistle, don't you?

THE MISSING PIECE

Colton Aalto

Since I had an upcoming triathlon looming on the horizon and the weather offered an unusually warm spring day, I had no choice but to get in a long training run. The air was chilly when I started, but the hot sun and clear skies meant the temperature jumped quickly, and by the end of my run, I was sweating and had stripped off my shirt. I was stretching and cooling down when Professor Sanders spotted me. "Do you have a minute, Skylar?" he asked.

A minute? Hell, I had all night for Liam Sanders. As if I would ever be so lucky! Sanders was hands-down the hottest professor on campus, the resident heartthrob for the straight coed/gay boy half of the University of Colorado student population. His classes were wildly popular, partly attributable to his being a great teacher, and partly because, as a group of drunk sorority sisters once articulated for me in vivid detail, Sanders was amazingly easy on the eyes.

I had a crush on Sanders but no reason to be optimistic about anything happening. Sanders was married, happily from all the evidence. I met his husband a couple of times at events sponsored by the gay campus group, and the man was as hot as Sanders. Had I been in Sanders's shoes, with a husband like that, I wouldn't have given me a second look. So, wishing Sanders was single and interested in me was a pipe dream.

Still, if Sanders wanted to talk, I was all over it. I could happily stare at the man for hours. "Sure," I replied, noticing for the first time a hint of gray in Sanders's jet black hair. To me, it made him sexier.

I was only wearing running shorts, and I thought Sanders gazed at me a microsecond longer than normal, maybe even paying extra attention to my bare chest. It was undoubtedly my imagination, but I made a mental note to lose the shirt after my runs if even a remote chance existed that I would see Sanders.

Normally, I would have welcomed Sanders's attention, imaginary though it probably was, but the wild idea of Sanders cruising me created a problem. My cock stirred to life. My thin running shorts wouldn't do much to mask an erection if I got one. I tried thinking about cold water.

Sanders pulled me to the side of the hallway and said, "I have an opportunity I thought may interest you. Some friends of mine have a huge, state-of-the-art house in Denver that's computerized to the hilt, but they've had nothing but trouble with the system. What they need is a troubleshooter. I thought of you because of your computer engineering degree and software expertise. Hours would be flexible, pay good, and I think you'd enjoy getting to know Kiel and Leland."

Kiel and Leland weren't the most gender-specific names, and I pondered the odds of my future employers being men and, beyond that, possibly gay. If they were friends of Sanders and his husband, they could definitely be a gay couple. But that was irrelevant. I desperately needed the money, so even if the job was pulling apart old computers on the night shift at a recycling facility, I would have jumped on it.

"I'm absolutely interested," I replied. "I really appreciate you thinking of me." The idea of Sanders thinking about me gave me a warm feeling, and my pesky cock stirred again. If thinking about cold water wouldn't do it, perhaps thinking about snow would. But fuck, Sanders was so close I could smell his deodorant or maybe his soap, and I wanted to dive into his dark eyes. His lips beckoned.

"Hopefully you can help Kiel and Leland," Sanders said. "They're great guys. I'll put you in touch with them via email." He smiled and clasped my shoulder, causing me to freeze and melt at the same time, and then drifted down the hallway. I was left to fantasize yet again about Sanders kissing me, staring at his slender figure while waiting patiently for my cock to go down so I wouldn't scandalize anyone on the way to the locker room.

At least I now knew the mysterious Kiel and Leland were men, but anyone wealthy enough to own a state-of-the-art house was likely to be three times my age, maybe four. So Kiel and Leland could be in wheelchairs. Still, the job sounded interesting, and the money would be a godsend.

Four days later, I made my way to Denver's Lodo district to meet Kiel. Lodo, short for lower downtown, is part of the trendy area of Denver. A largely desolate stretch of old warehouses thirty years ago, it blossomed when urban sophisticates reclaimed the brick warehouses for lofts. Upscale restaurants, bars, and boutiques, along with professional baseball, followed.

I found the address Kiel emailed me. The house was newly constructed but done tastefully, using old bricks on the façade to blend into the neighborhood. The red brick warehouses on either side had been converted into spectacular lofts. I hit the buzzer next to a massive, rusted steel door, and it swung open to reveal the most gorgeous man I had ever seen.

Full disclosure. In college, I stumbled upon a different "most gorgeous man I had ever seen" once or twice a week. But the man smiling at me in the doorway was incredible. He was three or four inches over six feet, perhaps thirty or thirty-five, with wavy blond hair, a long, straight nose, and a matching long, straight jawline. "You must be Skylar," he said, giving me a dazzling smile right out of a men's modeling magazine.

Stunned, I recovered enough to nod and mumble, "Uh, yeah." All I could think about were the thick red lips in front of me and how I wanted the stud in the door to sweep me into his arms and kiss me.

The Adonis introduced himself as Kiel. He shook my hand with a strong grip, and I fixated on the thick veins crisscrossing the back of his big hand. "Thanks so much for agreeing to do this," Kiel said. "My husband Leland talked me into installing a fancy computer system when we built the house, but there's something to be said for simplicity, reliability, and ease of operation, and this system fails on all three points."

I followed Kiel into the house, and he gave me a quick tour. I wasn't sure whether I was more in awe of the house or my host. I kept scoping out Kiel whenever I thought he wouldn't notice.

The house was massive, half devoted to public rooms and half to Kiel and Leland's private living quarters. The private quarters boasted a huge master suite, and I couldn't help but think about Kiel in the big bed and naked in the massive, four-headed shower. The public rooms were made for entertaining, with a giant kitchen graced by sparkling black marble countertops, a living/reception room big enough for a hundred people, a dining room with seating for fifty, and a gallery with wall after wall of expensive-looking modern art. The flower-covered rooftop deck had stunning views of the Rocky Mountains, Denver's recently renovated Union Station, and Coors Field, where the Colorado Rockies play baseball. The backdrop to the east was Denver's skyline, topped, at least for the moment, by billowing white clouds as an early spring thunderstorm rolled off toward the plains.

Kiel ushered me to the computer room, which was almost as big as the apartment I shared with three roommates, and I began tackling the system. It was devilishly complicated, a mishmash of differing hardware and incompatible software. Rather than integrate the components, the installers simply added redundant items. It was no wonder the system seldom worked.

I did what I could, solving three pressing problems, but after four hours of work, I had to tell Kiel it would take much more to get the system to run seamlessly. "Do it," Kiel said quickly. "Take your time, work when you want. You've already gotten some things to function that haven't shown life since the house was built. I'd give anything to have this system run the way it was supposed to run, even if Leland gets the last laugh."

It took me microseconds to agree. I loved challenges, and the computer system was more intricate than anything I had touched in college. I needed the money. And the chance to be around Kiel, even occasionally, sent a stab of desire to my cock.

Of course, I was getting a crush on a yet another presumably happily married man. I needed to stop thinking about Kiel. At least frequent trips to Denver would give me a reason to scope out some different guys on Grindr.

I worked off and on fixing Kiel and Leland's computer system. Within a week, Kiel gave me a key to the house and told me to come and go as I pleased. "You should text me your schedule, though," Kiel said. "Otherwise you could find we have a hundred society matrons for a charitable fundraiser, and they all think you're a waiter."

Leland traveled extensively, so I didn't meet him until I had been working for almost two weeks. I had a crush on Kiel until I met Leland, and then I couldn't decide between the two. Leland was a few years older than Kiel. He was Kiel's height and had the same toned, muscular build, but while Kiel was blond and smooth shaven, Leland had curly dark hair and a couple of days of scruff. Both Leland and Kiel could have walked off the pages of *GQ*. They could have offered workout tips and modeled designer duds on the way.

My schedule of classes and labs during the day meant I often worked at the house in the evenings and late at night, and Kiel or Leland began offering me a glass of wine as I finished. As I got to know them better, the glass of wine turned into glasses of wine with dinner. Leland started it, telling me one night he hated dining alone when Kiel was out of town. Soon my trips to Lodo involved dinner with either Kiel or Leland, or both of them.

And the trips became more frequent. I could work on the house's computer system remotely, but I found myself making the trip to Denver anyway, happy to spend what time I could with my employers, whether it was a quick conversation or a lengthy dinner.

I thoroughly enjoyed spending time with them, but the breaks meant I devoted less time to the computer system, which delayed progress. To my chagrin, the project ended up taking almost three months, consuming the spring and running past my senior year exams. Kiel and Leland weren't bothered by the delay.

I was one visit short of finishing the project when the three of us ate dinner one night and Leland proposed we retire to the big reception room at the front of the house. An impressive grand piano in the room caught my eye.

"Do you play?" Leland asked with surprise after I remarked about the piano. It wasn't every day I ran across a vintage Steinway.

"Not as much as I'd like," I replied. "But I did a double major in music and computer engineering."

"Play something for us!" Leland said. His dark eyes sparkled, and a smile lit up his face. Damn, the man was beautiful.

I sat down at the piano, wondering what to play. Spotting a signed poster of a Broadway musical, I played three songs from the show. I was surprised I remembered the music as well as I did, but hummable Broadway tunes are easy for me to remember.

"That was incredible!" Leland said when I finished. Sometimes the man was an open book, and I could tell he loved the music.

"You know any jazz?" Kiel asked.

I did. Jazz is great fun because it can be so creative and spontaneous. I played an old Frank Sinatra standard and a Cole Porter tune I had arranged myself. Kiel greeted the songs with a loud round of applause, and I couldn't help laughing.

"Do you hire out for events?" Leland asked. "We have a charity fundraiser this weekend, and it would be perfect to have you play for an hour or two before dinner."

I had never done anything like that and found the prospect daunting, but Kiel and Leland brushed away my reservations. Four days later, I found myself stuffed into a rented tux playing jazzed-up American Songbook standards. The audience of society couples, A-gays, and political types was wildly enthusiastic.

I planned to head back to Boulder after my stint at the piano, but Kiel and Leland insisted I stay for dinner, installing me between them at the head table. They wouldn't let me leave even when the crowd began to drift out.

Finally only the three of us remained. Kiel broke open a bottle of ice wine, and he and Leland rehashed the night, telling me stories about some of the guests. I hadn't realized I had entertained a U.S. Senator and a Congresswoman, along with a billionaire or two. The wine Kiel and Leland served at dinner had been wonderful, and I had guzzled far too much of it even before the three of us added two bottles of ice wine to the carnage. I was in no shape to drive and resigned myself to taking the late bus to Boulder and collecting my car tomorrow.

Leland asked if I knew *Chess*, a 1980s musical with a so-so plot and great music written by the two B's from the pop group ABBA. I played a couple of songs from the show, finishing with "I Know Him So Well," a duet sung by the two female leads. Leland knew the lyrics and sang it to Kiel as they slow danced. It was touching and romantic, and for the umpteenth time I wished I had a relationship like theirs. I added an extra-jazzy flourish to the end of the song, and when I finished, I remarked on how much Kiel and Leland had in common.

"Not as much as you might think," Kiel said, untying his bow tie and flopping down on a couch. He unbuttoned the top couple of buttons of his shirt, giving me my best view yet of his bare chest. Damn, the man looked hot in his tux with the tie dangling from his neck and his smooth chest exposed. My cock stirred. In the back of my mind, a voice said, he's married, you idiot! And his husband is right next to him!

"He drags me to Broadway musicals," Kiel continued, "but I'd rather read a book. In turn, I have to beg him for months to get him into a jazz club for an hour." Jazz or Broadway, I was good with either. Most of the piano music I knew fell into one camp or the other, and I would happily do both a Broadway show and a jazz club, even the same night.

"He'd rather work out in the gym than cycle outside," Leland added, "and I hate stationary bikes and would give anything to do long bike rides together when we're in town." The idea of seeing Leland pedaling in a spandex biking outfit sent chills down my spine and made my cock tingle. A second image popped into my mind: me spotting Kiel on a bench press, a sheen of sweat covering his muscles as he strained to lift the bar. Between the two images, I suddenly had weeks of jack-off material.

"The biggest problem is we're both tops," Kiel said, smiling at Leland and ruffling his curly dark hair. "An inconvenient fact meaning our sex life is confined to oral sex and mutual masturbation. Try as we might, neither one of us can handle a cock in the ass."

"Your fucking cock is too big," Leland replied, giving Kiel a sly look.

"Me? What about your fat beer can?" Kiel protested indignantly. The conversation was doing absolutely nothing to keep my dick under control. My image of Leland in a spandex bike outfit and Kiel in gym gear devolved into a vision of two big, stiff cocks, one pressing against bike shorts and the other tenting in gym shorts.

"Yeah, what we really need is a hunky little college bottom." Leland chuckled. "Even better if he would take both of us at the same time." Kiel opened his eyes and mouth wide, and he gave Leland a sharp frown. Leland took a moment to realize what he had said, and his face went white as his smile was replaced by a grimace.

Leland broke the silence, rushing to apologize. "I'm sorry, Skylar, when I said college boy, uh, college bottom, I, uh, pulled that out of the air. I wasn't being suggestive. Please don't take my comment wrong."

I had fantasized more than once—okay, constantly—about sex with Kiel or Leland. The thought of being in bed with both of them at the same time came like a blinding revelation. Too bad I didn't bottom.

It wasn't like I had never taken it up the butt, but my bottoming experiences hadn't been that great. I lost my virginity to a friend in high school who talked me into flip-flopping. He was older and I let him go first, but when it was my turn, he whined about it hurting before I was all the way in, and begged me to take it out. I didn't get to fuck and was suspicious because his cock was bigger, and I had taken it with no trouble.

Indeed, I had no trouble taking even an enormous cock up the ass. The dude with that monster between his legs was an older triathlon guy. My predilection for older men made me an easy target, and once the dude discovered I could take his dong, it rapidly became clear I was nothing more to him than a lubed hole. I didn't seem destined to enjoy bottoming, so I had avoided it during college.

But if bottoming meant I could sleep with the two gorgeous men staring at me…Who was I kidding? You bet I could bottom!

I was less sure about getting double fucked, but if that was what it took, I was signing up. No time like the present to learn a new trick. I broke the silence by mumbling, "Um…can I apply for the job?"

I thought it sounded lame. Kiel and Leland exchanged the briefest of smiles, and Kiel said, "Come here." In a fog, I sleepwalked from the piano bench to the couch Kiel and Leland occupied. Kiel pulled my head down and pressed his red lips against my mouth. I had fantasized about that moment since I first met him.

They both caressed me, and Kiel kissed me for a long time before Leland took possession of my mouth. "Damn," Kiel said, "I wanted to fuck your ass the first time I met you, when you showed up at the house looking like a lost boy. But I had to get Leland's permission."

"I thought he was crazy until I saw you," Leland added. "Then I wanted in your pants, too. We had a bet on who would bed you first. But this is better. It turns out playing to a tie isn't like kissing your sister, it's kissing your hot husband." He leaned over and French kissed Kiel while both of them worked on removing my clothes. I had the harder task, stripping two men, but I relished the job.

I'd fantasized about what Kiel and Leland would look like in the buff since the moment I met them. All it took was seeing a bare forearm under a T-shirt to make me wonder what the rest looked like. I finally got my wish, pulling off their shirts as they kissed.

Kiel's chest was smooth while Leland's had a spray of dark, silky hair. Snaking between Leland's six-pack was an intriguing treasure trail. I didn't have a favorite between the two ripped bodies. As soon as my focus riveted on one man's body, the other would capture my attention with the move of a muscle.

My curiosity wasn't sated by the two awesome torsos in front of me. I had waited long enough to see the two big cocks discussed moments ago. I pulled Kiel's zipper down, slipping my hands into his underwear and pulling out a long, straight tool. I stroked it a couple of times, distracted by Kiel's hands on my cock and Leland groping my balls. Like a kid in a candy store, I grabbed Leland's trousers and pulled them down. A thick slab of cock flopped out, pointed toward Leland's hip.

The rest of the night was a whirlwind. I had never been in a three-way, but I loved it, sandwiched between two men with beautiful bodies, awesome dicks, and pent-up desire. I discovered Leland was into slow lovemaking, cuddling, and snuggling. I could have spent hours in bed happily making gentle love with him, feeling his hairy chest pressed against me. In contrast, Kiel liked it fast, furious, and rough. His unbridled assault on my ass drove me crazy, leaving me hungering for more. And whether it was wine, euphoria, or something else, I felt only a twinge of pain when Leland and Kiel double fucked me. Once I loosened up, it felt amazing. High odds I was meant to be a bottom boy all along and hadn't known it.

I woke the next morning as Leland slipped from bed and announced he was starting breakfast. I assumed that was a call for Kiel and me to get up, too, but Kiel circled me with his muscular arms and said, "You're not going anywhere, stud. My cock has some unfinished business with your holes." The glint in his eye told me my ass was going to get pummeled. Again. I licked my lips in anticipation.

Despite a seriously sore and raw asshole, I was still horny when we finished breakfast two hours later. I assumed the night with Kiel and Leland was a one-night stand, and while I hoped for another chance to play with the two studs, they were happily married. I was under no illusions as to where that left me.

I showered, happily reliving the night and contemplating my roommates' likely reaction when I did the walk of shame, crawling home while still wearing my tux from the night before. As I got ready to leave, Kiel and Leland asked me to sit down in the kitchen. They were both shirtless, dressed only in basketball shorts, and their hot bodies were amazing in the early morning light. I hadn't gotten a chance to study the shirtless hunks in the daylight, and I resolved to make the most of the opportunity.

Kiel and Leland, however, seemed serious and it dawned on me what was about to go down. I was going to get "The Talk." It would be some version of "Yeah, we had fun last night, but we're married, so don't get any ideas. Hands off." I braced for the speech, telling myself not to make the situation awkward for Kiel or Leland. I was a big boy and could handle the truth, even if I hated the result.

"Leland and I have been talking," Kiel began. "We realize what we are about to say is unorthodox, and if it's not something you want to consider, that's fine. We understand completely. But having you around the last couple of months has been great. We both like you, like you a lot. I daresay we're both in love with you. We think of you as the missing piece to the puzzle of our relationship. And last night was, well incredible." He paused before adding with a smirk, "This morning wasn't bad, either."

Leland glared at Kiel and, impatient, interrupted. "What Kiel is trying to say, if he can get his mind out of the gutter, is we want you to move in with us. Travel with us, live with us, be a part of what we have going. Be a part of everything. Join our relationship."

Kiel smiled, reaching for my hand, and said, "Don't say no. Neither of us intend to let you leave."

My mind whirled, but I never had a doubt about my answer.

The idea of being in a threesome was weird at first, but within six months, it felt normal. Some of our friends and acquaintances have had a hard time getting their minds around it. To Kiel and Leland's irritation, a few of their friends still call me the houseboy. Because I freelance on computer systems from the house, it looks like my life involves nothing but taking care of Kiel and Leland.

Professor Sanders jokes that we owe him a finder's fee for being our matchmaker. We see him regularly because he's our fourth for bridge. Hard to complain about playing cards with the three most gorgeous men on the planet, but the eye candy makes it hard for me to concentrate on the cards.

Sanders's husband hates cards. He's a professional chef and would rather cook than shuffle and deal, so while we play bridge, he whips up fabulous meals. Try as I might, I've never gotten Sanders to come clean about whether he was scoping out my bare chest on the fateful day he asked if I wanted to work for Kiel and Leland. He's equally coy about whether it ever crossed his mind that we would end up in a threesome.

Kiel and Leland are great about telling me how much they love me but also letting me know that if I ever want a one-on-one relationship, they will understand. They suspect I want a relationship where I'm not exclusively a bottom, but that is unsaid. All I know is every one of my top ten sexual experiences have involved getting double fucked by Kiel and Leland. Never say never, but I can't imagine a one-on-one relationship as fulfilling as the relationship I have with the two men I love.

SECURITY BREACH

Evey Brett

The radio on my belt beeped, and the hotel operator's staticky voice came through my earpiece. "Hey, Joe, the banquet captain says someone's bringing outside alcohol into the reception. Can you go check it out?"

I sighed. Weddings were always my least favorite events to patrol because of the high incidence of stupid drunk people and the ensuing noise complaints. I held down the button on my collar mic. "Ten-four. On my way."

The throbbing music coming from inside the ballroom vibrated throughout the hotel. I poked my head inside, scanning for cartons and bottles that didn't belong. The activity was about what I expected from a gay wedding reception, bodies surging up and down to dance music, booze flowing freely from the bartenders. The grooms, or so I assumed, were both shirtless as they danced in a circle of their friends. My cock stirred at the sight of those hard, sweaty bodies, but window shopping at work was a bad idea.

Seeing no contraband inside the ballroom, I continued my patrol down the hallway and nearly blundered into a man exiting the men's room. My cock recognized him before my brain did.

Shit.

We both turned. Our gazes caught, locked. I stared, words lost as I struggled to figure out how the hell this gorgeous little hustler had managed to wander into my workplace.

"Joe." He looked me up and down with that searing gaze. "Nice duds."

Heat spread through my body, and it wasn't merely from annoyance. I'd only spent one night with him, but not a single cell of me had forgotten his touch. "What the hell are you doing here?"

"Big party." He nodded over his shoulder.

"Anyone you know?"

That slow, sly grin told me enough. He licked his lips. "I've made a few friends."

On cue, a man exited the restroom, adjusting his tie and pointedly ignoring my acquaintance. My cock and my annoyance swelled at the thought of what must have been going on in that bathroom. "I think it's time you found a different party to cruise."

"Make me." He held his arms wide, daring me to force him out. I couldn't. Hotel policy said security couldn't lay a hand on anyone unless it was self-defense.

"Go on. Or I'll call the cops and tell them what you're up to."

"Try it. I dare you." He shoved his hands in his pockets and began walking, taking a right down an empty corridor.

I followed. As soon as I rounded the corner, he turned around, grabbed my shirt, and kissed me. The taste of him went straight to my brain, as quick and addictive as crack. I was so shocked that I didn't move, not even when he thrust a hand between my legs and grabbed my crotch, fingers digging hard into my balls.

Then my senses returned. I shoved him away. "What the hell are you—"

He tilted his head toward the ceiling. I followed his gaze to where one of the CCTV cameras nestled in the corner.

"Son of a bitch." No one was in the security office right now, but if anyone saw that footage, I'd be fired. "What do you want from me?"

"Why don't we go somewhere a little more private where we can talk? I've missed you, Joe."

"I'm working."

"So am I." He studied me. "What's wrong? Don't your coworkers know you're gay?" He toyed with my tie, a cheap breakaway thing that made me look like a nerd.

I slapped his hand away. "That's none of your business."

He just laughed. "I like you, Joe. So innocent. So much fun to play with. Remember how much you liked it when I stuck my fingers up your ass?"

I had liked it. That was the problem. I'd emptied my wallet for this guy and it had been worth every penny.

He leaned in so close I could smell his pine-scented aftershave. "Want me to do it again?"

My briefs were suddenly too tight. I was screwed. I knew it. Jerking my head for him to follow, I went outside away from the cameras. The air was cool and scented with the ocean lapping at the beach a few yards away. From this vantage point, we could see the San Diego skyline lit up across the bay. "Look. I can't do this tonight. Not here. I don't have any money, anyway."

"This is a hotel. A nice one. There are other ways you can pay me. A room. A nice, hot shower. Room service." He shrugged. "Or I could leave a note at the front desk about suspicious activity in the south foyer."

Blackmail. Two could play that game. "I could turn you in for propositioning me."

A layer of toughness fell away, and he looked more like a weary teenager than a twenty-something man. "Please, Joe. Just get me a room for tonight. I don't have anywhere else to go."

I should have walked him to the edge of the property and shoved him over it, but his air of desperation provoked the protective instincts I was certain he was taking advantage of. I had an idea. "Stay here. Give me a couple of minutes."

I pointed him toward a stone bench with a view of the water and headed inside to my office. I accessed the hotel directory, found the room I needed, and made a card key set to expire in the morning. Five minutes later I went back, half expecting him to be gone. He wasn't.

Handing him the key, I said, "Here. The room is out of order. They're waiting on a part to fix the air conditioning. Don't call anyone and keep the drapes drawn so no one sees the light. That's the best I can do."

He stood. "Thanks. I owe you." He curled a finger around my

belt loop and tugged me closer, snugging our bodies together. "What time are you off?"

I'd already gone too far. "In a half hour or so. But I can't be here after hours. It's against the rules."

"Fuck the rules. There's a back staircase, isn't there?"

There was. And there weren't any cameras in the stairwells.

Forty minutes later, against my better judgment, I'd changed into street clothes and used a second room key to let myself into his room. The desk was laden with two bottles of beer, one of wine, and a basket full of finger foods, all of which must have been raided from the party.

The shower was running. He'd left the door open, making the room hot and humid. I waited, fighting the impulse to walk into the bathroom and watch the water cascade down his flesh. I gulped down one of the beers instead, needing something to steady my nerves. My brain insisted on leaving before I got caught, but my body had a mind of its own and refused to budge.

I sat in the desk chair and closed my eyes and thought of the first night I'd seen him and the sinuous way his body had moved beneath the flashing lights on the dance floor. I'd lusted after him from the start.

"You okay, Joe?"

I opened my eyes and he was there, sitting on the end of the desk wearing a fuzzy robe with the hotel's logo embroidered on the breast. "Why are you here?" I asked.

He grabbed the full beer and took a long swallow. "Told you. Got no place to go tonight."

"I mean here at my hotel. Tell me the truth." I grabbed his arm. He winced, and I let go in alarm. "What's wrong?"

"Nothing."

It wasn't nothing. I slid the robe from his shoulders, baring his chest. The bruises covering his ribs and arms were easy to see. "Shit."

He shrugged his arms out of the robe and gazed down at himself. "I've had worse."

"Were you mugged?"

"Sweetheart, get real." He took another swig.

It had been one of his johns, then. I ran my fingers over his abused skin. I wasn't a security guard because it was a cushy job. I had an instinct to protect people, even little hustlers who managed to track me down and threaten my job. "Who?"

"Doesn't matter. He was from out of town. I'll never see him again."

"It matters to me." I grabbed his wrist. "I don't have any money. All I've got in my wallet is a five."

"Just this once, I'll give you a discount."

My cock strained at my pants. It wanted him as much as I did. "Why me?"

"Why not?"

He was being evasive. Since his hand was occupied, he made do with his foot, sliding it up and down my thigh. Shit. He was half naked, skin still glistening from his shower, and he smelled of eucalyptus from the designer shampoo. I let him go, and he touched my cheek. I needed a shave, but his light fingers against the bristles sent a shudder through me.

"Close your eyes."

I shook my head. "I can't do this. Not here."

He pouted. "Where's that brave Joe who beat up an old man bent on taking my virtue?"

I choked back a laugh. He'd lost his virtue long before we met. "I need this job. I don't want to fuck it up."

"I don't let my guys get in trouble over me. Not if they don't deserve it. Trust me, Joe. You don't deserve it."

Alarm bells rang in my head at the thought of doing something so illicit. I closed my eyes anyway.

He wound the robe's fuzzy sash around my head to ensure I couldn't see him. He pinched my mouth open, but instead of his tongue, he slid in a cream puff. Before I swallowed, he kissed me, and together we shared the sweetness melting on my tongue. He tugged my T-shirt from my waistband and lifted it up over my head. Then he ran his hands up and down my chest. His fingers were rough and warm. He pinched each of my nipples and rolled them around in his fingers, which was half painful, half delightful.

Then he rested his weight on my lap, pressing his body against mine as he laid kisses along my neck and jaw. He tickled my skin with his hot breath as he nibbled my earlobe. He ground his hips against my crotch, sheer torture since my cock was still trapped in my jeans. I reached down to free it but he grabbed my wrist. "Hold on."

His pleasant warmth vanished. I heard the clink of beer bottles and the swish of baskets as he presumably cleared the desk. I didn't have long to wonder why as he urged me to stand and then sit on the edge of the desk. "What are you—"

"Shh." He laid his fingers against my lips, and then urged me to lie down. The sash around my eyes served to cushion my head from the hardness.

Something was intensely wrong yet highly erotic about letting him fuck me on a table with a perfectly good bed only a few feet away. I felt more helpless, more exposed, and he heightened that sensation by spreading my thighs wide. With practiced fingers, he undid my fly and pulled out my cock. I shuddered at the brush of cool air against my erection.

He removed my sandals, and then yanked at my jeans and briefs until my bare ass rested against the chilly wooden desktop. Something liquid and pungent hit my skin. The wine. Instead of being excited, I turned fearful. "Don't stain the carpet, or we'll catch hell."

He laughed. "Don't worry. There won't be a drop left."

I quivered at the touch of his lips against my belly. He swirled his tongue around my navel, licking every drop from the indentation. He traveled up my body, kissing and sucking with a deliciously hot wetness. I moaned, and he silenced me by driving his tongue deep inside my mouth. I tasted wine and the salt of my own skin, and him.

When he pulled back, I clasped a hand around his neck to keep him from going far. "Why'd you track me down?"

"You said we could see each other again."

"Not at work." Exasperated, I gave his cheek a light smack.

He batted my hand away and laughed. "Awfully convenient place for you to work. I bet you know this hotel better than anyone. All those secret, dark corners..."

I thought of all the places we could fuck. Up on the catwalk above the ballrooms. Any number of supply closets. The general manager's office. The pool pump room, which would be noisy enough to drown out any noise we might make. Out on the beach behind the breakwater. "True, but if I'm caught, I'll get fired."

"So, don't get caught." He disentangled himself from my grip then dragged the chair across the carpet. He guided my feet onto the arms, leaving my legs wide and my ass utterly exposed. When I bent my knees inward, I felt him, warm and firm and naked. He pushed my legs open then ran ticklish fingers down my thighs almost, but not quite, touching my cock. "The bed's too low for stuff like this," he said.

Like a good little hustler, he came prepared. I heard cellophane rip and soft, fleshy sounds as he rolled on a condom. I tried not to think about how many times he'd done this before, or with how many men. I choked, thinking of the last time I'd seen him and wondering why the hell I was letting myself in for another world of hurt. "I saved you from that raunchy old bastard in the club, took you home, cleaned you up, and you left. Without a word. Are you going to do the same thing now?"

"That depends." He pressed lube-slicked fingers against my asshole, circling it until the sphincter relaxed.

"On what?" He broached the tight entrance, probing inside me until he found that magic spot behind my prostate. I gasped at the sudden tightness in my belly. "Do you know what I make? Not much. I can't be your sugar daddy."

"I don't want one."

He didn't give me a chance to ask what he did want, because

he exchanged his fingers for his cock and jammed it inside so hard, I yelped. For the first few thrusts, it burned, but then it changed to a pleasurable ache. At the same time, he gave me a hand job, timing his twisting pressing fingers with his pumping hips.

I was reduced to pure sensation. I smelled his sweat and lube, felt my body stretch and clench around his. The desk squeaked and shook a little as we rocked together, and I gripped the edges, hanging on for dear life. His hands never ceased moving. They were slick and wet, up and down, back and forth.

A few more strokes, and I was close to bursting. My balls tightened and drew up, and then I tumbled over the brink.

I gritted my teeth to keep from shouting as loud as I wanted to. A noise complaint would bring my colleague to investigate, although I had to stifle a laugh at imagining the look on his face if he found me here, naked, being fucked by a cute little hustler in a room that was supposed to be empty.

He left me lying there, gasping. After taking a few moments to recover, I pulled off the makeshift blindfold and sat up. True to his word, not a drop of wine had reached the carpet. I looked over to see him guzzling the remains as he leaned against the wall, naked. The dim light enhanced the bruises scattered across his body. My jaw clenched. "Are you all right?"

He nodded. "Enjoy yourself?"

"I haven't gotten laid like that since..." I didn't have to finish. I got up and went over to him. "Tell me the truth. Why are you here?"

He wouldn't look at me. "I want a job, Joe. A real one."

I didn't make a joke. From his voice and demeanor, he was utterly serious and knew just how hard it was to get a regular job without references or previous work experience. I felt for him. Gently, I said, "You didn't have to fuck me to ask that."

It was hard to tell in the low light, but his skin darkened. "You know me. I don't do favors. Only trade." At last, he raised his gaze to mine. "I mean it. I want a steady income. I'm tired of..." He made a sweeping gesture to emphasize his battered skin.

I'd do anything to keep him from getting beaten, but I had to be sure he wasn't playing me. No way was I going to risk another broken heart. I rested my palms against the wall, one on either side of him, trapping him within a physical prison. "How do I know you won't cut and run like you did last time?"

"Because." He set the empty wine bottle on the dresser with a clunk.

"Because why?" I rubbed my hips against his semi-erect cock, naked of its condom. All that effort, and he hadn't come yet.

He groaned but didn't answer as I ground against him, hard. After a moment, he wrapped his arms around me and dug his nails into my back. I'd be lucky if I didn't bleed.

Hands locked under his ass, I scooped him up and carried him over to the bed. He bounced a little as I dropped him, but I didn't give him a chance to escape. I clambered atop him and grabbed his cock. I trembled as I felt the soft sacs of his balls and the smooth skin of his hardened shaft. I was afraid of hurting him, of pressing too hard on purpled flesh, but with his free hand he clasped the back of my neck and drew me down. He gave me a ragged smile. "Don't worry about it. You won't hurt me."

Maybe not, but I wanted to find the guy who had caused him such a world of pain. That, and I wanted to smack this kid upside the head for getting himself into such a bad situation in the first place. "Because why, you little bastard?"

Arms splayed above his head in submission, he turned his head aside. Damn, but this kid was frustrating. I should walk out and leave him. I couldn't. So help me, but he'd wrapped his hands around my heart and my cock and refused to let go. If trade was all he understood, then I'd have to barter for an answer.

Glancing around, I spied the bottle of lube sitting on the corner of the bed. I snatched it and squeezed a generous dollop onto my fingers. His body yielded easily to my two-fingered intrusion. He moaned softly and tilted his hips to accommodate me. He was slick and hot and tight. I loved the way he squirmed as I fingered him.

His body arched, tensing, but I didn't want him to come. Not until I had an answer. "What's it going to take to get you to tell me why you won't run?"

His cock was hard and stiff, the tip glistening with precum. I bent down and licked it, taking in the bitterness while I continued to wriggle my fingers inside him. Mercifully, he gave it in a hoarse, choked voice. "Because you were the only guy who ever came to my rescue."

The reply stunned me into silence. I couldn't move, not even to tip him over the edge. He just laid there, quivering and helplessly impaled on my hand.

"Please, Joe. Please." He fixed his gaze on me, as hard and penetrating as his cock had been.

My head spun as I tried to make sense of this turn of events. "You only want a job?"

"And maybe a bed. And someone to share it with." The words came out strained.

"I see. You only want me for my ass." I pressed against that spot behind his prostate.

He writhed, nails raking the sheets, and shook his head from side to side. "No. I want you." He took in a long, shuddering breath then whimpered. "Damn it. I love you, Joe. I can't get you out of my head. I won't run away again. I swear. Please. Please."

I may have extracted his confession under duress, but I believed him. I had to wonder what I'd get out of this deal. He'd be a needy kid, prone to sleeping around, but he was also someone to look after and care for. I was tired of going home to an empty, silent condo, of cooking for one and sleeping alone. He needed me, and I liked to be needed. That, and the fact that I was crazy about him, was enough to convince me. "I love you, too."

All I had to do was give his cock one little squeeze and he came, spurting over my hand. He clenched his asshole around my fingers. Arching back, he gave a low moan of satisfaction. "Damn."

After I cleaned up, I went back and spooned behind him. He clenched my arm to his chest as if it were his favorite stuffed animal. I held him tightly, though not so hard as to cause him pain.

As long as he stayed with me, no one would ever hurt him again.

❖

Two weeks later, I had to admit he looked sharp in a bellman's uniform. He had the perfect demeanor, both flattering and submissive, which earned him plenty of tips and more than a few propositions, some of which he accepted. He and I had a deal, though. I knew which rooms he went to, so if he got into trouble, I could bail him out.

Beyond that, I had keys to everything, and I knew where all the cameras were. If, by chance, we met in the luggage room and took a detour via the storage closet on the way back…well…I knew full well I was putting my job at risk, but after one illicit adventure had ended so well, I had a hunger for more.

"Ever been on the roof?" I asked him during one slow, lazy afternoon as we clocked out for lunch.

He grinned. "Not yet."

I pulled the hatch key out of my pocket and dangled it. "Shall we?"

I never had to ask twice.

CONTINUUM

George Seaton

The first people who lived in our old house surely gathered near the bright, orange heat of the small coal fireplace in the living room on one frigid night in November of 1893. I suspect, or so I would like to believe, it was then that they discussed and mourned the death of Pyotr Illyich Tchaikovsky, which had occurred that same month, that same year.

There is a continuum of sorts, a constancy of good feeling in the walls of this old house, and in the spirits who pass through them for the delicate genius, the tragic lover, Pyotr Illyich. Or, again, so I would like to believe.

❖

His attention is captured by something atop the dining room table. I find some little fascination in the knowledge that I still do not really know this man with whom I have lived for twenty-eight years. Oh, I can tell you, without even looking, he is reading yet another review of the merits of one or another audio component—speakers, amplifiers, connectors, cables. This, I know about him. I know also—evidenced by the six thousand compact discs that line the shelves, floor to ceiling, in the small study downstairs—that he is passionate about music, good music, the music of the masters, from classical to contemporary.

Do I love this man with whom I have lived for twenty-eight years? Of course, I do. Do I still wonder what the hell that word means? Yes, I do.

❖

"Let's go," I say, tying my tennis shoes.

He lifts his head from the magazine, and turns. "I'm ready," he says as he stands and walks toward me.

We step off the porch and begin the two miles we will walk this evening. The mama finch, which, along with her ruby-headed partner, have made a nest in the recess of the transom above the door, flutters frantically above our heads. "It's only us, mama," I say, trying unsuccessfully to communicate that we mean no harm to her or her eggs, her unborn children. Nevertheless, she breaks out from under the porch and flies to a low-hanging branch of the giant and ancient maple in front of our house. There, she examines our passage.

I close the white picket gate that opens into our small front yard and look back at our old house, which was built the same year Pyotr Illyich Tchaikovsky died. It is a two-story Victorian, a gingerbread house where, each time we leave it, the spirits who inhabit it smile at us from the upstairs window. David and I have lived in this house for twenty-four of the past twenty-eight years we have been together.

"Which way?" David asks, leaving the decision of our route to me. We have circumnavigated our northwest Denver neighborhood a thousand times, and any route I choose is not new. But now there is a newness to each walk we take. It is spring, and the whole world is new.

I turn right from our gate, and we embark on what we have come to call the standard route, which will take us south for nine blocks, two blocks west, and then back north for another nine blocks.

"Standard route," I say, and we both turn right at the end of our block like soldiers on parade, in step, and determined in direction. "How was your day?" I ask.

"Well…" he says, pausing, preparing me for his burst of jabber. "I had told you Scott was back with Jason. Well, let me tell you that it's the same old thing, and he doesn't admit it, but he goes over there to Jason's every night and they…Oh, sometimes they go to dinner or watch *Survivor* or some other inane series, and then, of course, they fuck themselves silly. And no, Scott says they are not boyfriends, and I tell him, 'Well, it sure looks like you are boyfriends, and if you are boyfriends, why do you always have to go over to his house? Why can't he occasionally make the effort, oh, the sacrifice to go over to your house?' I just don't understand why it's always Scott, Scott, Scott making the effort. It just doesn't make any sense whatsoever."

I smile. This is my David. This is my jabberer.

"I don't know why it matters to you anymore," I say, seeing the white Lab, our friend, tied to the porch in the yard ahead. "This is… what? The fourth time they've gone back together after having had a supposedly irreconcilable split?"

We stop and kneel down to the white Lab, who greets us, smiling and shaking. We scratch his ears and tummy. "Third time, actually. You are such a handsome boy," he says to the Lab, whose tail wags, his pink tongue hanging wet in the spring heat. We stand and continue our walk.

"You know what his therapist says?"

"No," I reply, knowing David knows I do not know what Scott's therapist says.

"He told Scott that he keeps breaking up with and then going back to Jason because he actually wants the stimulation of both events, that somehow his psyche feeds on the drama of it all. Can you believe that? Can you actually believe that?"

"Yes, yes, I believe that." I think what I always think when someone asks, Can you believe that? I think that nothing much that the world conjures has really surprised me for a very long time. It was the Big Party, that phantasmagoria of the time, of our time between 1969 and 1982, that was so truly amazing, so truly liberating, so truly…nasty, that, having come of age during that time, my credulity has forever been slightly skewed.

"Well, that's what he told them, and I don't think..." David goes on.

My mind is lost to the memory of the Big Party. How do I adequately convey a sense of what it was really like during those times of...revelation, liberation, and senseless primordial devotion to the fuck? I can only try. It was at the tail end, the closing days of the Big Party when my life with David began.

❖

David and I met one night in 1982, in a bar in downtown Denver where I'd found my niche, my comfortable corner. It, the bar—bare wood, leather/Levi's, strong drinks, men, and young men seeking men and young men. I was then brown-eyed and haired, always Levi'ed, cowboy boots, and stern but adorable. Well...adorably stern?

It was that time of our time, when we were being told that we should not have sex with men who were obviously ill: feverish, coughing, purple lesions on the skin. We had been reading in the gay press for almost a year about a hellish, exotic pneumonia, and a rare skin cancer that had appeared, proliferated, and infested the coasts, and was moving inward toward the center, toward Denver, where, on that night in 1982, I saw him: blond, boyish, blue eyes, smiling. David projected a bright and endearing gaze into the crowd of us. It was not the usual hungry, hard, brazen, straight-to-the-bone glare that each of us was so accustomed to receiving and, indeed, projecting. No, David still beamed with the wonder of us all, there, together in that dark and smoky space.

For several years before I met David, a narrow, wooden, rickety staircase led to the basement of the bar—an even darker and smokier space where we would pack ourselves in, ass to cock, each Friday and Saturday night. Our hands, in that place, were not left to ourselves. We were not beholding to any modicum of restraint, or fear of consequences, or care for...for anything other than the moment, the celebration of ourselves, the essential rite of passage, the tactile manifestation of delayed adolescence, that was the freedom that had come from Stonewall. It was a sexual freedom so intense, so overwhelmingly right, that to ignore it oozed a particular wrongness that belied the core of our very being. Oh, we reveled within the essence of the Big Party. It was the essence of the time, of our time. The baths. The parks. Cheesman Park. Every night, the quest. Most every night fucking a new lover or a new lover fucking me, because that was the fucking point of it all, of the time of our time; of the Big Party.

For me, the bar had become quite boring by 1982. TV monitors had been hung from the four corners of the ceiling, beaming music videos, and sometimes soft porn. No one touched anyone else they did not know then, there in that space where, a year before, touching a stranger had been the least of the intrusive but oh so pleasing, so welcome behavior that was expected, demanded by the imperative of the Big Party. Indeed, by 1982, luscious leers had become quick glances, not lingering, barely even coquettish in their intent. Men huddled within the convention of fuckbuddy coteries, sewing circles of matronly standoffishness.

By 1982, the bogeyman had certainly begun stealing the magic of the night from us all. We began to hear and understand the new words, and, oh sweet Jesus, our lexicon, our gayspeak became clinical—pneumocystis, Kaposi's, neuropathy, cytomegalovirus, T-cells, crystosporidiosis, lymphadenopathy, retrovirus, candidiasis, cryptococcus and on and on—the litany of the boogeyman's ferocious baggage, a vernacular that beautiful young men should not have to assume as their own. It was assumed, though. Necessarily. "Yeah, Ronnie seemed to kick the pneumocystis, but that fuckin' lymphadenopathy—even the nodes in his groin, man, hard as fuckin' rocks." Yes, and by 1982, many of us were teetering on the cusp of a stark and insidious epiphany that would soon be revealed to the world, a gut feeling that we just simply had not reckoned much with the consequences of the time, of our time. That the Big Party could not just simply go on forever.

Then along came David.

I was thirty-three. He was twenty-two. He was my...type. He was a "Music major at CU. In Boulder."

"Oh," I said, realizing that his eyes were not blue, but green, which was not a bad thing. Just not totally my type. The ones with green eyes usually had more hair on their ass than I liked. I could deal with it. I was not getting married, for Christ's sake. I liked the name, though—David. "I was a music major for a while, too," I said, wondering about that ass. "Finally graduated with a B.A. in history. From CU, too."

"Wow," he said, looking at my eyes or my nose. I wasn't sure. He smiled. "Can I buy you a drink?"

"Hey, you're the poor college kid. Let me do it." I grabbed his right hand, in which he was holding his drink, and lifted it to the light. "Looks like a screwdriver to me?"

"Yes," he said. "Thank you."

I had sidled up to him as he stood with his back against the wall that faced the heavily traveled hallway from and to the dimly lit meat rack, where a waist-high wooden shelf bordered one wall upon which you could place your drink, or sit and watch the crowd saunter past. A chain-link fence covered the opposite wall, floor to ceiling. Beyond the meat rack was another room with two pool tables and three pinball machines. Beyond that room was a large outdoor deck with its own bar. David had strategically placed himself where I often did, a place where you could see much of the comings and goings through all sections of the bar. From his vantage point, you could also see the new arrivals coming through the front door, and also the traffic headed down the stairs to the video bar.

I came back with our drinks, and David and I moved into the intimacy of the meat rack room. We talked. We felt each other. We kissed. More drinks. I suggested we go out onto the deck, for no other reason than I really wanted to get a close look at his ass, at the movement of cheeks through the thin stretch of his faded and oh, so tight Levi's. And urging him to lead the way, I saw enough to know I was definitely interested, definitely determined to pursue the fuck.

❖

"What a fucking mess," I say, snapping out of my reverie, and it is usually what I always say as we pass the corner house that provides what I am sure the owner of the property would call a xeriscaped yard. You call this xeriscaping, I would like to say to the young married couple who we know live here. This is lazyscape. This looks like shit. No, this looks like somebody's idea of a fucking joke! That's what I'd like to say to the young couple. As we pass the house, their white-haired little girl, who must be at least five and who is still sucking on a pacifier, waves frantically at us from the porch of the house and screams, "Hi! Hi!"

"Hi," we both say as we wave back at what we've both observed is a very ugly little girl.

We walk in silence for two blocks. Sometimes we cover the entire two miles in silence. Have we said everything to one another during the past twenty-eight years that really needs to be said between two people who might as well be attached at the hip? Because that is as close as we have become to one another, day in, day out, year after year. And no, it is not the banter about work or someone's yard, or the brutal truths we share about an ugly child that I am thinking about. No, it is the verbalization of those things that have kept us together for so long, that have made us comfortable with the silences between us. Have we really said all there is to say to one another? Have we really?

"Oh, look," David says, pointing to a yard about a block away. "The black dog is back." I look and, sure enough, the black puppy of indeterminate lineage, who, months ago, excitedly greeted us as we passed his fenced-in front yard, is back. We saw him only that once, when he must have been only three or four months old. Now, there he is looking full-grown. "Do you think he will remember us?"

"Of course. We are...memorable," I say, smiling, feeling good about seeing the black dog again. We have so often seen new puppies in the neighborhood one day and, after a week or two, the new puppy disappears. Gone. Well, we didn't realize he was going to shit on the rug or keep us up all night. And he ate the fucking couch! Not just a cushion or a pillow. The whole fucking couch! We can't put up with that. We simply can't! And then, of course, there are so many more in our wonderful neighborhood who cherish their animals with a devotion akin to adoration, good parents taking the good with the bad, good parents loving even the ugliest of children.

We stop, pet, and talk to the black dog, who is as excited today to see us as he was months ago. And yes, we can believe that he remembers us as we share the joy of this moment.

We begin the ascent back toward our home.

Our northwest Denver neighborhood is called West Highlands because it sits on a substantial rise that overlooks downtown Denver, barely three miles to the southeast. Our standard route takes us down the rise, and then back up. Again we walk in silence, and my thoughts return to...

David's ass was hairier than I preferred. But damn it! How was I supposed to know that it wouldn't matter? How in the hell could I have had any inkling that that twenty-two-year-old kid who had still not lost all of his baby fat, and who had trouble taking me seriously, and who laughed at my sternness, and who loved my dogs as totally as I, and who could perform Mozart from memory on the piano, and play every single woodwind instrument flawlessly, and who loved opera, and who had grown up on a farm, and laughed sweetly as he stared into my eyes—placing my head between his hands as he kissed me softly—and said, "No, honey, no you don't," when I told him I would love to move to a farm and raise cows and pigs that would never be slaughtered or sold, and horses that would be named after the dogs I had loved and buried, and...Goddamnit, how was I to know that this blond, green-eyed kid who grew up on farms in eastern Washington and detested the thought of ever returning, would be the one? The forever one? And if I had known, what would I have done? What?

I asked David to move in with me in November of 1982.

It was only a week or two after David had moved in with me that he dialed his parents' number and told them he would not be coming home, that he had moved in with a…friend. I was sitting in the living room, and David was in the kitchen. I was flipping through a magazine, attempting not to appear to be listening to his conversation. It was obvious his parents weren't letting him off the parental hook easily. He was only twenty-two, for Christ's sake! What did he know about the world? And who the hell was this older man he was moving in with? Soon, David's entire body erupted in a sob that surely—yesiree, without a doubt—was the result of a laser-directed belly punch from the good folks at home. "Don't call me that," he sobbed. "I am not a queer. I am not…" I moved to him, took the phone, and hung it up.

From behind him, I locked my arms around his body and held him tightly, so tightly against his sobs, and I said the words, over and over again, "I love you. I love you, baby. I love you. I love you." Yes, I really said it, and lord—what was this world coming to?—I meant it. Yes, I, such an adorably stern picture of few words and careless passions, I had said it. That was the first time I told David that I loved him.

And as I loosened my lock on his body, he turned to face me, and through those lovely greens washed by such intense grief, he smiled slightly and said it also: "I love you, too."

As some of our friends and acquaintances, young men, beautiful men, commenced their dying then in that same year, 1982, David and I dug in hard to what I had previously thought were absurdly stupid core principles that provide the basis for solid relationships: monogamy, eating at least one meal a day together, sharing what he called the chores. It was easier for David because that, the relationship, is what I believe he truly wanted in his life. I, oh, I, on the other hand, had been a performer in the Big Party for so long, I had loved so many men for at least as long as it took to complete the fuck, and had accepted, oh, even reveled in what was then the transitory nature of love that the job for me, yes—now I understand it as I write it—yes, the job for me was never to forget that first nonsexual embrace when the pain in David's soul passed into mine, when his sobs were captured by my embrace, and when the truth of the words we spoke to one another, "I love you," had somehow, for the first time, made sense.

My job was also to remember that young men were dying, and that, most likely, David and I had saved each other's lives then, in 1982, then, amongst the detritus the bogeyman had made of the Big Party, then, in the face of the bogeyman's insidious snicker, "You ain't seen nothin' yet, baby."

❖

"Bob and Norma will be here the last week of June," David says as we stand at the intersection of 32nd and Lowell, the center of our West Highlands business district, waiting for the light to change.

Bob and Norma are his parents who, twenty years ago, arrived at our old house towing their fifth wheel behind their Ford 250. I guess almost eight years of silence between them and their son had been enough. They had come to reconcile. They had come to evaluate the older man who had captured their son's heart. Yes, and I guess that almost eight years of silence between them and their firstborn son had convinced even them that if this was a phase, it sure as hell wasn't ending anytime soon.

They've visited once, sometimes twice, every year since then.

"You taking time off?" I ask.

"Yes. So are you. Mom wants you to take her up to Blackhawk. She's been saving her quarters for the slots."

"We can do that," I say. "Are they going on to Missouri this time?"

"No, not this time. Mom's still weak from the chemo."

We cross the street in silence. His parents usually visit with us, and then head down to Missouri to visit family. The chemotherapy for his mother's breast cancer ended just weeks ago.

The aroma of the best pizza on the face of the Earth wafts from the little restaurant on the corner. The liquor store across the street is crowded this time of the day with the young professionals from the neighborhood who believe profoundly that each dinner must sport a new and exciting wine. The smell of scented candles oozes from the open doors of the three knickknack stores, which, apparently, have captured their fair share of the market in our little neighborhood business district. The little bookstore remains so pitifully small.

"Are we doing Pride this year?" David asks.

"Oh, I don't know. What's the point?"

"The point," he punches my arm, "is the boys, almost naked boys…everywhere."

"I know. I know. But the pride part…I suppose if I were to really reflect on that, the pride thing, I'd just think about us. All these years. All these ups and downs we've had together. Hell, I'm proud of us."

David is silent for a moment. He grabs my hand. "Yes," he says. "Me, too."

"What's for dinner?" I ask, both of us smelling the baking pizza.

"Don't know. Your choice."

"No, I chose last night. It's your turn to choose."

"No. Wrong. Your turn."

"All right. Let's wait a while, though," I say. "Give me time to think this through."

And this verbalized ritual of the dinner plans takes us to our street, where we turn the corner onto the last block of our walk. I remembered then that…

❖

The first time I told David about the Big Party, his response was that he had been born too late. "I was just getting started," he said as we lay naked together shortly after he had moved in with me.

"I was just beginning to understand the...the game, the excitement of the search. Jesus, I'd been to the baths only twice, before you... captured me."

"What a lovely way to put it. Captured?"

"You know what I mean."

"I think your mother would know what you mean."

"No, no," he said, turning his face to mine. "I think I wanted to be captured. I think I wanted to be...encircled, held, loved, bound together by something more than the sex."

He was so serious then, and his eyes, his green eyes were so large with the truth of what he was telling me that I wrapped my arms around him and pulled him closer to my body. I kissed his eyes as I told him what, for me, was beginning to be easier and easier to say, "I do so love you, baby."

❖

As I open the gate to our front yard, I notice two things almost simultaneously: the spirits at the upstairs window await our return with their impish grins. They have probably turned on a light or two, or moved my reading glasses again from where I always put them. And the mama finch is alerted to our return, her little gray head perked well above the rim of her nest. As we near the porch, she flutters desperately away to the limb of the maple where, as I unlock the door, she watches our passage beneath her unborn children.

I pass through the living and dining rooms, and on through the kitchen to the back of the house where we keep the food for Melissa and Calvin, our Alaskan Malamutes. They stare at me from the porch through the back door window. They both sit, side by side, their eyes and ears perked, pleading for their dinner. I fill their bowls: half dry, half meat, and a goodie or two on top. Melissa, nine years old, also gets a hormone pill, a thyroid pill, and a baby aspirin. Calvin, who is five years old, gets just his food. I open the back door and serve them, chattering as I always do about doggies in China going hungry for days, and fortunate doggies, say, for example, Melissa and Calvin, who haven't missed a meal since they were born and...

And they ignore me as they quickly devour the best dog food money can buy. Tomorrow, David and I will run/walk our two miles in the park with Melissa and Calvin leading the way.

David has taken his magazine into the living room. He sits on the love seat and flips to the page with the creased corner. I don't even think he notices me pass as I cross the living room to the stairs. When his stomach begins to growl, he will remember that we have yet to eat dinner.

I climb to my second-story study, which faces the front yard, and from which our spirits watch our comings and goings from our old house. I believe they are elsewhere right now. I sit down in my big, black leather chair.

I have been reading lately about Tchaikovsky. Last night I read that his death from cholera on November 6, 1893, was most likely caused by his decision to intentionally drink a glass of cholera-infested water, seeking the comfort of death rather than living with the painful knowledge that his beloved nephew, Vladimir, had forsaken their relationship by associating with female prostitutes.

Love hurts, or so the song says.

Yes, and love laughs and love cries and love is silent and love is cacophonous and love is ugly and love is pretty and love is all there is and love is lacking and love is fulfilling and love is a tear and love is a smile and love is a nod and love is a mystery and love is known and love is unknown and love is brilliant and love is stupid and love is bright and love is dull and love is tough and love is easy and love is…a many-splendored thing. And, yes, enduring love is a prideful thing.

❖

Love? No, I still don't know exactly what the hell that word means. I just know that the years David and I have had together have been…lovely.

And I guess that's really all that needs to be said, except…yes, except that the spirits have returned. They whisper in my ear, their breath a cool wisp against my cheek. "Continue," they say in a voice as old as the walls of this house, but as vibrant as the new spring. "Continue," they say as softly as the creak they make as they pass through the floor to surround David sitting on the love seat below. "Continue this," they say softly, sweetly, as they leave me to kiss David's eyes with their smiles.

Or so I would like to believe.

AFTERWORD AND ACKNOWLEDGMENTS

I don't know about you, but I have a little tear in my eye about now. It's gotten dusty in here, hasn't it? Unless we're more sentimental than we'd like to admit. We hope you've enjoyed our looks at love and romance and will seek out more of these fine writers.

My thanks go out yet again to Radclyffe the Magnificent, the inimitable Sandy Lowe, Cindy Cresap, Stacia Seaman, and the rest of the Bold Strokes Books staff for putting some very fine stories into print. And, of course, I have to thank the authors of those stories, whose creativity once again astounds me. On a personal note, I'd like to thank, as usual, Ryk Bowers and our dogs, the noble Duncan and the Lady Lexie as they slept at my feet.

And, of course, my late partner, Jamz, who showed me what romance was all about in the first place. Thanks, bigbear. Miss you.

CONTRIBUTORS

'NATHAN BURGOINE (nathanburgoine.com) lives in Ottawa with his husband Daniel and their husky Coach. He appears in dozens of anthologies, has a novella in *On the Run* (Wilde City Press), and his debut novel *Light* (Bold Strokes Books) was a Lambda Literary Award finalist.

JERRY RABUSHKA, from St. Louis, MO, is a novelist, playwright, and musician. His novel *The Prophecy* is published by Bold Strokes Books. He has many plays published with Brooklyn and Heuer Publishers, which are produced nationwide and internationally. He's also produced several albums of original music.

DALE CAMERON LOWRY (www.dalecameronlowry.com) lives in the Upper Midwest with a human and three cats. Dale enjoys writing and publishing stories, wasting time on Tumblr, getting annoyed at Duolingo, and reading folktales.

MICHAEL BRACKEN is the author of several books and more than 1,100 short stories published in *Best Gay Romance 2010* and *2013*, *Best Gay Erotica 2013*, *Hot Blood: Strange Bedfellows*, *The Mammoth Book of Best New Erotica 4*, and many other anthologies and periodicals. He lives and writes in Texas.

ERZABET BISHOP is the author of *Sigil Fire* and *Club Beam*. She is a contributing author to *The Big Book of Submission*, *Slave Girls*, *Bondage Bites*, and many other anthologies. She lives in Texas with her husband, furry children and often plays at local bookstores. Follow her on Twitter @erzabetbishop.

Thom Collins is married and lives in North Durham, North East England. His novel, *Closer by Morning*, a racy, romantic thriller, is due for publication in 2016. He loves creating strong, sexy characters in a world of glamour, excitement, and danger. He's currently working on the first novel in a trilogy of thrillers. Contact him at ThomCollinsAuthor@aol.com or Twitter: RealThomCollins.

Matthew Bright is a writer, editor, and designer who often has to debate about what order those words come in. His short fiction has appeared in *Queers Destroy Horror* (*Nightmare* Magazine), *Queen Mob's Teahouse*, *The Biggest Lover*, and *Manchester: Revolutions*. He is also the editor of the anthologies *The Myriad Carnival* and *Threesome* (Lethe Press). By day, he pays the bills as a book cover designer. He lives in Manchester, England, with his partner John and a dog with a taste for eating valuable hardback books. Find him on Twitter at @mbrightwriter or online at matthew-bright.com.

Megan McFerren revels in exploring queer history through erotic romance. She lives in NYC, and when not writing, can be found photographing pigeons, sampling good whiskey, and reading Evelyn Waugh. She can be followed on Twitter @inarcadiamegan and has shared stories in anthologies from Cleis, Torquere Press, Insatiable, and more.

Kevin Klehr lives with his long-term partner in their humble apartment (affectionately named Sabrina) in Australia's own "Emerald City," Sydney. He has written two novels, *Drama Queens with Love Scenes* and *Drama Queens and Adult Themes*, and one ebook, *Nate and the New Yorker*, which are published through Wilde City.

Born to a military family just outside the nation's capital, Kassandra Lea has been reading since she could hold a book. Growing up, she wanted to be a horse or Batman, then she discovered writing and realized she could be whatever she wanted if she lived vicariously through her characters. Her short stories have appeared in a number of anthologies. When not writing, she can be found hanging out with her dog, driving flashy cars, pursuing her love of horses, and cheering on the Packers. She lives in southern Wisconsin in an old house with her mother, a gang of furry monsters, and a ghost lovingly dubbed Bob.

R. W. CLINGER writes gay romantic tales and thrillers for JMS Books. He is the author of five Stockton County Cowboy novels: *Chasing Cowboys*, *Riding Cowboys*, *Roping Cowboys*, *Branding Cowboys*, and *Saddling Cowboys*. His novel *Cutie Pie Must Die*, a gay mystery, is published with Bold Strokes Books. When R. W. isn't writing, he enjoys football, the cowboy life, and the nature of domestic cats. When he is writing, he creates tales about manly bears and beachside tales set in Florida (*Barefoot Beach*, *Barefoot Kill*, and *Barefoot Storm*). R. W. Clinger also has a love for football and its hardcore sexy players on and off the field: *Torso Tackle*, *Off Season*, and *Back in the Game*. Currently R. W. is writing a new gay novel called *Sugaring Ben*. He resides in Pittsburgh with his husband of twenty-one years and can be reached on Facebook and www.rwclinger.com.

VINTON RAFE MCCABE is the author of ten books of nonfiction and one novel, *Death in Venice, California*, which was shortlisted for the Lambda Literary Award for Debut Fiction in 2015. An award-winning poet and playwright, and lifelong journalist, McCabe also works as a literary critic and reviews for *The New York Journal of Books*.

RICHARD NATALE is a Los Angeles-based writer whose short stories have appeared in such publications as *Gertrude*, *Wilde Oats*, *Chelsea Station Magazine*, and the anthology *Off the Rocks*. His most recent novel, *Love on the Jersey Shore*, was published in early 2016 and his previous novel, *Café Eisenhower*, received an honorable mention from the 2015 Rainbow Awards. He also penned the novella *Junior Willis* and the YA adventure *The Golden City of Doubloon*.

MARYN BLACKBURN has written short erotica for the anthologies *Power Play: Sex and Politics*, *Love Me Tender*, *Ageless Erotica*, and *Underground Erotica*. Her novels include *Taming the Wilde* and *Brick by Brick*. Maryn lives near the Great Lakes, drives a minivan, yet refuses to buy a golden retriever.

Entertainment journalist **GREGG SHAPIRO** is the author of *Lincoln Avenue* (Squares and Rebels Press, 2014), *GREGG SHAPIRO: 77* (Souvenir Spoon Press, 2012), *Protection* (Gival Press, 2008), and the forthcoming *How To Whistle* (Lethe Press, 2016). His interviews and reviews run in a variety of regional LGBT and mainstream publications and websites. He is the co-winner of Seven Kitchens Press's Robin Becker Chapbook Prize, and his chapbook, *Fifty Degrees*, will appear May 2016. Shapiro lives in Fort Lauderdale, Florida, with his husband Rick Karlin and their dog k.d.

COLTON AALTO lives in a century-old brick warehouse in Denver with his husband and two spoiled cats. After collecting college degrees for a decade and a brief criminal justice career, Colton left the East Coast for the sun and ski slopes of Colorado. He practices law, except on powder days.

EVEY BRETT lives in southern Arizona with two cats and a Lipizzan mare. She's written queer romance and erotica for Lethe Press, Cleis Press, Loose Id, Pathfinder Web Fiction, and elsewhere. Visit her online at www.eveybrett.wordpress.com.

GEORGE SEATON lives and writes in Pine, Colorado. He shares his life with his partner, David, of thirty-three years (husband of two years), and Kuma, their Alaskan Malamute rescue. "Continuum" originally appeared in his collection *American Stories* (Wilde City Press, 2014).

ABOUT THE EDITOR

JERRY L. WHEELER has been shortlisted for the Lambda Literary Award three times for his editing work (*Tented: Gay Erotic Tales from Under the Big Top* and *The Bears of Winter*) as well as his writing (*Strawberries and Other Erotic Fruits*). He has three other volumes of erotica available from Bold Strokes Books (*Riding the Rails*, *The Dirty Diner*, and *Tricks of the Trade*) and a four-novella anthology from Wilde City Press, *On the Run*. His short fiction has appeared in numerous anthologies, both print and online, and he is currently working on his first novel, *The Dead Book*, due from Lethe Press in 2016. He lives and writes in Denver, where he makes his living doing freelance editing.

Books Available From Bold Strokes Books

Death Comes Darkly by David S. Pederson. Can dashing detective Heath Barrington solve the murder of an eccentric millionaire and find love with policeman Alan Keyes, who, despite his lust, harbors feelings of guilt and shame? (978-1-62639-625-8)

Men in Love: M/M Romance, edited by Jerry L. Wheeler. Love stories between men, from first blush to wedding bells and beyond. (978-1-62639-7361)

Slaves of Greenworld by David Holly. On the planet Greenworld, the amnesiac Dove must cope with intrigues, alien monsters, and a growing slave revolt, while reveling in homoerotic sexual intimacy with his own slave Raret. (978-1-62639-623-4)

Final Departure by Steve Pickens. What do you do when an unexpected body interrupts the worst day of your life? (978-1-62639-536-7)

Love on the Jersey Shore by Richard Natale. Two working-class cousins help one another navigate the choppy waters of sexual chemistry and true love. (978-1-62639-550-3)

Night Sweats by Tom Cardamone. These stories are as gripping as the hand on your throat. (978-1-62639-572-5)

Soul's Blood by Stephen Graham King. After receiving a summons from a love long past, Keene and his associates, Lexa-Blue and the sentient ship Maverick Heart, are plunged into turmoil on a planet poised for war. (978-1-62639-508-4)

Corpus Calvin by David Swatling. Cloverkist Inn may be haunted, but a ghost materializes from Jason Dekker's past and Calvin's canine instinct kicks in to protect a young boy from mortal danger. (978-1-62639-428-5)

Brothers by Ralph Josiah Bardsley. Blood is thicker than water, but you can drown in either. Jamus Cork and Sean Malloy struggle against tradition to find love in the Irish enclave of South Boston. (978-1-62639-538-1)

Every Unworthy Thing by Jon Wilson. Gang wars, racial tensions, a kidnapped girl, and a lone PI! What could go wrong? (978-1-62639-514-5)

Puppet Boy by Christian Baines. Budding filmmaker Eric can't stop thinking about the handsome young actor that's transferred to his class. Could Julien be his muse? Even his first boyfriend? Or something far more sinister? (978-1-62639-510-7)

The Prophecy by Jerry Rabushka. Religion and revolution threaten to bring an ancient civilization to its knees…unless love does it first. (978-1-62639-440-7)

Heart of the Liliko'i by Dena Hankins. Secrets, sabotage, and grisly human remains stall construction on an ancient Hawaiian burial ground, but the sexual connection between Kerala and Ravi keeps building toward a volcanic explosion. (978-1-62639-556-5)

Lethal Elements by Joel Gomez-Dossi. When geologist Tom Burrell is hired to perform mineral studies in the Adirondack Mountains, he finds himself lost in the wilderness and being chased by a hired gun. (978-1-62639-368-4)

The Heart's Eternal Desire by David Holly. Sinister conspiracies threaten Seaton French and his lover, Dusty Marley, and only by tracking the source of the conspiracy can Seaton and Dusty hold true to the heart's eternal desire. (978-1-62639-412-4)

The Orion Mask by Greg Herren. After his father's death, Heath comes to Louisiana to meet his mother's family and learn the truth about her death—but some secrets can prove deadly. (978-1-62639-355-4)

The Strange Case of the Big Sur Benefactor by Jess Faraday. Billiwack, CA, 1884. All Rosetta Stein wanted to do was test her new invention. Now she has a mystery, a stalker, and worst of all, a partner. (978-1-62639-516-9)